For
For belie

◊ ◊ ◊

Dedication

To Mr. P and all the kids who played on his fields, and to the 4 kids who made it to the show and walked through the player's tunnel and up the steps into the dugout and looked up to see the bright lights.

◊ ◊ ◊

I would like to thank the following for their help in bringing this book to life: Rebecca Foster, Paul Braunton, Victoria Joy Sacino, Linda Allen Jessica Kent, David Kent, Russ Marlow, Andretta Schellinger, Bill Green, Hank Conger, Pat Crawford, Rich Penjoyan and Jon Waterson.

◊ ◊ ◊

Based on Jon Waterson's first sermon at CUMC Methodist Church, where he preached about his love of baseball and what if God forgave Cain for killing Abel?

MUTINY IN THE DUGOUT

BEING ON A BASEBALL TEAM WAS THE **ULTIMATE** ACCEPTANCE

Rod Kent

ISBN 13: 978-0-985-47960-2
ISBN 10: 0-985-47960-4

Library of Congress Control Number: 2021910101

All characters and events depicted in this book are entirely fictitious. Any similarity to actual events or persons, living or dead, is purely coincidental. And is not based on experiences witnessed by the author coaching Youth Summer League baseball for ten years.

CHAPTER ONE

This is what Charlie Maddox lives for — baseball. It had taken him over ten years away from home to play professionally. Even if it is the minor leagues, he'd made it. At the age of thirty, his whole life is geared toward playing the game, having fun, and making the most of this chance. He left his family behind in a move to Albuquerque, and with them, the self-doubt that once upon a time told him he'd never be good enough to play for *any* team. Trying to escape his past, he ran far, far away to fulfill a dream he could never achieve back home.

Charlie still had mixed feelings about his hometown. Sometimes he itched to return, but after more than a decade of abandoning all he knew, he felt it had been too long. Over what seemed like a lifetime, a lucky chance had given him what he needed to get out, and Albuquerque became his home.

Here he is now. Finally on the field, one foot safely touching third base. The next move — steal home. The crowd is loving him like no one has ever before. Their anonymous cheers warm his heart, and he performs for their adulation. Charlie brushes his messy blond hair out of his face and dances off third base, taunting the pitcher, who looks torn between giving chase and playing on. The pitcher stares down at Charlie before beginning his windup. With one leg positioned slightly back, the pitcher holds the ball in his hands, his glove fixed halfway between his chest and waist. He nods to the catcher across the way and takes a small step backward, intent on getting that last strike to end the game. Charlie senses the pitcher's frustration and takes a large lead off third. The pitcher breaks his windup and throws to the third baseman. Charlie dives under the pickoff just in time to avoid being tagged out. He loves the play. The teasing twinkle in his eye fuels more frustration from the pitcher, whose only goal is to wrap up and go home. Charlie stands and dusts himself off. As the third baseman throws the ball back to the pitcher, Charlie once again leads off the base. This time the pitcher ignores him, trying not to get intimidated by the shenanigans, and releases a pitch gone wild — the ball cranes high over the catcher's head and slams into the backstop. As the catcher scrambles to retrieve the errant ball, both Charlie and the pitcher race for home. They meet at the base simultaneously, with the catcher zipping the ball into the pitcher's glove in the nick of time. Despite being cartwheeled by Charlie's slide into home, the pitcher holds the ball high in the air for the umpire to see.

"Safe," the umpire yells. The pitcher slams down the ball and argues with the umpire as if he had just thrown a perfect game. Both team managers take to the field and get in the umpire's face. Normally the umpire would let the pitcher make his case, but he's been shown up one too many times over the years of his lackluster career, and today he's taking a stand. The two managers and the pitcher get ejected from the field.

With no regard for the debate going on a few feet away, Charlie soaks up the sun and unending praise from his adoring fans. He glances over at the scoreboard:

RENO ACES — 4
ALBUQUERQUE ISOTOPES — 4

Charlie is in heaven. Nothing can shake his spirit in this moment. He takes in the crowd and then his own team, and the sense of knowing that he's finally where he belongs — here in this diamond with the rest of them — floods his soul. Savoring the moment, he looks down at the fresh-cut grass with all its brown spots, pleased to be playing on real grass that smells alive. In fact, the whole place is alive and teeming with goodwill.

Charlie looks back at the crowd to satiate his need for love, hoping to accept just a little bit more while he can. But he shouldn't have stolen that second glance. It was selfish of him, and instead of love, he gets reminded only of its absence. He looks to one side of the bleachers and notices a dad sitting with his two sons. This image holds him as captive as the photographs he once took, effortlessly sweeping him away from everything good that has happened that day. The little family seems to be loving the moment and the time spent together, savoring one of the most simple pleasures of American life. The dad holds a hotdog in one hand and a beer in the other while the boys enjoy their lunches. He seems relaxed, enjoying the outing on this warm spring day. Charlie watches him laugh along with his sons, as though laughing and loving life were the easiest things in the world. In that moment, Charlie knew that the love he received from anonymous fans couldn't compare to the love of someone who really knows you — knows you and still loves you, despite everything. But right now that's all he had.

He abruptly turns to face the other side of the bleachers. His heart rewarms at the cheers of other adoring fans as he joins his teammates, who offer up high-fives. This was his life now, and there was no going back. From out of the dugout, a golden retriever named Shoeless Joe Jackson runs onto the field. The dog, zoned in on Charlie alone and oblivious to the crowd, takes a leak on home plate and leaves a mess behind. Noticing the dog's inspired efforts, the fans go wild and break out into laughter.

"Why the hell does he do that?!" the umpire booms at Charlie, annoyed.

Charlie shrugs and smiles. "Just making his mark like the rest of us."

◊ ◊ ◊

It had been a good day, and getting a cold beer and spending some time with even better company to celebrate was the icing on the cake. Charlie has a soft spot for the local sports bar. The bouncer there knows his rouse — he walks around with his tall frame of defiance and cockiness, trying to denounce the big chip on his shoulders. For some reason, he can't yet claim the semi-celebrity status and reputation he was slowly creating and often hides behind dark glasses, feigning blindness. He likes it when women feel sorry for him. He craves the soft, feminine, sort of motherly attention he has never known. The bouncer greets Charlie and Shoeless Joe with a nod as they approach. Charlie wears dark glasses and uses a white cane.

"Evenin', Pete. Any potential in there tonight?" Charlie asks.

"Real stunner at the backbar, man," Pete answers. "Tall. Blonde. Miniskirt. Coulda been made to order. I think her name is Sasha, or maybe Sara."

Charlie grins and enters the establishment. Customers inside make way for 'blind' Charlie and his "Seeing Eye dog" as they move through to the back of the bar.

Upon closer inspection, Sara is even more attractive than Pete described. A drop-dead babe. Tall, with wild blonde hair, a sexy miniskirt, and dazzling wind chime earrings. A perfect ten, if he ever did see one. She stands with her back to him, and Charlie does the same, looking out at the Saturday night crowd. Looks like the usuals haven't piled in yet, but Charlie isn't one to wait until the end of the night. His strategy is to get the action early and often; make his move and then move onto another later that night.

Shoeless Joe looks up at Charlie, who nods. Joe licks the back of Sara's leg. Shocked, she twirls around, spilling her drink. Right on cue, "It Girl" by Jason Derulo plays through the bar as she faces Charlie, her eyes filled with rage. Charlie stares past her, oblivious.

"Hey! What the—" Sara's face suddenly softens. She beams at the gorgeous golden retriever at her feet. Joe wags his tail at her, and her anger completely fades away. "Oh, what an adorable puppy dog!" Bending to pet the dog, she takes in the combo package in front of her. Charlie does his best not to stare down in her direction and gives a self-satisfied smile. Sara straightens up and sees Charlie still looking past her but now smiling.

"Sorry 'bout that. The little guy just can't help himself around a beautiful woman. Neither can I, for that matter." Charlie keeps smiling while Sara eyes him suspiciously.

"Oh, yeah? And just how does a blind man know who's beautiful?"

Charlie shrugs. "Well, me 'n Shoeless Joe Jackson here, we got the same taste. You pass his test, you pass mine," he explains as a smile creeps across Sara's face. "What say we get ourselves a table?"

"Sure." Sara hooks her arm through Charlie's and leads him through the bar. They settle on a booth at the back. Sara helps Charlie find his seat before taking her own. They order a round of tequila shots and a round of beer with the first server who comes by. Joe lies underneath the table, an empty travel-sized dog bowl beside him. Once they get their drinks, Charlie unsteadily pours a little beer into Joe's bowl.

Sara gives him a weird look. "You always give him beer?"

Charlie downs his tequila shot. "Not always. He prefers tequila. But tonight he's the designated driver, so he can't get drunk." They share a laugh. "Hey, you a baseball fan?"

"Baseball? Oh, I love it," Sara exclaims. Charlie's eyes widen with interest. "Sometimes I'll catch a game on TV, and by the start of the third inning, I've already got half the housework done. It's such a great motivator."

Charlie laughs before breathing a sigh of relief. Luckily his cover still holds. "Very funny." He seizes every opportunity to enlighten someone new about his favorite sport, and so he begins. "Baseball is the sort of game where you play as a team but can also shine in your own right. You know, I was almost a pretty big deal once..."

Sara inches her hand across the table to rest hers atop Charlie's. "*So* considerate. *So* talented. What happened?"

Charlie loves the attention. He milks it for all it's worth. "Fastball, up and in. Unconscious for two days."

Sara strokes Charlie's hair as she downs the tequila shot. "You've suffered so much," she says, her voice oozing with sympathy.

Charlie motions to the server for more shots and more beer. "MVP one year—"

"MVP?"

"Most valuable player—"

"Wow," Sara says, smiling wryly.

"Blind as a bat the next." Charlie sighs deeply. "But hey, life is full of unexpected turns." They sit in an awkward, sad silence for a long moment. The server brings over more drinks.

Sara picks up a tequila shot and holds it in the air. "Shots," she announces before tossing her glass back. Charlie follows suit. "To unexpected turns." She slams down the empty shot glass in commiseration on the sorry state of being human and all its trials. Under the table, Shoeless Joe slurps up more of the beer amid the silence. Sara refreshes her own glass. "So, what do you do these days, Charlie?"

"Well, I'm not the sorta guy who gives up so easily. Fate may have taken my sight, but you don't need eyes to dream." Charlie cooly takes a sip of beer before he quips, "I'm training to play with the Los Angeles Dodgers."

Sara stares at him in disbelief. She hesitates. "I'm no expert, but I'm pretty sure you'd need eyes for that."

Charlie leans down and pets Joe. "That's where ol 'Shoeless Joe comes in. We have a system. One bark for a fastball. Two for a curve." Sara looks doubtful while Charlie grins convincingly. "You wanna know what he does for a screwball?" Sara ponders that one for a moment. She looks suspicious, slowly wising up to the façade. Charlie offers up something honest. "I actually play winter baseball for the Albuquerque Isotopes right here in New Mexico," he brags.

Charlie's manager Earl approaches the booth from behind. Only Sara sees him coming. Dressed in an expensive tailored suit with a stern look to match, he places a hand on Charlie's shoulder like he means business. He knows precisely where and how Charlie spends his Saturday nights. Earl acknowledges Sara with only a nod. Accustomed to these flirtatious shenanigans, he doesn't bother introducing himself anymore.

Charlie sniffs the air. "Hmm. Old Spice..." He sniffs again. "Halitosis..." Then he laughs and says, "There's an unmistakable stench of an old man's desperation. It's gotta be Earl."

"Ha-ha, funny boy." Earl places a handwritten note on the table, smiling pretentiously at Sara, sizing her up. She returns a smile but looks away uncomfortably, expecting an introduction that doesn't come. "Got a message from your brother." Earl bends down to pet Shoeless Joe. "He's been trying to reach you for days. Sounds serious."

Charlie urgently sheds his dark glasses and reads the note. He turns solemn, like a dark cloud has just descended over him. Sara's eyes widen and lock onto Charlie, a confused look on her face. "Hey! What the— You can see?!"

Panic briefly flashes in Charlie's eyes. Busted... He tries playing it off. "Rejoice. Praise be to God. You have just witnessed a miracle," he intones robotically before shooting her his sweetest smile.

Sara jumps up from the table, resolutely not having it. She picks up her beer and for a moment internally debates dumping it on his head. "What a jerk," she spews, her head shaking from side to side with disgust. In a last-minute switch, she chugs the beer and grabs an expensive pen that just barely sticks out of Earl's pocket. "*I've* just witnessed a miracle?" The vexed woman writes her phone number on the blank side of the note and tosses it, along with Earl's fancy pen, onto the table. "This is the miracle. Call me." Sara gives a mischievous smile as she turns to walk away.

Charlie eyes the note, half-amused. He gets this sort of retaliation mixed with admiration all the time, so it's nothing new. As he turns over the note to read Earl's chicken scratch on the other side, Earl slides into the seat occupied by Sara just moments ago. He looks across at Charlie, who now stares back with a destroyed look in his eyes. "I think I've got to go home."

CHAPTER TWO

Charlie opens his eyes to the painful throbbing of a hangover-induced headache. He eases out of bed and skulks into the bathroom for a shower. In lieu of breakfast, he grabs a Coke from the fridge, cracks open the can, and takes a deep swig. The persistent calls from his brother, and now the note from his manager, signal that something must be *really* wrong at home. He hadn't given much thought to his family over the past few years — not until yesterday, when he witnessed that dad in the bleachers. The anonymous dad with his two sons. It had been a sign. Something telling him that life as it should have been could have been... Let's just say, the unhealthy relationships he had with his own dad and brother needed some attention. He'd spend enough years away from it all, and by now, part of him knew that success on the field would not — in fact, could not — be achieved while feeling like he didn't deserve any of it.

So many times over the years, Abe had left messages asking for Charlie to call. Saying that he had forgiven him. That Gordon, their father, had forgiven him. Couldn't they just move on with their lives, they'd ask. *Really?* It wasn't Abe or Gordon who had to forgive him; that didn't even matter at this point. What mattered more is that Charlie couldn't forgive himself. He couldn't let go. The shame he felt about what he had done back then was still too powerful. He loved the game, and the game was the one place where he felt safe, free, joyous, and loved, but deep down inside he always knew. He could never squash the nagging reminder that he had stolen what was meant to be his own brother's life. He didn't deserve it, and there was no way to share it with Abe. That much was clear to Charlie. What would he do? Call him up each week to talk about how amazing the game has been? Could he shove the sheer madness and joy of the game in his face?

Charlie walks down the long hallway toward Earl's office. He stops when a poster hanging on the wall catches his attention, reading, 'Los Angeles Dodgers — Major League Open Tryouts.' Gavin, an eleven-year-old batboy, approaches Charlie. "My dad says you're gonna chicken out again this year," he remarks snidely.

Charlie's eyes never lose sight of the poster, unfazed by the kid's attempt at an insult. He replies, deadpan, "Oh, yeah? Are you calling me 'chicken'? Get me a side of mashed potatoes to go with that comment." Gavin rolls his eyes and continues on his way down the hall. Charlie stares after the boy, thinking back to when he was that age. It was around that time that his own dad stopped talking to him. Evidence that dads still talked to their kids bemused him since he had been deprived of such a thing for most of his childhood. Charlie sees Gavin as one of the lucky ones. "And bring some coleslaw too," he teases, his voice booming, just as Gavin slips through the exit at the end of the hall. Charlie shakes his head before walking into Earl's office.

The last thing he wants is a confrontation or a lecture, so he simply watches as Earl heads to the coffeepot on the side table. Finally, the older man says in a welcoming yet serious tone, "Nice of you to drag your butt outta bed, Charlie. Take a seat." Charlie cordially obliges. Earl grabs two whiskey tumblers, pours coffee into one, and into the other he dumps a healthy shot or two of Jack Daniels from the half-empty bottle sitting nearby. He offers both to Charlie. "Hair of the dog that bit ya."

"I'm taking the seat, Earl," Charlie states. A frown settles across Earl's face. Charlie downs the whiskey, and in a faint attempt to ease the tension, begins lightly, "Hell, I've been bit so many times, it's a miracle I ain't got rabies." The coffee sits untouched on the desk. Earl's frown remains. "What did you want to see me about?"

Earl drops into his seat and sighs. "I gotta tell ya, bud. Going home right now... I don't think it's a smart move. You gotta focus on the tryouts. Could be your last shot."

Charlie shrugs. "And this could be my last chance to see him, Earl. I gotta go. I have no choice."

Earl pounds his fist on the desk. "Damnit, Charlie. You're not a young buck anymore. You gotta decide what you want out of life. What's really important… Family aside." Charlie takes in Earl's words. Had he put baseball on a mighty pedestal for too long? He loves it, though; hence, the dilemma. But the whiskey had begun to stir up some fresh logic. He knew Earl was on his side and just wanted what was best for him.

Charlie speaks after a long silence. "But I'll come back here for the tryouts. I don't *want* to leave, but— Or maybe I can try out in LA? Somewhere closer to home, anyway? Can you find out?"

"Yeah, I'll find out, but can *you* find out where your head is at? You've been playing well, and you have the potential to move on. We both know that. But lately, you've hit a wall."

"Yeah, yeah. That's what I'm trying to do. So, I'll go home —just for a week. You'll see. I'll be back before you know it."

"I don't see you bouncing back from this," Earl challenges.

"You know what? You could be right." Charlie stands up and turns to the door. "But so am I." He walks out of the office, being careful not to slam the door on the way out.

◊ ◊ ◊

Charlie sits in a claustrophobic airplane aisle seat in economy, far back on the plane. He still has a long way to go before reaching first-class. A statuesque brunette flight attendant places a dark-tinted drink on the little tray in front of him. She seems timid, if not a bit nervous, having recognized him from TV. Meanwhile, the surrounding passengers are oblivious to Charlie's semi-famous status. Charlie doesn't notice her hesitance nor her beauty. He's too busy staring down at the handwritten note that Earl had slipped him just the night before: *Dad's had a stroke. It's serious this time. I think you should come home. —Abe*

Charlie turns the note over to reveal Sara's number. Should he call? Her number *was* a miracle, after all. He'll only be gone for a week. Couldn't hurt to give her a call once he's back. He notices that the flight attendant already brought his drink, and boy, does he need it right about now. The thought dawns on him: he's going home. It's been a long time coming, and besides, Abe has never asked for much. All Charlie has done is take, take, take. The time has come, along with the guilt he'd tried for so long to keep swept under the rug. Charlie picks up his drink, and the moment he tastes it, he spits it out.

The flight attendant, now a few aisles down, comes running back to Charlie when she sees the commotion. With eyes wide, she asks, "Something wrong with your drink?"

"Diet Coke, *really*? And you have to ask?"

"I'm sorry about that, sir. Just a moment." The flight attendant hurries back to her cart, locates a mini bottle of rum, a can of Coke, and a fresh glass with ice. She sets it all down on his tray. "Sorry about the mix-up, sir. Enjoy your flight."

"No, no, I'm sorry," Charlie begins. "I'm a little nervous, I guess. Just got called up by the LA Dodgers. It's my first time getting called by them for the show."

"Really? How exciting is that!"

"You have no idea. I used to play in the Youth Summer League near that stadium. I knew one day I'd play pro ball, but I never expected it would be for the Dodgers. A possible dream come true."

"So, a local boy grows up to be a Major League Baseball player for his home team. What's the marketing angle?"

For the moment, Charlie's all smiles. Is this what he really wants? He empties the bottle of rum into his glass, topping it off with Coke, and stares at it before downing the lot.

◊ ◊ ◊

The flight had been a good one, despite the onslaught of fears surrounding his return home for the first time in over a decade. Charlie and the flight attendant walk into the baggage claim room together. He spots her name tag for the first time. "*Beth*, baby, just let me grab the last of my luggage, and then I'm all yours until the big game." Charlie opens an aluminum kennel and out runs a happy Shoeless Joe. The dog lifts his leg over the stack of surrounding luggage. Charlie looks briefly but ignores him, so Joe moves on to sniffing Beth's leg.

"Sorry... The dog's always been partial to attractive women," he quips. Beth looks up at Charlie with half-lidded eyes and a smirk by lips that beg to be kissed. What's a guy to do?

Afterward, they make their way out of the airport and hail a taxi. The driver gets out and loads the small mountain of luggage into the trunk as Charlie, Beth, and Shoeless Joe get in the backseat. The taxi soon pulls off and fights its way through the dense airport traffic. Charlie stares out the window on the way toward Catalina Island, watching the peaceful ocean as they drive by. It's like another world... By the time they reach the city streets of Huntington Beach, Beth is cozied up to Charlie, using his arm as a pillow.

Charlie notices a photo stuck into the driver's visor — a young boy in a baseball uniform. He catches the driver's eyes in the rearview mirror. "Your kid?" The driver nods. "He looks happy," Charlie remarks. "He likes baseball?"

"Dylan? Yeah, loves the game," the driver replies. "Who doesn't?"

"I used to be like that. That's the main thing. You must be really proud."

"I am proud of him. Not so sure he's proud of me. Just a cab driver. He might be proud of me if—"

"Why don't you get Charlie's autograph?" Beth interrupts. "He's a rising star, right? Just about to sign with the LA Dodgers." She smiles up at Charlie. "Your kid would love that, wouldn't he?"

Charlie eyes Beth playfully, wishing she'd tone down the admiration. "Sure." He pulls out one of his many A5-sized photos and signs it before passing it over the front seat.

The driver takes the signed photo. "Thanks. He's been down on himself lately. Has yet to hit his first homer. That's all the coaches care about these days. They put a lot of pressure on those kids. Never good enough, you know? I'm still proud of him, but I want him to shine like the others."

Charlie nods in understanding. "Yeah, coaches can be tough." Something outside the window catches his eye. The taxi rolls past a Youth Summer League field. With the sun shining its last rays of the day overhead, the field beckons to Charlie like an old friend.

Beth seems to notice his interest and pipes up, "Maybe you can show him, honey? How to hit a home run?"

"Hey, yeah, can we pull over real quick? I'll give you a few pointers to share with your son. Make you the best team dad of the season..."

"Well," the driver starts, unsure about the deviation. He momentarily pulls into the field's parking lot. Charlie, Beth, and the driver get out of the taxi, leaving Shoeless Joe to lounge in the backseat. The driver peeks into the open car door. "Hey, this ain't no doggy daycare." Joe whines and hops out onto the field with the rest of them.

Charlie steps up to home, taking in the view. Joe immediately cocks his leg over the plate. "Not here, Joe. This is sacred ground." Charlie swings an imaginary bat and watches the imaginary ball sail out of the park. He circles the bases to the tune of the cheering fans going wild in his head. Along the third baseline, he comes to a slow walk, focused on a billboard that screams: 'Welcome to Mr. G's Fields: Home of Ocean Youth Summer League World Champions.'

Charlie skips to home plate, the defiant clown of his youth. This display of the family name on his home turf instantly reverts him into the joker character he always played back in the day when he had to fight for even a shred of attention. Then he remembers that Beth and the driver are waiting on him. Doing his best to rein in the clowning, he asks the driver, "If he never hits a home run, would it ruin your taxi business?"

The driver looks confused. "Well... No."

"Is the kid still going to get up every morning, eat his breakfast, and play with his friends?"

"I suppose."

"Is the sun still going to rise the next day?"

"Isn't it pretty to think so?"

Charlie laughs. "Look at the cabbie quoting Hemingway now." Then he forces a more serious tone. "Hey, but don't worry about it, then. Besides, every professional player will tell you the same thing — home runs don't win games. We just do it to please the fans."

They all return to the cab after their detour. Although Beth invites him up to her hotel room, Charlie decides to call it a day. It has been a long one, indeed. He promises to call her over the next few days before she flies away to a new destination for work. Funny… It was usually him doing the flying away. After Beth gets dropped off at her hotel, Charlie comes to terms with his reality. It's time to face the music. See his old man and get the status updates in-person. He goes silent as they drive through the familiar suburban streets. It almost feels as though he had never left.

One of the houses in the old neighborhood makes him lean forward in his seat. "This is it. Just up here." The driver pulls up in front of a two-story home in Huntington Beach and retrieves the remaining luggage from the trunk. Charlie looks frozen to his seat momentarily, but soon enough he gets out, followed by Shoeless Joe. "Thanks for going out of your way," Charlie tells the driver while gripping his lone suitcase.

"Thanks for the autograph."

"Anytime. Oh, and tell your kid to forget about hitting home runs. Singles win ballgames." The driver thanks him with a nod before returning to the taxi. Meanwhile, Charlie musters the courage to walk up those porch steps once again, letting himself into the house he once called home.

CHAPTER THREE

Pastor Abe Maddox, Charlie's brother, stands facing a trestle table at one end of the long church fellowship room. He is lanky, athletic, and deeply devoted to his faith. A large banner hangs just above him: "Say No to Drugs." On the table, Abe arranges a few candles that surround a framed photo. From the frame shines the smile of a teenage boy. A newspaper clipping sits beside the photo… It's an obituary with the headline "Town Mourns Youth's Death From Drug Overdose." Abe prides himself on the unspoken bond he had managed to build with the church's youth. While he isn't necessarily someone the teens look up to, they do allow him access into their world — even if just a smidgen. Formally trained as a high school science teacher, Abe had felt called by God to enter the ministry, where he worked to incorporate all the scientific whiz-bang tricks in the book to secure the attention of the rowdy teens.

Tonight would be different, though. He wanted to soften the noise and distill the spirit, establishing a calm space — something that many of the attending teens had never known, neither at home, school, nor out on the sport field. The past week was a hectic one for the troubled teens. One of them landed in a bit of trouble with drugs, following news that flooded the community about a teen who had died from an overdose. Most of the teens that showed up to youth group every Friday night were only there by necessity. The teens' attendance was part of their "warning" from the cops; either shape up or ship out. Abe fed them well; that they couldn't deny. Despite their begrudging attendance to the weekly meetings, the home-cooked meals prepared by volunteers in the church kitchen, and the occasional fast food runs or pizza nights were more than enough to keep them coming back.

Most who came tried to hide the hurt, pushing it down as far as it would go, instead of addressing the pain and sadness they had experienced over the past week. Abe tends to sidestep the past and instead focuses on the here and now. He urges everyone to look to the future and imagine the possibilities it can hold. Jack Ross, an athletic, scruffy-haired teen, walks in for the last few minutes as usual. Meanwhile, the others are busy lounging around, playing cards, eating and drinking to their heart's content, or texting their friends.

Jack struts over to Abe. "Evenin', preacher. What's the Bible quote of the day?"

Abe, standing at the trestle table, looks over his shoulder before turning around to face Jack. "Corinthians, chapter fourteen, verse forty. 'Let all things take place decently and by arrangement.' You like that one, Mr. Ross?"

Jack responds with, "It's a bit, uh, Biblical for my taste." A few of the teens laugh, suddenly interested in the conversation.

Abe doesn't back down. "How about this one? Mark, chapter fourteen, verse sixty-two. 'Sit down and shut up.'" Now, everyone laughs.

Jack goes to sit down, and without looking back, he says, "Yes, sir. I'm good at multitasking." The boy slinks away and fist bumps with a few of the guys as he takes a seat.

With his open Bible balanced in one hand, Abe lights one of the candles at the table in honor of the teen who lost his life to drugs. "I'd like us all to spend a moment in silence for Riley now." The teens ignore him, chatting among themselves. Frustrated, Abe slams his Bible shut and stares down at the teens. For the first time, all eyes are on him. "Let God change your life. Let God be the strength. You can do it. Listen up — repeat after me, 'Just say no.'"

The teens chant in a zombie-like fashion, each with the same monotone, "Just say no."

Abe smiles gracefully, seeing right through the teens' obedient façade. "Ah. If only you meant it. See you next week."

The teens run at the first chance of escape, pushing and shoving each other out the door, leaving behind soda cans, chip bags, and general mess from the fast food they had devoured scattered on the tables and floor for Abe to clean up. He would get to it soon, but right now, he needed another sort of cleaning up. A sort of confession perhaps.

He walks out of the room and into the chapel. It was during times like these that he felt stuck. Maybe he wasn't cut out for this… He quickly remembers that this sort of thinking wasn't worth his time. It had nothing to do with his *own* abilities. Perhaps he needed to take a bit more of his own medicine, and let God do the work. The teens would come around soon enough. He truly believed that. Just like he believed that his brother would come around too. He bent his head in prayer for the lost souls. For those who had wandered, however far away. Although he would never stop believing, Abe sometimes couldn't help but wonder when God would finally hear his prayers. The same prayers he has been praying for so long. He keeps reciting them, hoping, knowing, and holding fast to the notion that things would all work out in His precious timing.

Charlie climbs the steps to the porch of his childhood home. He hesitantly eyes the doorbell before thinking better of it and instead retrieves a spare key from under the doormat. Using the key like old times, he enters. The house looks dark and seemingly empty, lacking any hint of a woman's touch except for the photos and memorabilia still on the sideboard — images of Abe and Charlie from when they were young, and medals, statues, and trophies celebrating the boys' success in baseball.

Abe quietly comes down the steps, catching Charlie off guard. "Well, well, well. The prodigal son has returned."

Charlie glances at Abe before returning his attention to the baseball memorabilia lining the dusty shelves. He wants to reply, "Where?" But all grown up, he thought it in poor taste to speak to Abe with such sarcasm and jokes now. He was no longer the kid brother, and such a tone didn't seem to fit the moment. Charlie pipes up, "How is he? Is it bad?"

"The doc says he's got a few years left. Whether that's good or bad depends on who's hearing it."

Charlie shakes his head and releases a deep breath. "Damn, a stroke at fifty-three. That's a little young, ain't it?"

Abe nods solemnly before pointing his eyes upward. "He wants to see you, you know."

Charlie's gaze slowly matches Abe's. "He— God?!"

Abe takes a step back up the staircase. "No, idiot, the other Mr. G. You coming?" Charlie moves closer to the stairs. He stops suddenly, his heart filled with dread about what's coming next. Shoeless Joe stands at Charlie's side and whines, holding a leash in his mouth.

Charlie looks down and ponders the idea for a moment. "Good call, Joe." He decides to take the dog for a walk, disappearing out the front door while Abe walks down the hall.

◊ ◊ ◊

Gordon Maddox, pushing fifty-three, has run the local Youth Summer League for the last twenty-five years. Now, he's bedridden, with slurred speech and a paralyzed right arm after suffering a stroke. Abe sits by his side, reading the Bible. In this moment, he wondered if he had surpassed his hundredth reading of the Bible yet. Sometimes he would read it from start to finish — the process was an elixir to his pain. He felt as though reading through even the worst of the events, including Genesis, chapter nineteen, and the Book of Judges, would see him draw closer to God, calling up His angels and the Holy Spirit to be encamped around the room.

Abe reads aloud in a soft, smooth voice. "And Cain knew his wife; and she conceived and bore Enoch: and he built a city and called the name of the city after the name of his son, Enoch."

It takes a while, but Charlie eventually makes it up to see Gordon. After a gentle knock, the door slowly opens into the room, and Charlie steps inside. He takes one look at Gordon, and his face crumbles. Gordon lies there, asleep. He doesn't look half as bad as Charlie feared he would, but the aging process was undeniable compared to the last time they had all been under one roof. Gray hair and deep wrinkles etched in his face cover up any signs of the sprightly man he once was — full of vigor and enthusiasm for getting on the field of life. Charlie redirects back to the hallway and slumps to the floor. Abe eases out of the room, going after Charlie. He looks down with sympathy, feeling his brother's internal burden of having missed so many years, so much time with their dad. But it wasn't too late for either of them yet.

"Sorry, I—" Charlie starts.

Abe puts a hand on his shoulder. "It's okay. It's hard seeing him like that."

Almost as if on cue, Gordon's voice booms from the bedroom. "You idiot, bunt!" Charlie stares up at Abe, confused.

Abe nods knowingly in response. "He's been sleeping a lot since it happened."

Again, Gordon bellows. "Hustle, boy! Hustle!"

"And he babbles about baseball while he's doing it," Abe adds.

Charlie avoids Abe's gaze, almost as if looking through him. "When didn't he?"

Abe lets go of Charlie and smiles, trying to lighten the mood. "A man doesn't win nine Youth Summer League Baseball World Series Championships without being at least a *little* obsessed."

"He also made it his job to ensure *every* kid had a memorable time." Charlie sarcastically counters.

"Now, now... He's your dad too."

Charlie snorts. "Since when?" Trust is not a familiar phenomenon in the Maddox household... Charlie heads down the stairs.

Gordon grumbles from overhead, "Ahh, you run like you got a piano in your pocket. Don't let him dig in. Brush him back."

Abe calls after Charlie. "He'll be okay. Just give him some space. And I'm sorry about the messages... I was worried. Just thought it was about time we got together. He caught your last game, you know. Good ol' ESPN."

As Charlie retreats to the living room, Abe returns to his post in Gordon's bedroom. He silently watches the older man sleeping. The sudden urge to clobber his father with a baseball cap becomes overwhelming, so he removes himself from the situation and joins Charlie in the living room, stopping to retrieve a pair of beers.

Abe takes a seat at one end of the couch, with Charlie at the other. Abe passes a beer across the middle couch cushion. The brothers drink while a baseball game quietly plays on the TV. "You should've heard him when you hit that double in the bottom of the eighth," Abe tells Charlie.

"Yeah? Let me guess." Charlie clears his throat, preparing an imitation of his father. "'A player worth his salt would've made it to third.'" He takes a swig of beer.

"Don't be so hard on him, Charlie. He was proud of you. I could see it in his eyes."

Charlie turns to look at Abe, his eyes showing nothing but doubt. "He'd never say it to my face."

"Maybe not — but he's not that sort of man."

From upstairs, Gordon's voice reverberates through the house. "Run for third base, boy!"

Abe drains his beer and stands up. "Anyway, I'm gonna hit the hay. Gotta be up early for T-ball."

"You're playing T-ball? Aren't you a little old for that?"

"Not playing, doofus. Coaching Nicky and her team."

Charlie looks confused. "Nicky?"

"My daughter." Abe smiles proudly.

"Sorry — I've been a horrible uncle."

"It's cool. We haven't—" Abe brushes off the rest of the words he was planning to say. "Anyway, I coach T-ball most Saturdays. Maybe you can help out."

"Maybe," Charlie starts. "But I'd rather have a root canal while squirrels run up my leg, looking for nuts."

"Well, think about it. There's another field across the way

if you want to get in some practice." Abe starts toward the staircase. "Oh, Nicky and I are staying here with Mr. G to keep an eye on him, so if you need anything, just let me know. A nurse comes every morning to distribute his meds and help with rehab."

"Good to know. Night."

◊ ◊ ◊

Still fully clothed, Charlie lies on the bed in his old room. Not much has changed from how he left it all those years ago. He pulls Earl's note from his pocket and stares at Sara's phone number. The events of the day left Charlie feeling wired. In fact, sleep was the last thing on his mind. His thoughts wandered to how he could have been making out with the gorgeous flight attendant from earlier that day. For a moment, he thinks about calling her — but deep down, he knows that his body, mind, and heart needed another sort of release. It had been a long day, but the thoughts in his head had gotten more of a workout than his body.

Eventually, he finds his way onto the front porch. He sits there for a while, taking in the peaceful silence of the neighborhood and thinking about the life that could have been — had he stayed. Would his relationship with Gordon have healed? Would it have been worth those absent ten years to heal a relationship? How much were relationships really worth in terms of time? And was time the arbiter of peace or something else? Charlie's thoughts wander to a moment in time with a girl he knew back in high school — Teri. They had something once. She was the only girl he had ever been serious about, even after all these years. He had felt rejected by her uncertainty, followed by her refusal to follow along wherever he went. After all, he was the man in the relationship... Wasn't he *supposed* to be the leader? Wasn't she *supposed* to have followed him? Giving up her dreams for his own? But women no longer wanted men to be the ones to take charge and take care. The casual flings he'd experienced over the years had served him well enough. Those experiences are what led him to give up taking charge or taking care of anyone. The women were free and so too was he. No one was tied to anyone else, and the only commitment given to each other was the fleeting moments they spent together.

Walking the familiar streets helps Charlie clear his mind of the racing thoughts as he goes over the flings he'd had most recently. Was he really up to calling the flight attendant? The streets from his youth were devoid of people at this hour, lacking the pulse and life it once had. He felt lost in an eerie time warp. Had these streets, the homes and the people who filled this neighborhood, stayed the same while he had chosen to move on? Or was it in fact himself who was stuck in the past? No matter how much his life had changed on the outside, no matter how far away he got, the same interior monologue remained. Some chapters of his life still hadn't come to an end. They gnawed at him, refusing to let go. Or was he the one who needed to let go?

Charlie walked and walked until he reached the ocean — finally, a place filled with *life*. The jetty was all lit up. Groups of young people lined the beach with their bonfires, their singing and laughing echoing into the night. Everyone was having the time of their lives. As Charlie walked by, he felt like the world's biggest outsider. He had given up so much by leaving, even though he had fulfilled his childhood dreams of playing professional baseball. He had surely received a lot over the years, but he had also managed to lose some along the way. His last time around a bonfire had been the start to a romantic night with the girl he couldn't forget. Even now, none of the casual flings he had engaged in could compare. He wondered what she was doing now and where life had led her. They hadn't stayed in contact over the years. What was the point? He had asked her to leave town with him and come along for the ride — become a part of the semi-professional baseball circuit. It was a massive blow to Charlie's self-esteem when she turned him down in favor of studying and getting a "real" job.

He settles into the sand on the beach and watches the waves roll in for a while, thinking about his life and reflecting on the choices he had made. That was something he rarely did. He had spent his life filled to the brim with movement and action, leaving little time to think and be alone with his thoughts. This moment of self-reflection was foreign to him. He felt it in his spirit… This was something he had needed for so long; to slow down and be alone, simply sitting and staring up at the distant life above. The stars seemed to wink down at him, as though saying that happiness was still out there, within his reach.

From his wallet, Charlie removes an old photo. Two teenagers, a boy (Charlie) and a girl with long brown hair, sit around a bonfire on this very same beach so many years ago. The girl smiles up at Charlie, beaming with an unshakable confidence. Charlie sighs with regret.

CHAPTER FOUR

Charlie managed to sleep well despite his restlessness from earlier that night. Sleeping in his old room with his dated Pearl Jam, Nirvana, and Soundgarden posters on the wall transported him right back to his teen years. He had spent so much time right here in this room, just imagining the day he would finally leave this place behind. Now, he had fulfilled the goals he could once only dream about and felt a wave of contentment wash through him. He was content to be in a different emotional space rather than the angst-fueled space to which he had once belonged. Although the father-son relationship between he and Gordon wasn't yet mended, it was somehow comforting to be back. Even if the rest of the home was unshaken by his presence, this room was still his own; still his one escape route for solace. The fact that Gordon had left his room untouched for all those years gave Charlie an idea that perhaps his father had hoped he would come home one day.

The next morning was a Saturday. It felt nice to sleep in without having to worry about the clock; no appointments, no game plans, no *nothing*. Usually, there were places to go, people to see. Everything revolved around baseball but it was never truer than on game days, and Saturdays were game days. That's what Charlie and Abe had known all their lives — Charlie, with his current commitments to playing professionally, and Abe, coaching a T-ball team during his downtime from ministering to the youth of his church. After a fast dunk in the shower, Charlie checks in on Gordon. The older man was still sleeping like a baby. Abe had told Charlie that the nurse would arrive at 10 a.m. and let herself in, so on this rare occasion, he was free to spend the day however he pleased.

Charlie finds himself down at the Youth Summer League baseball fields, practicing for the LA Dodgers tryouts. He hits ball after ball from a pitching machine that sits up on the mound. It was nice to be alone for a while. Baseball was one of the few sports where you could almost get away with being a "lone ranger" — but no one wins that way, and he knew it. Being a lone ranger meant losing out on becoming a vital asset to the team, but for the first time, it was doing Charlie some good. It suddenly became clear to him that he was indeed acting the part of the lone ranger, despite having Shoeless Joe and an entire team behind him. Long ago, he had decided he would no longer depend on anyone. Life was about what you made it *for yourself*, and you couldn't trust anyone to support you through any of it.

It's a beautiful day, he realizes, staring out over the field from home plate. His kitbag sits on the ground nearby. Beer cans peek out from the zipper compartment, while an open one sits beside the plate. The pitching machine sends a ball his way. Charlie makes contact, belting the ball straight into the gap of centerfield. Shoeless Joe was having the time of his life, running after the ball, fetching it, and then returning it to his best mate like the loyal soul he was. Charlie smashes the ball again and again, silently thanking Joe each time because without him, he'd be running himself ragged to retrieve each ball himself. With Joe by his side, he could feign having a best friend but not worry about anyone other than a dog and himself. Charlie had adopted Joe as a pup when he first moved west to New Mexico. He was the only master Joe had ever known. When Charlie found out the dog shared the same birthday as his hero baseball player Shoeless Joe Jackson, he had to have him, and thus, the name stuck. When the next ball flew over a high fence, into the T-ball field next door, Charlie decided to call it a day. He whistled Joe over so that they could check out the game going on next door and fetch the ball together.

From Charlie's spot on the empty field, he could see Abe with his T-ball kids in the distance. Charlie's love for baseball began on the T-ball field. The first time he stepped up to the plate, he felt free. A feeling of embarrassment bubbled up as he recalled that his game-playing had somehow taken a backseat to every one of Abe's performances. It wasn't a bad time; at least he was still given a chance to be on the field. It was before the crazy competition and screams from Gordon — coach of every team Charlie and Abe had played on as kids — took over. Gordon soon enough had Charlie relegated to a seat in the dugout, with nothing to show for himself. It was cruel for any child to have a coach as a father, and Charlie wouldn't wish it on anyone. Too much pressure to perform. Too many expectations that the apple could never fall too far from the tree. Unfortunately, Charlie had fallen so far from the tree that he recognized nothing from Gordon in himself except for their innate love of baseball.

Some of the parents loved the Youth Summer League, while the others always looked angry to be there. It was understandable, though. The games could sometimes take hours, and they were frequent. Day games on Saturdays, day games on Sundays, and night games during the week. Can't forget the constant training when games weren't on. Of course, then there were the parents who made use of the time while their kids were on the field, reading the news or working through emails on their phone or tablet. Each season, the parents were either passionate, patient, or peeved about the league games.

T-ball, on the other hand, was tame — so tame that Charlie couldn't stand the sport. It only made sense that Abe had chosen to coach the team of little sluggers. Something in him had changed back then after the accident. A switch went off, and by the time he returned to the field, he no longer lived a life committed to the chaos and competition of the Youth Summer League. He had given up. T-ball was supposed to be about having fun. It's the simplest form of baseball, where two teams of five-year-olds play their little hearts out to no avail — while most of the parents cheer them on with passion and futile pressure to hit the ball out of sight. Charlie watched Abe's team playing for no longer than thirty seconds and got lost in the thought that twenty kittens on the field would do a better job. Yet, the parents never stopped pushing their kids out onto the field, believing that if you didn't learn how to play baseball by the age of five, you'd have zero chance at playing professional ball down the road.

◊ ◊ ◊

At five years old, Abe's adopted daughter Nicky is a poster child for innocence, effectively concealing her devilish demeanor from the adults. From the pitcher's mound, she fields a grounder and runs to first, where she comes face-to-face with the grinning batter — safe.

Nicky yells at the batter, "What's wrong with you? Run! You hit a home run!"

"No, I didn't," the batter responds.

"Did so! Good grief. Don't ya know the rules?!" Nicky does a dramatic facepalm. The confused youngster takes a hesitant step off the base. Immediately, Nicky tags him with the ball.

"You're out," shouts a parent, who's poorly dressed as an umpire. The batter bursts into tears and races for his mom in the bleachers, passing by Abe, who pats him on the head. Nicky trots back to the pitcher's mound, laughing at the trick she had just pulled.

Abe storms toward the mound. "Nicky, what have I told you about playing fair?" Nicky half-ignores the reprimand and shrugs.

Her face brightens suddenly as she sees Shoeless Joe trot toward the dugout, stopping to take a leak on a kid's ball bag. "Oh, what a cute doggie. Daddy, can I keep him?" Nicky runs over to pet Joe. Abe follows.

"Sorry, kid, but he's spoken for," says a distant voice.

"Oh, balls!" Nicky manages to tear her eyes away from Joe just in time to see Charlie walk up to the diamond. He has a bat in one hand and a beer in the other. Joe squirms away from Nicky and fetches the lone ball he came to retrieve before running back to Charlie. With the ball now in his hand, Charlie pats Joe, giving him the love and affirmation he deserves.

Abe clocks the beer in Charlie's hand. He frowns. "Beer for breakfast?"

Charlie ignores his brother's comment. "Tough game?"

"Hilarious." Abe sets a loving hand on Nicky's shoulder. "Charlie, meet Nicky, my daughter."

Charlie crouches down to Nicky's eye level and shakes her hand. "Pleased to meet you, Nicky. My apologies that it's taken so long." He calls Shoeless Joe over to his side. "This here is Shoeless Joe Jackson, named after one of America's best Major League Baseball players. Heard of him?"

Nicky looks thoughtfully at Charlie for a moment. "Are you an alcoholic?" The question left her mouth just as it would any five-year-old — with honesty and confidence.

Charlie's smile droops. "Are you a pain in the a—"

"—Charlie!" Abe cuts him off.

"You missed all of my birthdays, so you owe me a present. Your doggy will do just fine."

Abe answers quickly, "Nicky, a dog is a man's best friend. We'll get you your own friend one of these days." Nicky doesn't look pleased with Abe's response. More interested in the dog than Charlie, Nicky wanders onto the field with Joe and throws him the ball, leaving the men to chat while the T-ball game concludes. The parents thank Abe as their kids trudge off the field, excited to be heading home. Despite Nicky's cheekiness to the other team, the kids are all quite cordial with one another, much to the amusement of Charlie.

Everyone quickly clears out, leaving Abe, Charlie, Nicky, and Shoeless Joe with the field all to themselves. On such a beautiful day as this, there was no rush to head home. Nicky continues doting on Joe and picks up where Charlie had left off — smashing the ball into the outfield while Joe chases after it.

Charlie and Abe sit in the bleachers, watching Nicky and Joe. It had been so many years ago that the two of them played T-ball right here on these fields, long before the stress and competition of the Youth Summer League kicked in.

"I clocked your fastball at ninety-four miles per hour," says Abe.

"And?"

"You mean, the pitch?" Abe asks.

Charlie chuckles knowingly. "If you're lucky, maybe I'll show it to you."

"Gee, thanks, I'll add it to my list of things to hope and pray for." Abe looks out at Nicky having the time of her life with the friendly dog. "You know, you've proved you can play the game. You've made it. There's nothing left to prove; not to anyone. Why Gordon shut you out from the league, I'll never know, and trust me, I've been thinking about it. I never understood why he favored me over you. I mean, you *were* Mom's favorite. You look like her, act like her... Maybe Gordon didn't want to be reminded—"

"Really? That's the best you could come up with?" Charlie asks with a smirk. Abe shrugs his shoulders. "Well, how about you? Doesn't Nicky remind you of her mother?"

"Sure, sure, but it's different with me. Nature, nurture. Who truly knows how our personalities are born? I believe that God knows us before we even exist. He knows us intimately. When I look at Nicky, I see God's love in her. That's what I hold tight to — not memories of her mom's death. Nicky's been living with me for a year now, and I've known her since she was a toddler. Although I show her pictures of her mom and do my best to incorporate those memories into her life, she's picking up some of the Maddox ways too."

"Oh, no, not the Maddox ways..." Charlie and Abe laugh. They turn back to the field and watch in silence for a few moments.

"She's got some arm on her, huh?"

Charlie cracks open another beer and takes a swig. "Some mouth too."

Abe glances down at the watch on his wrist. "Speaking of which, it's about that time to go check on the oldest Maddox..." Abe stands up. "Time to go, Nicky," he calls toward the field.

Abe and Charlie begin walking to the only truck left in the parking lot. Nicky and Joe soon catch up to them. Nicky pulls a wagon piled with an ice chest and all her gear. Charlie helps pack everything into the back of Abe's truck while Nicky and Joe settle into the backseat. The brothers stand around awkwardly for a few seconds.

"Oh, hey," Abe starts, "there's a Youth Summer League board meeting tomorrow night."

"And that matters to me because..."

"Come along. Catch up with all your old buddies." Abe pulls out a folded sheet of paper from his back pocket — a flyer for the meeting. Charlie gives him a look as if to say, *What old buddies?* When he ran away from this place, he left no "buddy" behind.

Abe holds back a smile. "Herbert will be there."

Charlie almost chokes on his beer. "Oh, yeah, what's ol' 'snot nose' been up to?" The two had been friends for a short while back in the day. They bonded over their mutual ousts from the field, being stuck in the dugout for most of the games. But then Herbert decided to start selling photos that he, Charlie, and Teri had taken on Teri's camera and pocketed the money for himself. Charlie was furious when he found out. Herb never conceded that the cash, in fact, belonged to the three of them and should have been shared.

Abe responds, "He and the rest of his pals on the city council want to tear down our fields and build a Home Depot."

"That sounds about right," Charlie says, shaking his head in disgust. "Money was all he ever thought about, even as a kid. He didn't mind being stuck in the dugout with me as long as he could figure out a way to make it worth his while."

◊ ◊ ◊

Charlie made dinner for everyone that night. It had been a long time since he'd made dinner for anyone — including himself — and it felt novel for him to do so now.

"I actually followed a recipe. Had to — wouldn't know how to make it otherwise. Roast chicken with halloumi and honey.

Baked veggies too." Nicky had brought up some pureed food to Gordon, who was still confined to his bed. They prepared to sit around the table, ready to enjoy their meal without distractions from their phones or the TV.

Nicky pipes up. "Can I say the Superman grace?"

Charlie cocks an eyebrow from across the table, looking at Abe. "The Superman grace?"

"Sure. Why don't you teach Uncle Charlie the movements?" Abe answers with a smile.

Nicky stands up like a superhero, beaming confidence. She places her hands on her hips, signaling for Charlie to do the same. He slowly follows.

Nicky extends one arm into the air as she chants rhythmically. "Thank you, God, for giving us food." She extends the other arm. "Thank you, God, for giving us food." She mimes the motion of flying through the air, now both arms extended. "For the food we eat and the friends we meet." Her hands go back down onto her hips. "Thank you, God, for giving us food." Nicky shifts her hands into a prayer position out in front of her. "Amen... Nuh-na-na-nah... Amen. P.S. Help my uncle's laziness in the kitchen next time. I know I would have done better." Charlie and Abe both let out good-natured chuckles. Everyone sits, happy and content to eat their first meal together.

"It's good," Nicky confirms with a hint of surprise in her voice. She was thrilled to have two additions join her family "team." None of the impossible questions ever came up, like, "Where have you been all my life?" And for a girl who was quite bold, not yet having acquired the filter of a grown adult, she never made any accusing judgments, much to Charlie's relief. All Nicky knew was that she suddenly had more family — and better yet, a dog — to talk with and entertain. While Abe and Charlie discussed boring grown-up stuff, she quietly fed Shoeless Joe the "funny cheese" under the table.

After dinner, they all zoned out in the living room to a sitcom on TV. Nicky fell asleep on the couch soon after. Abe put her to bed and retired himself right after, exhausted after a big day on the field. Meanwhile, Charlie wandered into Gordon's room, resolved to spend time with the man he hardly knew.

Charlie cozies into the chair next to Gordon's bed and flips through a baseball magazine. Gordon was in the midst of feigning sleep, tossing a bit and then cocking his eye open, just enough to catch a glimpse of his son, who was none the wiser. It's been a long time... He tried to sneak a peek at Charlie's reading material, when suddenly the magazine slipped from Charlie's fingers and he awkwardly slumped over in the chair, sound asleep. Gordon soon enough gave into the pressing fatigue and drifted off also — for real this time.

Sunlight awoke Gordon first the next morning. He had always been a morning person, so it pained him that he couldn't just hop out of bed and go for a run like usual. The older man glances over at Charlie, still asleep, softly snoring, dribbling, and crumpled in the chair beside him. Was it really his son in the flesh? He struggled to remember why he had always been so harsh on this one. Had his own son merely served as a painful reminder for all he had lost? Not once, but twice.

Gordon puts on his actor face and opens his eyes as if for the first time. His voice sounds feeble, with none of its familiar oomph behind it. "Charlie? Is that you? I thought I was dreaming last night."

Charlie stirs and slowly awakens. He rubs his eyes and throws out a yawn for good measure. "It's me — in the flesh. What, thought you'd never see me again?"

"Thought it."

"I'm s—" Charlie contemplates apologizing but stops himself before the word "sorry" can escape. "I'm starving. Can I get you something? Need anything?"

Gordon eyes Charlie, pondering, sizing him up, wondering whether or not his son was up to the challenge he had in mind. "Yeah, I need something." He beckons Charlie to come closer." "Yeah — I need you to coach the team."

Charlie stumbles backward in shock. Coaching the team

was the last thing he would ever have expected Gordon to ask from him. "Me? No way. I—"

"Please, Charlie," Gordon begs.

Charlie's head begins to spin. He isn't prepared or willing to give up his life in pro-ball to be a coach. The old phrase runs through his mind, "Those who can — do. Those who can't — coach." He spews, "Can't Abe do it?"

Gordon scoffs. "Abe?" He shakes his head dismissively, a frown setting in on his face. "I'm taking about baseball here, Charlie. I don't need a preacher for this. I need someone who can really do God's work. They don't listen to him… Some preacher man." Gordon scoffs again, sounding disgusted this time. "He coaches T-ball; not *real* ball."

"So, you're not proud of either of us?" Charlie asks, wide-eyed, his mind still reeling from the disappointing request. Gordon feigns sudden sleep and rolls over, snoring. Charlie shakes his head. "I'll get you some breakfast," he says before excusing himself from the room.

Charlie enters the kitchen, anxiously in need of a caffeine fix and some food. Afterward, he gives his manager Earl a call. This visit was already feeling too long. It hadn't been what Gordon said but rather the way Charlie felt, being close to Gordon — instantly, he was back there, in the same place he had been so long ago, feeling small and incompetent. Earl never made him feel that way, even when Charlie made the wrong decisions for himself or his team.

Earl's gruff voice speaks on the other end of the line. "Charlie, my boy, how's home?"

"Well, Gordon is still as stubborn and cranky as ever."

"What can I do for you?"

"Any chance of talking with the Dodgers? Going to bat for me? I don't want to just give it all away — might as well make the most out of my chances while I'm here."

"Just go to the open tryouts."

"Sure. Okay. But can you talk with them about me?" Charlie asks earnestly. "You know, spill the beans on how great

I am?" He chuckles while Earl sighs into the phone. "Maybe just send over my stats and some footage from past games. Just so they know who I am."

There's a long pause before Earl speaks. "I'll get some things together over the next few days. How does that sound?"

"Sounds great. You're a legend."

"Have fun at home. Don't do anything I wouldn't do."

"Thanks." Charlie ends the call with a small smile. It was nice to have someone go to bat for him. That's what parents were supposed to do. Too bad Gordon had never seemed interested in supporting Charlie with anything, especially when he was young. Gordon had his own agenda all those years ago, and he still had it now, as a frail, sickly old man. Charlie was only a hack ballplayer to him — or Abe's brother. Never a son. Never *his* son.

CHAPTER FIVE

Charlie sifted through the stash of photos he had stowed away in his closet years ago. Did anyone else keep a collection of their own photos? He hoped so. Visual memories always beat out mental memories, especially in his experience. Photos are one of the few ways to pinpoint a moment in time of long-forgotten events and long-gone people. He was proud to have a keepsake box that held the secrets to his own private past. With a coffee in one hand, he sits on the floor, pawing his way through the old metal box's contents, now scattered on the floor. He hoped this might help him drum up some memories. What had caused he and his dad to emotionally part ways? What was the defining moment that spurred the title change from "Dad" to "Gordon"? It happened before the grenade that tore through Abe's world. Way before then, in fact, but for some reason, Charlie's recollection otherwise was nothing more than a blurry memory.

While sorting through the photos, he found one of him and his mom... Followed immediately by one of him *without* his mom; him in a suit, just standing there at her funeral, alone. Who had taken the photo? Surely not Abe or Gordon. They had been buried in their own private grief at the time. There was no one who cared to observe his loss. Or was there? Then he remembered. Teri was his best and only friend at ten years of age. She should have been born with a camera in her hand. A constant observer, she was, and he loved that about her. Teri was the one who started the trend of taking team photos when they all had nothing better to do than watch the star players out on the field while they sat sullenly, banished to the dugout.

His hand lands next on a photo of him as a real youngster,

maybe four or five years of age, clinging onto his mom's skirt. He was so small and shy back then, and Gordon hated that about him. Gordon held strong to the belief that his sons should be big, brave, and strong — not cowardly weaklings clinging to their mom's skirt. No matter how much time passed, Charlie never stopped feeling the absence of his mom. He missed her more than he could express. She had listened to him. She understood him. Most importantly, she loved him. To her, it didn't matter if he played well that day or if he had upended the house with his toys. She would pick him up and hold him tightly in the warmest embrace. It was there that he felt safe. He'd been waiting to feel that same way for over a decade.

Although he had his fair share of embraces from female fans, none of them had been able to fit the mold for the empty space left in his heart when she left. Gordon didn't start relating differently to Charlie until after her death. None of them were ever the same. Abe found comfort in his faith, but Charlie struggled. He transformed overnight into a challenging, combative version of his former self, combined with the attitude that people were disposable. It didn't matter how you treated anyone — because who knew when they would just up and leave, whether by choice or through no fault of their own. He grew despondent, but at age ten, he hadn't a clue how to explain those feelings. How to express his grief and loss... The emptiness was all-consuming. Equally difficult for a child was to understand that Gordon was also dealing with his own grief — and the way he did that was to pull away.

Charlie's eyes returned to the photo of his mother. She was of Swedish heritage. A statuesque, soft-spoken women with the warmth of no other and a knack for melting hearts everywhere she went. Studying the photo, it was only then that he noticed how strongly he resembled her. The distinctive cheekbones, plus her cheeky grin, complete with enchanting dimples... Charlie's smile indeed *was* his mother's. No wonder Gordon couldn't bear to look at him. Every moment must have been like looking death in the face. But was it the cause behind

Gordon's choice to put so much distance between them? Or had it been solely due to Charlie's perceived character flaw that led Gordon to see him as nothing more than a weakling? A weakling so dependent on his mother that he couldn't eat normally for months after she died? Gordon refused to accept that he had a weak crybaby for a son.

What had Charlie's mother seen in such a hard, tough man as Gordon? It was hard to think Gordon even capable of falling in love. Charlie heard the whole spiel as a child, but it had been a long time since he recalled how they met. As the story goes, his mom grew up in Sweden and had come to the states as an exchange student. That's when Gordon met her — back in high school. When she returned to Sweden, they kept in touch by writing to one another. That went on for a few years before she decided to leave her homeland and become Gordon's wife. What a courageous woman, to have traveled across the world and start a new life, without the only family and friends she had ever known. She truly left *everything* for love. In Charlie's mind, that made his mom someone to revere and respect. He knew that she had loved his father, and Charlie was blessed to have been born into that union. His one regret was that he couldn't make Teri love him enough to follow him. If only she had left this place with him... But then again, was it fair to compare the two? He could only imagine the intricacies of Gordon and his mom's relationship and what each of them had to give *and* give up just to be together.

◊ ◊ ◊

Charlie enters the living room with his keepsake box and a few other pieces of memorabilia from his childhood. He spreads it all out onto the coffee table, giving the items a once-over. When he looks up, his gaze momentarily locks on the family trophy case standing nearby. He stares as though seeing it for the first time. The trophy case was special, containing several autographed baseballs, a worn fielder's glove, and an old cap from the LA Dodgers, his dream team from the start. Charlie and Abe's baseball photos — yearly team photos and some action shots from the field — hung on the wall, in the same spots as when they first went up. Aside from this particular wall, there were no signs of Charlie's existence anywhere else in the house. One photo shows Charlie hitting a baseball out of the park, with a neatly handwritten caption underneath that says, "Game-winning home run!"

Charlie's mind flashes back to that moment captured in time. He was twelve years old then and happy to be playing in the Youth Summer League World Series. It was the first chance Gordon's team had gotten to compete for the title. Young Abe, age eleven, hits a line drive to left field and safely reaches first base. Batting next is their teammate Luke. The pitcher forces him to take a walk, automatically loading the first two bases. Back then a young buck, Gordon was in his mid-thirties or so. He talked strategy with Charlie in the dugout.

Gordon dramatically takes in a deep breath. "You smell that? That's the smell of our first World Championship. It's close. It's ours. We just gotta reach out and grab it."

Charlie pipes up. "Let me knock one out of the park, Dad. I can do it. I'll win us the game."

Gordon shakes his head. He already has it figured out as always. "We don't need heroics, Charlie. Abe's gonna steal third, and you're gonna bunt."

"But, Dad, I want to knock one out of the park!"

"I said you're gonna bunt, you idiot! Bunt!"

Charlie shakes off the memory like a moth-eaten blanket that no longer kept in the warmth. He steps away and turns back to the coffee table piled with stuff. He'd be back later on to take care of his mess. For now, he needs to clear his head.

He quietly meanders through the house, taking it all in. Not much has changed even after all these years. Charlie wanders into the garage and pulls the cover off a pristine blue 1967 Mustang. With a smile, he lovingly runs a hand along the bodywork. He's missed this old beast. If only he had taken it with him… Luckily, Abe had kept up the maintenance, so the old car was still in working condition. Charlie hops in behind the wheel and starts the engine. It purrs to life.

Charlie proudly cruises through the neighborhood in his classic Mustang, windows down, his hair blowing in the breeze. Eventually he finds his way to the beach and parks facing the water. From the car, he silently watches the waves roll in. After a little while, Charlie reaches across the seat to open the glovebox. It's nearly filled with an array of cassette tapes, most crudely labeled with handwriting, along with a few old 90s rock albums thrown into the mix. He looks pleasantly surprised by his latest discovery.

After he clears away the old tapes, he continues rifling through the glovebox's contents and soon produces a handwritten letter attached to a mixtape. He looks down and reads it: *Trying to study, but all I can think about is you. Can't wait 'til school's out. I'm scared though… About the future. I feel so close to you, and I don't ever want to lose that — but I know you want to get out of here. Make something of yourself. Show the world who's boss. Just remember, Charlie. Life is full of unexpected turns… See you at school. Loads of love. —Teri*

Charlie smiles sadly. He inserts the cassette into the vintage Mustang's modified audio hookup. Teri had made him a mixtape, the first song of which was Robert Smith's 'Strange Attraction.' Although Charlie hadn't been a fan of The Cure, Teri was. Hearing the song now felt weird. It was about lovers writing to each other across the distance — something that he and Teri never did. He had left quickly, leaving their issues unresolved. Both were angry and neither had gotten what they wanted. Compromise just wasn't in the cards; not back then, anyway.

Charlie kept playing the tape, drifting back into his teen years. Some of the songs were ones he loved, a unique setlist she had made just for him. After leaving the beach, he drives around for a while without any destination in mind. He eventually pulls to a stop alongside another car in the parking lot of an abandoned school. The lot sits directly next to the Youth Summer League Fields. With 90s music still blaring through the speakers, Charlie slowly rolls up the windows and picks up the flyer Abe gave him the afternoon before, reading, 'Monthly League Parents Meeting, this Sunday at 7 p.m. We will be discussing the future of the Ocean View Youth Summer League. Punch and cookies will be served after the meeting.'

◊ ◊ ◊

A large auditorium-like room buzzes with the murmur of parents. Rows of chairs, most occupied, sit facing a podium on an elevated stage platform. Charlie and Abe sit all the way at the back. They watch as Judy Ross, a no-nonsense businesswoman in her late 30s with well-manicured nails, perfect makeup, and not a hair out of place, flits past them on her journey from the small set of stairs to the podium. When she settles in front of the microphone, the murmurs abruptly die down. The parents rest their eyes on Judy, most of them patiently waiting for her to begin the meeting.

One angry dad in the front row stands up. "Say no to Home Depot," he shouts, looking to his compatriots for encouragement. The crowd voices their support, backing him up.

Judy lifts two fingers in a request for silence. "Thank you, Mr. Harris." She gazes at the faces in front of her. "I know you're all very angry about this—"

"Damn right we are," yells Mr. Harris, the angry dad. Once again, the crowd resumes their boisterous murmurs, which quickly turn into shouts.

"Please, Mr. Harris. Let me speak—"

Another angry parent jumps up from their seat. "You tell those bastards down at Home Depot that this is *our* neighborhood. Those fields are *our* fields! They're not gonna get their filthy, greedy, money-grubbing hands on 'em without a fair fight!" At this, the crowd goes crazy, multiple parents now on their feet in support of the others. Abe and Charlie exchange a grin, enjoying the fiasco.

Back on the stage, Judy steps away from the microphone and approaches the edge. She screams at the top of her lungs, "Ladies and gentlemen, please—" The crowd goes silent, watching as Judy walks back to the podium. "Thank you," she calmly says into the microphone.

Charlie scans the room from the back, curious to see if he could recognize any of the kids, now parents, who used to be on the Youth Summer League with him way back when. Through the years, he had done his best to block out the memories of those who were more interested in Abe and Gordon than himself at the time. Most of the people whose faces he could see, he didn't recognize. But who knew if the peers he once played with were parents now, anyway. Maybe they had chosen a different path in life like he had and were now miles away from this place. Charlie laughed to himself for a moment when he realized how unlikely that would be. Then he spots Herbert, the little nerd who grew up to be a bigger jerk and now threatened the future of their sacred fields.

Judy commands silence before beginning her speech to the group of displeased parents. "Home Depot is set to demolish our fields. So far we aren't sure if we will be able to finish out the current season. The school district owns the land, so they can technically do anything they want." In the midst of the crowd, Herbert stands. The confident, cheerily chubby man wears a three-piece suit, wingtips, and horn-rimmed glasses to demonstrate his "high standing" within the community.

His voice booms, crisp and clear, "Madam President, may I?" Without a response, Herbert strides to the podium, almost jogging up the steps to the microphone.

Judy awkwardly looks at Herbert, slightly uncomfortable and surprised by the interruption. Regardless, she takes a step back, allowing Herbert some space at the podium. "I yield the floor to the honorable city council member, Herbert Turner."

Herbert looks out at the crowd with an awkward half-smile, half-smirk — his trademark. Some of the parents boo, but he's unfazed by the backlash. He grabs for the microphone and switches into politician mode. "Well, now, folks. It looks like we got ourselves a problem, don't we?" More boos resound through the room. "We all want to keep the fields. None of us want to see them dug up for yet another Home Depot." Now, an overwhelming amount of boos fill the room. Judy winces, but still, Herbert remains unshaken and continues his speech, "Luckily, ol' Herbert T. Turner's here to save the day." He holds his arms to either side, waiting for the praise from the crowd; none comes.

In the back, Charlie leans over and whispers to Abe, "My hero." He then stands and gives a slow clap, the sound echoing through the momentarily silent room.

Back on the stage, Herbert's eyes widen — he recognizes Charlie. The incessant boos did nothing to shake his confidence, but the mere sight of Charlie causes him to lose his train of thought. He stares across the room at his arch nemesis for the first time in over a decade. After a long pause, Judy clears her throat. Herbert suddenly remembers he's in the middle of a speech, not to mention up for re-election in a few months.

Herbert centers himself and turns back to the crowd. "You see, folks, that land is owned by the school district, yes — but the school district needs a permit from the city in order to demolish the fields." The concerned parents whisper to one another as the room buzzes with anxiety once more. Herbert continues. "I, however, can slow down that process so your kids can continue to play. Until the end of the season, at least." His grin oozes self-satisfaction. He's offered them what they want: salvation; might as well start counting the votes already.

Judy's face warps into a look of confusion as she takes in Herbert's words. Maybe he's not the enemy after all. But then she looks around the room and thinks otherwise as she sees the parents' faces. Some look confused, some concerned, and others still, angrier than ever. Everyone is clearly wondering the same thing… Will it be that easy to stop the steady wheels of progress and capitalism?

Herbert shouts into the microphone one last phrase that changes it all: "Let the games begin!" He peers over the crowd, triumphant as he sees a shift in the room's demeanor.

Happy murmurs and applause slowly follow and quickly grow. Grinning, he accepts the accolades with a few awkward bows and waves — and can't forget his signature smile-smirk. Charlie smiles along with the rest of the crowd, feeling a bit stunned. It was hard to believe, but he guessed even Herbert could change. Or had he?

Judy takes Herbert at his word and returns to her place in front of the microphone. "Thank you, Herb. That is reassuring to all of us who care so much about the game. Perhaps now is a good time to reveal more good news for our community. I'd like to take a moment to welcome our old friend and local hero, the famous and fabulous Mr. Charlie Maddox!" Judy points at Charlie and he stands, gratefully acknowledging the adulation and standing ovation from the parents around him with smiles, nods, and waves.

Herbert looks back Charlie's way from the stage, but there is no adulation from him. He doesn't smile nor clap. Charlie notices the reaction and gets an eerie feeling in the pit of his stomach as he locks eyes with an unwavering Herbert.

After enough time has passed, Judy holds up two fingers, again signaling her demand for silence. Charlie wraps up his fleeting celebrity moment and sits down, followed by the rest of the crowd. Herbert makes his way back to his seat in the front.

When everyone settles, Judy resumes. "Alas, on a sadder note, Charlie's father, our beloved Mr. G, is still recovering from his stroke. Please continue to keep him in your prayers." Some of the parents bow their heads solemnly. "There is a get-well card for anyone who wants to sign at the table in the back." Slight murmurs run through the crowd. Judy's volume raises just a touch as she continues. "And one last item before we adjourn. I was recently contacted by the head office. They want to honor Mr. G for his twenty-five years of service in the league. On his behalf, they have guaranteed our team a wildcard slot in this year's playoffs…" She pauses, waiting for everyone to give her their full attention. "…in *the* Youth Summer League World Series!" Everyone suddenly applauds. Some of the parents hop to their feet with joy. Loving her role as the bearer of good news, Judy cheers along with the crowd and then leaves the stage as everyone starts to mingle. Some of them approach Charlie and shake his hand, a bunch of unfamiliar faces welcoming him home. Meanwhile, others eat the homemade cookies one of the parents brought, washing them down with some off-brand fruit punch.

◊ ◊ ◊

Charlie and Abe sit on the hood of the Mustang in the old school's parking lot amid the warm breeze of the nighttime air. They both sip a beer. "Where does 'snot nose' play his games these days?" Charlie asks before nibbling at the chocolate chip cookie in his hand.

Abe shrugs. "All over. He's set up a kind of professional league for kids."

Charlie nearly spits out his cookie in shock. "The kids get paid?!"

"Yeah, right," Abe says with a chuckle. "Herbert gets paid. Parents give him a bundle to get their kids on his team. He bills it like it's some kind of early pathway to the majors."

Charlie looks off into the distance, nostalgic. "What I wouldn't give to be a kid again, traveling…"

Abe breaks his brother's reverie. "Who said you grew up?" He smirks. "Plus, you travel all the time now." A woman crosses the parking lot, walking past the Mustang. Abe gives Charlie a nudge. "Old flame at one o'clock."

"Jesus… That's Teri?" There she is — Teri, a beautiful blonde woman, Charlie's former lover and now a kindergarten teacher and single mom. Charlie catches her eye for a moment. She smiles politely, clearly recognizing him. Neither makes a move to speak, but Charlie desperately wants to — if only to remind her of the letter she once wrote him and their promise to stay together. He does his best not to stare and fails miserably.

Abe jabs him in the ribs. "Why don't you go say hi?" Spellbound, Charlie can't tear his eyes away. He watches but still makes no move to approach her. Abe takes a bite of his cookie and chews amid the awkward silence, quietly laughing to himself.

Charlie manages to break his gaze only after Teri gets into her car and drives away. That's when he turns to Abe. In an attempt to change subject, he asks, "How about you? Gonna give it a go? Coach the As?"

A look of dejection flashes in Abe's eyes. He bows his head slightly. "Gordon would never ask me. That's one of the things that changed when you left. Ever since the... Accident... I've been as good as dead in his eyes."

Charlie winces and looks away, suddenly uncomfortable. He notices Herbert approaching from across the lot. Charlie nudges Abe and says, "Doofus at doofus o'clock." Abe looks slightly amused upon seeing Herbert. When he stops in front of them, Charlie does his best to smile.

Herbert approaches with one of Charlie's official team photos and a permanent marker in hand. "Mr. Maddox. So good to have you back. It would be an honor if I could get your autograph." He holds them both out to Charlie.

"Don't interrupt me while I'm ignoring you," Charlie quips.

Abe gives Charlie a disapproving glance and whispers to him, "Charlie."

Herbert looks slightly offended, if not enraged, but tries to conceal it. "You are cruelly depriving a village somewhere of an idiot."

"Why don't you do some soul-searching? You might just find one."

Herbert fakes a laugh. "Right... Good one. But hey, seriously, I need an assistant coach for my travel team. You interested?"

Charlie responds with a blank stare, as if looking right through Herbert. Any potential offering of peace just flew out the window, and not to mention, this one was patronizing at best. Herb looks at Charlie with a smile. A smile that said he wasn't planning on acknowledging the events of the past. A smile that said he wanted to play best friends again. But why?

"It pays sixty grand for the year, with medical benefits," adds Herbert.

Charlie puffs out his chest. "I'll give you a reason to use your medical benefits." He stares down Herb, and if his eyes could speak, they'd be saying, "Back off." Abe sets a hand on Charlie's shoulder, trying to pull him back before things get too far. Something was brewing, and Charlie knew it. Any offers of partnership with ol' "snot nose" was a no-go, as far as he was concerned. Decidedly done with this conversation, Charlie turns away and goes back to his cookie, savoring the delights of homemade goods. He washes it down with a gulp of beer.

With the clicking of heels to announce her presence, Judy walks up to the trio, directing her attention solely on Charlie. She smiles, her gaze purposefully wandering up and down his body, taking it all in. Tipping her head to one side, she asks the question she's been dying to ask all night. "Mr. Maddox. Here to take your father's place, I presume?"

Charlie continues eating his cookie and drinking his beer. His eyes shift from Judy to Herbert. "As much as I'd like to spend some quality time with you fine folk, I have tryouts with the LA Dodgers next week, and then I'll head back home to play pro-ball." Judy runs her eyes over Charlie's body again, taking in his chiseled features and athletic physique. Herbert watches with more than a slight tinge of jealousy.

Judy's eyes finally make their way back up to Charlie's face. "Glad to hear it. Maybe without a coach, we can finally disband the A-Team. I never did like the idea of a team stacked with all-stars."

Abe pipes up. "It did help us win nine World Series, let's not forget."

Judy ignores Abe. "Herbert," she says, still holding eye contact with Charlie, "may I have a word?" She walks off, her heels again clacking against the pavement. Herbert follows Judy like a lost puppy to a secluded area of the school's parking lot.

"Be straight with me, Herbert," Judy says, cornering him.

"What's it going to take for you to bury the building permit, and what's it going to cost to keep the fields?"

Herbert's smirk creeps across his face. "Let one of my travel teams join the league for this season," he counters.

"Out of the question. The teams have already been selected."

Herbert's eerie grin makes a reappearance. He leans in close to her. "You are president of the League, are you not?"

Judy sighs. "If I do it, you'll deny the permit?"

"Scout's honor," Herbert replies. As Judy turns away, he grabs her arm and whispers into her ear, "Or you could just show me this fabled basement of yours…"

CHAPTER SIX

It was weird, this relationship Charlie had forged with Abe over mere days, when so much time had gone by with no more than a yearly call around the holidays — if nothing else, to maintain the slightest acceptable link with his past. The brothers managed to create a sort of relationship both had yearned for all their lives, but it was different from how Charlie imagined it would be. Abe had changed over the years. Without his competitive spirit to fuel Charlie's resentment, the fiery jealousy once battled during their youth was no longer palpable. All this time, Charlie envisioned himself as the villain who had stolen his brother's future. He certainly wouldn't blame Abe for being the jealous one now, but the man that Abe had grown into didn't seem to have the ability for animosity. No ill will, no grudge — none of it.

In Abe's mind, his future was something that couldn't be stolen. He found safety in the refuge and security of the Lord. In fact, Abe told Charlie that over time he became grateful for the accident that occurred back then. Having his baseball career cut short at an early age was discouraging, but it had acted like a sharp curveball, redirecting his entire life. The new destination to which he was en route ended up being somewhere he never would have imagined nor chosen for himself. It had never even been a thought, yet he fell into it by default. Looking back, Abe shared that he owed it all to the Man upstairs. It was He who worked in mysterious ways, and He knew from the start that Abe was destined to be one of His own. Abe's livelihood was now rooted in a safe, comfortable, sort of *mediocre* position, Charlie thought — but did Abe see it like that? Avoiding mediocrity didn't seem to be a goal for him. Charlie, on the other hand, feared mediocrity. Being "average" would never satisfy him. He always wanted to be at his peak, both mentally and physically; to master the art *and* mindfulness of the game.

Charlie rolls up to the edge of the main field in his Mustang and exits the vehicle. Baseball fields... They were like a magnet for him. He stayed on top of his practice, no matter the geographical location or situation. Shoeless Joe trots behind Charlie as he walks across the field, over to Abe, who sits in left field, staring down at the grass. He could be praying, Charlie supposed.

"Gee, you live an exciting life," Charlie says, interrupting his brother's meditative state. "Watching the grass grow?"

Without looking up, Abe responds, "I'm waiting for it to reach optimal height before I mow." He sticks a ruler into the field's greenery.

"And you get paid for this?"

Still, Abe doesn't look up. "The league pays me three hundred and fifty dollars each month to keep the grass at the right height."

"Wow... Gardening *and* preaching. Living life at Mach 10 there, bro."

"It's my job, idiot. God works in mysterious ways, and what you sow, so shall you reap."

"Wanna see something slightly more interesting? I've been working on a new pitch."

"You finally perfected it?" Abe asks.

Charlie bows his head for a moment and then surges with renewed confidence and a smile. "Come watch." Without waiting for an answer, he's halfway to the mound by the time Abe decides to follow. It's not like he has any better plans awaiting him right now, anyway. Nicky's at a playdate, and writing his sermon can wait.

An oversized bucket filled with balls sits near the dugout. Charlie jogs over and brings it to the mound with him. Abe stands on the side, observing. Then Charlie winds up... He throws the ball. As the pitch hurtles toward home, a strange curveball-slider hybrid, Abe looks stunned.

"Holy cow," he exclaims. "What in the Father's name was that?"

Charlie has a satisfied grin on his face. "Half slider, half curveball. I call it the 'slushie.'" Happy to have impressed his brother with the new pitch, Charlie delivers a few more across the plate. Abe watches, pondering his strategy to get a piece of that thing.

Shortly after, Abe steps up to the plate with a bat in hand. He takes a practice swing. It had been a long time, with him on the plate and Charlie on the mound. Charlie winds up for the pitch. He looks at Abe, who stares back at him, suddenly frozen. Change of plans... Charlie pitches it nice and easy over the plate. Abe connects and sends the ball straight into the outfield. Now, a second ball sails into the outfield, and soon, another one. Shoeless Joe fetches the balls as they rain down onto the field, one by one. Abe's game picks up with every pitch. Then comes the home run.

On the adjacent field, bumbling groundskeepers Norm and Patrick had been sending poisonous gas down the gopher holes to eradicate a new case of pests. Abe's homer lands on the field, barely missing the two men. They seize the opportunity for a break and cross the field to return the ball to the other side. Norm, always the nosy one, wants to know who the star player could be.

"Nice hit, Abe." Norm's booming voice attracts the attention of the brothers. Charlie looks amused; Abe, not so much.

Norm's buddy Patrick can't bear to be left out. "Even I could've hit that outta the park."

"You take an at-bat, Paddy, you'd better hit it outta the park," Norm comments before slapping his friend in the gut. "'Cause you ain't runnin' nowhere with all those cupcakes under your shirt." Patrick's face turns sour while Norm diverts his attention back to Abe. "How's it going, Abe? Need a real—"

Patrick's jaw drops as he looks to see who's on the mound.

"Charlie Maddox," he exclaims, staring in awe. Norm turns to look, his eyes wide. The men walk up to Charlie and nervously force handshakes, gazing upon him like he's a rockstar. Although they both have the sudden urge to kneel at the feet of their hometown hero, they recite his history instead.

"Summer of '93," Norm begins. "Our first World Series Championship game. Score tied. Last inning. One out. Runners on second and third. Count full—"

Patrick jumps in. "You look over at your dad. He signals you to hit one out of the park—"

"And you hit one out of the park and win us the championship," Norm concludes proudly. They continue to stare in awe.

Refusing to be left out, Abe storms over to the mound. "Hey, what about me?" His question comes out with a defensive tone, out of character for the man he now prides himself on being. "I was on third base. That makes me the *winning* run."

"Still trying to steal the glory from your brother?" Norm asks, eyeing Abe with a smirk.

Patrick scoffs and looks at Norm. "You know what they say. Those who can play, play ball. Those who *can't* — coach."

Norm chimes in, "And those who can't coach, *coach T-ball*." He and Patrick exchange a high-five and boisterous laughter.

Amid the raucous commotion, Abe turns to Charlie and says, "And those who can't *do either* trap gophers on a T-ball field." Now, Charlie and Abe laugh while Norm and Patrick look sourly at them.

No one notices Judy approaching from behind until she calls out, "Oh, boys…" Norm and Patrick turn around to face the woman. She follows up as firmly as a school principal. "Are we all playing nice?"

"Yes, Ms. Judy," Patrick confirms. "We're all taking turns and sharing real nice… Aren't we, boys?" Abe sneers in response.

"Boys, boys, boys. If you can't play nice, I'm going to put you all in time-out." Judy's now all business, having grown tired of playing "mommy" with the "boys." She looks down at her phone and squints. Her critical gaze soon enough returns to Norm and Patrick. They look away. "Finished early today, have we, Norm? Patrick?"

Norm looks down, purposefully avoiding her gaze. "Gopher traps are all set, ma'am."

Patrick does his best to avoid eye contact, looking everywhere but at Judy. "That's right, ma'am — nothing more we can do 'til tomorrow."

Judy gives them a penetrating glare before turning to Charlie. She bites her bottom lip, her eyes running over his handsome physique. "Are you busy, Charlie?"

Charlie looks caught off guard at the question. "I was just about to leave, actually. Got a hot date with a cold beer."

Judy leers at Charlie like a wolf eyeing its prey a moment before pouncing. "Well, do you mind if I chaperone? There's been a development I need to talk with you about."

"Only if the boys here can join us," Charlie replies, pointing his head in the direction of Norm and Patrick.

Norm tries to mediate. "Yeah, it's happy hour, and I'm buying. Got my residual check yesterday, and it's burning a hole in my pocket."

"It's been a long time between drinks," Judy murmurs, as if to herself. Then, louder, "I'm in. Let me tell the hired help to pick up the kids from school." She barely finishes speaking before she steps away from the group, her phone pressed to her ear.

Charlie and his new friends look to Abe expectantly. "I'll pass. Still got a lot to do out here," he says, motioning to the field, more than happy to stay behind.

◊ ◊ ◊

Judy and Charlie, with Norm and Patrick lagging behind, walk into the local sports bar. The group heads to a table in the back. On their way past the dimly lit bar, Norm and Patrick acknowledge the bartender.

"Hey, Frank," Patrick calls.

"Norm, Paddy, good to see ya," the bartender responds

cheerily.

Once the group settles in their seats, Judy wastes no time. She cuts right to the chase. "Boys, I added one of Herbert Turner's teams, the Giants, to our roster."

Patrick nearly spits out his beer but thinks better of it and swallows. He then grabs a glass of water instead, drinks it, and does his own spit-take. "Why would you do that?!"

Charlie picks up his beer and answers for Judy. "Obvious — he wants our wildcard slot." He takes a big gulp.

"What about the As? They're the ones who deserve the slot," Patrick spews.

"It's the only way he can get his team in the championship," Charlie adds with a shrug.

Patrick, needing to buy all the vowels, continues. "But why allow it?"

Charlie refrains from hitting Patrick upside the head, thinking that one more blow to the cranium was the last thing the goof needed. "He's holding our fields ransom," Charlie responds calmly. "If his team doesn't play, neither will ours."

Judy smiles at Charlie with approval. "Not just a pretty face." She turns abruptly to Norm and Patrick. "Dummies. No field, no play baseball. No play baseball, no wildcard slot. Get it?"

The bar door opens suddenly, casting a stream of light over the darkened room, and in walks Hank, a short man in an umpire's uniform. In his mid-fifties, ulcer-ridden and grumpy, Hank holds tightly to his dream of living in another era and playing baseball with the New York Giants on the Polo Grounds with greats like Babe Ruth. He takes a seat at the end of the bar, his face set into a perpetual scowl from umpiring the Youth Summer League over the last twenty-five years. It had been so long, but still, Charlie instantly recognizes his reclusive uncle. He had been a fair man who seemed to understand young Charlie's emotional journey back then more than Gordon ever could.

Glancing down at his watch, Charlie grins. "One o'clock on the dot. Guess some things never change." Being Charlie's late mother's brother, Hank had once been a warmly welcomed member of the family. When she passed, that connection faded away, and he became known as nothing more than his first name, without the title of 'uncle.' In fact, since his mother's passing, no one in the family retained their titles. 'Dad' became 'Gordon,' almost as though without a mom, there could be no dad. It didn't help that Gordon, the team coach, had always been at odds with Hank, the one to call the shots as umpire. Hank had become a bit of a recluse who always seemed to be carrying the weight of the world on his shoulders. Charlie excuses himself from the table and takes a stool next to Hank, wondering if his uncle will recognize him since he had been away from home for so long.

"Uncle Hank," Charlie says. Hank graces him with a quick glance, no acknowledgement otherwise, before turning back to his beer.

"It's me, Charlie Maddox. Mr. G's son."

"I may be an umpire, but I'm not blind. I know who you are," Hank replies. Taking a swig of beer, he looks Charlie up and down, barely recognizing the confident man he's become. "Your father's not doing too well. He wants you to coach the As."

"I know, Hank. I know." Charlie nods solemnly.

"So, why won't ya?" Hank makes brief eye contact with Charlie for the first time. He goes to take another drink of beer but stops and sets the bottle on the bar. "Those kids don't just need a coach, Charlie. They need a Maddox behind them. Heck, most of them don't even know how to wipe their own nose, let alone play ball."

Charlie lets out a sigh. "I don't pander to Gordon anymore. I've moved on with my life."

"What life? The one he wanted your brother to have?" *Bastard.* "You still think I've got all the answers? I don't. I never did." Hank bows his head. "I'm sorry, kid. I should have been there." The mood turns somber as the man recounts his failures. Would Charlie feel that same way in thirty years? He tries to shake it off.

"I finally got my shot at trying out for the Dodgers," Charlie says after an extended silence. "I'll hear back in a couple of weeks." No response from Hank. Charlie scoffs, his brows furrowed. "Does that not mean anything around here? It's a real shot at the bigs for me."

"Well, how-de-do. Would've thought you'd have aged out of that dream by now." Hank takes a sip of his beer. Nothing would shake that overwhelming feeling of sadness from the broken man's soul. He reaches into his bag and pulls out a ratty baseball. It has handwritten initials on it in faded but still legible ink: "CM." He sets the baseball down in front of Charlie. "It's yours. You carry it." Charlie picks up the ball and a taste of Hank's guilt along with it. "You ever think it might be time to heal an old wound?"

Frank, the bartender, motions to Charlie — but Charlie doesn't feel like another drink. He *feels* like drowning his memories in an entire bottle of Jack Daniels. But not here. Well, what do you know? The first time Charlie tries smoothing over the jagged lines of history, he ends up getting cut on the sharp edges instead. Charlie's phone vibrates on the bar. He seizes the opportunity to step away, with the ball reluctantly clutched in his hand, leaving his recluse of an uncle to wallow in his own sorrow. Being an umpire for so many years had taken a toll on Hank, forced to stand by and watch as the innocence of countless children turned corrupt.

Charlie walks out the bar to answer the phone call — it's Earl. "Hey, thanks for calling back. How'd it go with everything? Hype me up? Hadn't heard from you for a while."

"Yeah, been busy here. We could really use you. When do you think you can make it?"

"Soon. I'll see what I can do. Just trying to find someone to coach Gordon's team before I leave. He's a bit stuck right now. Wants me to coach, but I don't think I'm up to it."

"You're not tempted?"

"Me coaching a bunch of whiny preteens? No way. Not my cup of tea."

"Good to hear. We had a few injuries, and your coach is pressuring me to fill your shoes... Might need you to cut your plans short and get back to the game here."

"I'll wrap things up ASAP. But you know, I really want that gig with the Dodgers, Earl."

"And it might take a few more years of playing out here — but nothing is ever wasted."

"Sure, yeah, I know the drill."

CHAPTER SEVEN

Today is Field Appreciation Day. A colorful banner drapes across the main field's batting cage. Team spirit fills the air, with plenty of hands on deck ready to make this day a success. Some of the parents work to pick up random bits of trash, while others paint the dugouts in bright, cheerful colors of blue and red. In that moment, it didn't matter that the fields may or may not be demolished within the next few months or even weeks. All that matters is seizing the time they have left and making it nothing short of a celebration. There was no time to let the worries of the future affect their ability to enjoy the *now*.

Charlie and Abe sat in left field, pulling weeds by hand. So many people Charlie had known once upon a time would be there today. His anxiety was kicking in, but in all honesty, he was proud to have come back with his head held high. As a pro-ball player, he wasn't the most well known, but he certainly was no longer an unknown either. The day was off to a warm, sunny start, and taking care of the grounds was not an easy task under the beating sun. Sweat already poured from Charlie and Abe like a fountain.

Abe stands and wipes his brow. "I'm parched… Break for a drink?"

"Yeah, sure." Charlie stands, squinting as he looks over at the nearby snack bar. His eyes widen — he sees Teri manning the station. "Actually, I'm not all that thirsty, but you go ahead."

Abe turns to the snack bar and chuckles, shaking his head. "Scared, doofus?"

"I ain't scared. I'm just…" Charlie says, eyes still locked on the snack bar. "She was the first, Abe. First crush. First kiss. First steady girl. First—"

"Heartbreak?"

"That too."

Abe puts a hand on Charlie's shoulder. "Well, maybe it's time to heal an old wound." It wasn't the first time Charlie had heard that.

Over at the snack bar, now twenty-nine, a caring kindergarten teacher and single mom with a heart full of love and patience, Teri had taken over the role of "team mom." Her responsibilities included securing the team trophies and keeping the snack bar fully stocked with food and beverages. Right now she was in the midst of organizing the other moms as they prepared sandwiches, desserts, and drinks. Some of them were in the process of decorating the snack bar with ribbons and motivating posters to amp up the team spirit.

Teri looks out across the field and sees the two brothers. Should she be the one to break the ice? She'd need to talk to him eventually... Teri's gaze locks onto Charlie, who appears to be returning the look, as she wipes down the bar of the concession stand. She lifts a hand to her necklace and fidgets with a heart-shaped pendant.

Silva, one of the volunteer parents, notices Teri's almost robotic state and asks, "Old flame, huh?" Teri doesn't answer; she's too lost in thought. Silva gives her a nudge. "Why don't you go say hi?"

Teri quickly looks away from Charlie and blushes. "I... I couldn't do that."

Meanwhile, Charlie gives into his need for hydration and makes his way toward the stand. He needs to swallow his pride, that's all. Just get it over and done with. Baseball was the one thing they still had in common, and they'd be running into one another all summer. It would be even more awkward if they were both actively avoiding each other. Someone needed to say something, and today was the day.

Still behind the bar, Teri looks up and sees Charlie approaching. Her eyes widen in shock. She quickly hides the heart pendant under her shirt and nervously fluffs her hair.

Sure, she used to know the man who was fast approaching. She knew him very well, in fact, but that was a long time ago. So long… How much had he changed since they last met?

Teri's eleven-year-old son Seth, and a solid left-handed pitcher who loves everything about baseball, practices on the side with one of his teammates. Seth suddenly drops the ball when he notices Charlie and takes off running toward the snack bar. He must alert his mom that someone amazing is about to grace them with his presence.

Unreservedly excited, Seth reaches the stand and yells to Teri, "Mom, it's him! It's Charlie Maddox!" Moments later, Charlie reaches the snack bar, smiling awkwardly at Teri. She returns an equally awkward smile. Seth stands by, starstruck, jaw almost to the floor.

"Hey," Charlie says, frozen in place. It takes every bit of motivation not to turn and run.

Teri stares back at Charlie. After a long delay, she replies, "Hey."

"Mom," Seth butts in, "this is Charlie Maddox! The best baseball player ever to come out of this town." Awkward silence between the two adults while Seth continues to stare in awe.

"I know who he is, Seth," Teri says, never once breaking her gaze from Charlie.

"Mom, huh?" Charlie questions. He gives Seth a pat on the head. "How are you doing, buddy?" The boy looks overjoyed by his hero's recognition.

Teri pulls her son close. "He's about to start a twelve-step program for baseball addicts." The adults chuckle for a moment until another awkward silence descends. Charlie and Teri avoid eye contact, but Seth doesn't seem to notice, still beaming up at Charlie. Teri clears her throat. "Did you, uh, need anything?" Teri begins. "From the snack bar?"

Charlie comes back to the present. "Oh. Yeah, uh — two Cokes. Please," he stammers. Teri smiles and turns to the mini fridge that houses the beverages. As she hands the soda cans to him, the two lock eyes.

Charlie diverts his gaze suddenly. "Well, I'd better get back to fixing up the fields. It'll be a busy day…"

"Good to meet you, Mr. Maddox," Seth blurts. "Hope to see you again."

Charlie smiles. "Sure. Good to meet you too. Nice to see you, Teri." The small talk was awkward as expected, but they had to start somewhere. Besides, Seth's jubilance had helped.

"You too," Teri says with a smile.

Charlie returns to Abe with the drinks in hand, thinking how the encounter went better than he had imagined it would. Teri was as beautiful as he remembered, with the same smile that could still melt his heart. What a fantastic precursor to the season…

The clusters of parents and kids worked hard to get the grounds into good shape for Opening Day. It was one of those few days on the field that lacked the usual competitiveness and angst, where the parent simply relaxed and supported their kids. Something had changed on his home turf, but Charlie couldn't quite put his finger on it. Gordon was still coaching the team, despite his current absence. Was the lighter mood due to Gordon being MIA or had his coaching ethics miraculously changed over the years? He would have to ask Abe.

As the day comes to a close, Charlie, Abe, and Teri find themselves sitting on the hood of the Mustang, admiring the fruits of their labor. The camaraderie between he and Teri almost reminds Charlie of old times. Empty Coke cans litter the pavement below the Mustang. Shoeless Joe dutifully picks the cans up one by one, bringing each to the trash until none remain. On the field, Seth and Nicky play together, along with a few other kids whose parents are still hanging around, simply enjoying the afternoon and catching up with the other parents they only see during the Youth Summer League season. Meanwhile, the trio of old pals sits there, reminiscing about their days as teens. Back then, their priorities were simple and the highlight of the day was playing pranks on the neighbors around town. They were able to just have fun without worrying about the consequences of their actions.

Charlie looks out at the kids playing on the field. His gaze lands on Seth. "He's a good lookin' kid."

"Thanks," Teri answers. "I made him myself."

"Oh, yeah? How does that work?"

Teri laughs faintly. "Well, I had a hand. Obviously."

"Obviously. Where is he?"

"Not in the picture." Teri evades Charlie's gaze for a moment.

Charlie conceals a smile. "How'd you end up doing at UCLA?"

"I dropped out."

"Really?" Charlie asks, his eyebrows raised in question. "You were so into it. I remember when you got in. You didn't talk about anything else for weeks... Annoyed the hell outta me." Teri laughs, brushing it off, but something gnaws at Charlie. He vividly remembered how much UCLA had meant to her. Certainly more than going on the road with him. Why would she abandon the one thing she had quit their relationship for? He had to know. Teri can sense Charlie's mind racing as he holds back from asking why. Finally, she assuages his curiosity.

Teri slides off the hood of the Mustang and turns to face him. "Got pregnant." A moment of silence passes. She waits for him to realize... To count the years... But he doesn't get it.

"Tough break."

"Yeah," Teri says, trying to keep the disappointment from showing on her face. She quickly changes the subject, refusing to get caught up in the past she had spent so long trying to forget. "Those were the days. Almost feels like we should go TP someone's house now, huh?"

"Sure. Just let me stop home and grab my Letterman jacket," Charlie says with a laugh. Even back then, when they were nothing else but free and impulsive, there had been a sort of pride, a trendy "uniform" for all to wear. Abe's pastoral life nowadays didn't leave him with much interest for mischief.

Actually, the most mischievous thing he'd gotten into recently were his weird and wonderful science experiments that had the tendency to get out of hand every now and again.

Always the more sensitive one, Charlie's most affected by the nostalgia bug that's going around. He shakes his head. "Things weren't so complicated back then."

Teri doesn't give into the melancholic meanderings. "But it's better now. We're grownups… Or at least I am," she jokes, casting a flirty look at Charlie for the first time in a long time. She holds his gaze and continues, "We can do what we want when we want. Well, as long as we put in a fifty-hour work week, pay the bills, play mother and father, *and* get up every day just to do it all over again."

Overwhelmed by Teri's dose of reality, Abe reflects on his own current life choices and the responsibilities that come along with them. "Preach sermons, counsel teenagers, listen to married couples complain about money, mind the flock, feed the homeless, aid the sick, *and* pray for the dying."

Charlie chimes in. "Hit a fastball going ninety-two miles an hour…" Whose life was the hardest, really? Reflecting on the various burdens and responsibilities of their individual lives, Charlie realized his own was pretty good. He says coyly, "So, am I some kind of local hero around here or what?"

Abe confirms with a nod. "Not only are you a legend in your own mind but the kids around here worship you too." Charlie unconsciously stands taller due to the ego boost but consciously stops the words from going to his head and possibly endangering his renewed connections. He wants to know more about Teri and asks about her life. She gives him the basics and glosses over the details for now.

◊ ◊ ◊

Later that night, Charlie returns to the field alone except for the company of Shoeless Joe. Something was nagging at him deep down inside, but what? Everything had gone so well earlier that day. Maybe it was something Teri or Abe had said, or was it Hank and that godforsaken ball? Why had his uncle held onto it for so long, anyway? What did it matter to him? Sure, he was an experienced umpire, but not everything that happened on the field was his business. He needed to keep his eyes on his own paper for once.

Shoeless Joe watches Charlie as he obliterates ball after ball from a pitching machine on the mound. Still in the zone of reminiscing, Charlie replays the fateful event that occurred on that very same field.

Twelve years ago, Charlie, at age seventeen, was in the middle of warming up his pitching arm, while Abe, sixteen, busied himself with putting on his catcher's gear.

A younger, more tenacious Gordon approached them. "Listen up, boys, and I mean, *listen up*. Do you see that bald guy over there? That's a scout from UCLA. He's here to watch you two play." Gordon paused to focus on Charlie. "Charlie, this is a big moment. Don't mess this one up too." Charlie's body tensed ever so slightly as he worked to stand his ground.

Abe was the one they watched. Abe was the one they wanted. And there Charlie went, throwing a temper tantrum like a two-year-old and blowing the most important opportunity of Abe's life. After all these years, Charlie thinks about everything he had messed up during the first seventeen years of his life — his relationship with Gordon, his relationship with Teri... So many years had been lost. Years that could never be brought back. If only he had known then what he knew now. Gordon's words from long ago rang in Charlie's head. *Don't mess this one up too.* It felt as though Gordon had put a sort of curse on him with those words. As though each day moving forward would be dictated by his constant screw-ups and the repercussions he experienced while cleaning up the messes he had made. Charlie silently wishes away those words and their ill intent.

Darkness has descended over the lonely baseball field. Charlie stares up into the starry sky. "There to watch *us*, hey, Dad?" He shakes his head in frustration and rummages around in his gear bag, hoping to find a beer can that isn't already empty.

When he removes his hand from the bag, he instead pulls out the old baseball with the faded initials. The one Hank had held onto for all those years.

"More like there to watch *Abe*." Charlie tosses the ball into the air and slams it out of the park. Shoeless Joe diligently takes off to retrieve it, leaving Charlie on pause, leaning on his bat and drinking a beer. Joe returns the ball to Charlie, who takes it. "Could've been me and Teri, tearin' up the campus..." Charlie tosses the ball high into the air. "Together." A loud crack resounds through the open field, and the ball again sails over the fence.

Two beers and plenty of hits later, Charlie yells at Joe, upset. "Just leave it where it lands already!" The misdirected anger has been a long time coming. It doesn't take long for Charlie to realize that his loyal mate, his precious pup had only been doing what he was trained to do. Charlie was the one refusing to do what needed to be done. He could have stopped hitting the ball at any time. Chucked it into one of the nearby trash cans. Just let it go. All of it. Charlie sits on home plate, empty beer cans surrounding him. Shoeless Joe stands patiently beside him, holding the ball in his mouth. The dog whines, confused.

"Give it a rest, Joe," Charlie says as he gets to his feet with some effort and slinks into the dugout with his gear bag in tow and Joe right behind him. Charlie takes a seat on the bench, a familiar spot for him, and opens his bag to pull out another beer. Something catches his eye inside the bag. He pulls out his wallet and opens it, revealing a faded photo — the one of him and Teri, sitting around a bonfire, their arms linked. This is Charlie's favorite. He smiles wide into the camera while Teri smiles cheekily up at him. Suddenly, the past rushes back like a wave, and Charlie has no choice but to surrender and let the ocean pull him further off-shore. Eyes frozen on the photo, he pops open another beer, and another, and another...

CHAPTER EIGHT

J ack, resident troublemaker of Abe's youth group, stands at the head of a line of kids that wraps around the dugout the next afternoon. It all started with Jack's early morning (or late night) stroll, when he noticed Shoeless Joe wandering alone nearby the fields. The dog led Jack to Charlie, passed out on the small dugout bench. All it took was one photo posted to social media of the now *infamous* Charlie Maddox, passed out, seemingly unconscious. Naturally, the hometown "scandal" goes viral, resulting in the long line of kids, each waiting for their own selfie with Charlie at two bucks a pop. Complimentary uploads of each photo goes straight to the new Instagram page Jack has set up just for the occasion.

When the next kid in line steps up, Jack encourages a cheeky pose just like a pro photographer and quickly snaps a pic of the kid alongside a still unconscious Charlie.

"Next," Jack calls out. He takes the two bucks offered up by the next kid in line. Further down in the line stands Casey Ragsdale, a newly-turned twelve-year-old, and Seth. Shoeless Joe sits behind them, two one-dollar bills tucked in his collar. The boys are in the middle of a Charlie-centric conversation. Casey looks impressed when Seth mentions that he and his mom are "friends" with the pro-ball player.

"You think he's gonna teach you how to pitch?" Casey asks, wide-eyed.

"I think so," Seth answers with a smirk. "Pretty sure he's got the hots for my mom." Casey gives Seth a fist bump of approval.

Meanwhile, Charlie begins to stir on the dugout bench just a few feet away. He looks around in a drunken haze, slowly piecing it all together as he watches Jack snap a photo on his phone before one of the kids happily trots out of the dugout.

Charlie blurts out, "What's going on? Who are you?" Panic visibly begins to overtake him. "Where— Where am I?" He sits up too quickly and grimaces in pain. His hand goes straight to his head, cradling it.

Jack seizes the moment, turning to the remaining kids in line, who stare excitedly, mouths agape. "Everybody, stand back!" He looks back at Charlie reassuringly. "Don't worry, Mr. Maddox. I have everything under control." Jack takes a step toward the kids and opens his mouth to issue another warning — but all hell breaks loose as the kids clamor over to Charlie, climbing, jumping, and piling onto him while he does his best to maintain his temper, brushing them off one by one.

Jack looks at the onslaught of overexcited children. He had tried to stop them, after all, so he moves onto the next best thing. Turning back to the handful of kids still waiting patiently in line, Jack yells, "Okay, now that he's awake, that'll be four bucks a piece!"

Shoeless Joe bursts through the crowd with a water bottle in his mouth. He nudges it toward Charlie, who lunges for it and pours the water over his head, dousing the kids in the process. They screech and giggle happily.

"Good boy." Charlie gives Joe a pat on the head — and then notices the two dollars stuck into his collar. "You too, Joe?" The dog whines in response.

Jack makes another futile attempt at crowd control. "Relax! Give the man some air!" Charlie manages to break free from the onslaught and escape the cramped dugout. Seth and a few others follow after him. Without turning around, Charlie says, "Later, boys."

Seth hurries to catch up. "Mr. Maddox, wait! We want you to run the clinic today."

Charlie stops and turns to face Seth. He sighs. "Sorry, kid, but the only clinic I'm interested in is one that can cure a hangover. I've got to be ready for tryouts."

Seth doesn't give up so easily. "Please. We gotta get some practice in."

"That's not my job. I *play* ball, not watch from the sidelines." Charlie grimaces as a wave of nausea washes over him. He shakes his head and walks off the field. He whispers to no one, "I don't belong here."

A few of the kids had been following behind Seth and Charlie. One of them yells out, evidently crushed to see Charlie leaving, "My dad says you're just a third-rate hack with zero chance of making the majors."

Charlie hears the comment but keeps walking, summoning every ounce of willpower to stop him from going off on the kid. Instead, he mutters to himself, "Well, I got news for ya, buddy. Dads don't know jack." Realizing he should be proud of what he's already achieved, Charlie visibly swells with pride, unwilling to let his poor decisions make a fool out of him. He glances back at the kid. "Your dad would give up everything to trade places with me." The kid stares back with a sour look, his arms crossed over his chest. Charlie stomps off, leaving the rest of them watching, disappointed.

On his way through the parking lot, Charlie notices Brian Ragsdale, Casey's father, who leans against a huge luxury RV. The Ragsdale family is old money, and Brian's the biggest deal in town. As Charlie approaches the Mustang, Brian forcefully offers his hand for a shake. Charlie tries to ignore him.

"Brian Ragsdale, Casey's father. It's an honor to meet you, Mr. Maddox." Charlie walks straight past the man, without any acknowledgement. Brian doesn't seem fazed and continues. "I see there's some confusion about who's running the clinic for today."

"No confusion here," Charlie replies as he reaches the driver's side of the Mustang. He unlocks the Mustang, and by the time he looks up, Brian is standing beside him and physically forces a handshake onto Charlie — with a few crisp one-hundred-dollar bills inside.

"That oughta clear it up," says Brian. He nods toward the

money in Charlie's hand.

Charlie peers down briefly and lets out a scoff. After a long pause, he makes eye contact with Brian for the first time. "I'm gonna need a *hell* of a lot of aspirin today..." Brian chuckles, and just like that, he slaps another hundred into Charlie's hand. Charlie pockets the cash and heads back the way he came.

The kids gather around on the field. Seth jumps up and down excitedly and points at Charlie as he steps back onto the field. "Guys, look!" A joyful murmur runs through the crowd of kids as they whisper to one another, waiting to see what's going on.

"Alright, kids," Charlie starts. He winces up at the sun beating down over the field, already regretting it. "Let's go." The kids cheer loudly, eliciting another wince from Charlie (this time, of pain), and disperse across the field. Jack quickly falls into line beside Charlie, who slowly walks toward the mound.

Jack throws an arm around Charlie's shoulder as if they were old pals. "You look like you're gonna need some help, man."

Charlie keeps walking. He doesn't even turn his head. "And you are?"

Jack steps directly in Charlie's path and offers his hand. Charlie stops but doesn't shake his hand. "Jack D. Ross. Consider me your assistant coach for the day. Twenty bucks, and I'll help you run the clinic."

Charlie looks the cocky teen up and down. Jack looks bright-eyed, athletic, and enthusiastic... He certainly knows how to command attention, what with the hubbub earlier that morning (granted, a hubbub Jack himself had caused, unbeknownst to Charlie). A good leader makes a good assistant, Charlie pondered. "Well, Jack D. Ross... Consider yourself hired —for today."

The day progresses, with Charlie and Jack working together to coach the kids. Jack tosses a tennis ball high into the air, and Charlie hits the ball up toward the sky with a tennis racket. The kids race to catch it. Meanwhile, another group of them practice sliding techniques with Shoeless Joe leading them up and down a makeshift Slip 'N Slide.

Later, the kids stand in the outfield, except for one at-bat and another on third. Jack pitches from the mound. The batter hits the ball and runs to first base as the runner on third rockets toward home. Those in the outfield practice their speed and endurance, trying to tag the two runners out. Soon, those acting as runners join the kids in the outfield for a practice swing session. Charlie and Jack work with the kids, correcting their batting stances, some much worse than others. For the last activity of the day, Jack calls everyone off the field, and they practice hitting the ball with the help of an air-powered batting tee.

Finally, when the day comes to a close, Charlie treats the kids (courtesy of Brian Ragsdale) to food and drinks at the snack bar as a reward for their cooperation and hard work. Charlie can't wait to get his hands on a Coke to re-caffeinate his exhausted mind and body. The snack bar's hours are limited, only open for lunch and the last half-hour of the day. Teri runs the snack bar during today's afternoon shift. She hands over two large trays, piled high with food and drinks. Jack takes the first tray, and Charlie takes the second.

Teri's eyes linger on Charlie. "You're doing a good job," she says with encouragement, smiling. "You look right at home. Who'd have thought you'd turn out to be so great with kids?" Teri laughs. That laugh of hers could still give Charlie goosebumps.

Charlie smiles. "Well… It *is* familiar territory."

"Oh, really? I didn't—"

"I meant the field. I've watched a lot of games here. Right there in that very dugout," Charlie hooks a thumb toward the dugout. "Remember?"

Teri's just about to say something when the kids race over, wildly grabbing snacks and drinks off the trays before darting away as quickly as they came. Nothing remains for Charlie and Jack. The guys turn back to Teri with a sad look on their face and an empty tray in their hand. Charlie's goosebumps overtake once more when Teri laughs again, putting an end to any further conversation between the two — for now.

◊ ◊ ◊

It's been a long weekend. Exhausted and ready to call it a day, Charlie trudges through the parking lot, toward the Mustang. He passes Brian Ragsdale's RV, still hanging around despite the field now being devoid of children. Just as Charlie slides his key into the Mustang's door, Brian emerges from the RV.

He holds open the door and calls out to Charlie, "Mr. Maddox, can I have a word?"

"Depends," Charlie says. He looks up at Brian. "You got any more of that aspirin?"

Moments later, Charlie steps into the RV. He looks around curiously. The RV's walls are fully decked out with baseball memorabilia — tour photos and other relevant merchandise from countless games throughout the years. Clearly, the man has love for the game.

Charlie spots a photo of Brian posing alongside the current Dodgers coach. "You know the coach?"

"If they're important, Charlie, I know 'em," Brian answers.

Charlie nods, trying to look neutral and rather unimpressed. "Nice machine. You travel a bit?"

Brian shakes his head and cracks a smile. "Nah, this here's my wife's two hundred thousand dollar commode. She doesn't like using the ones on the field." Brian turns to the RV's compact fridge. "Have a seat," he urges. Charlie makes himself comfortable on a luxurious couch while Brian pulls out two expensive, exotic-looking beers. He hands a bottle to Charlie.

Charlie takes a swig and grimaces. "Got any *real* beer? This fancy stuff makes me want to paint my nails and get my hair done." Brian laughs and takes a seat opposite Charlie. He sips his beer, studying Charlie intently, and then reaches into his suit jacket, pulling out a check. Brian casually hands the check to Charlie, who stares down at the slip of paper, his eyes wide.

"That's five large," Brian says.

"I can't accept this. I'm not—"

"You take the As all the way this year, there'll be another waiting for you when they lift the trophy."

Charlie sips his beer with another grimace, inspecting the bottle before focusing on Brian. "The LA Dodgers are giving me the chance to tryout."

"There will be time for that," Brian says with an encouraging smile.

"Not until next year." Charlie shakes his head, annoyed.

"C'mon, Charlie, coach the team. What do you want? Another grand? Two? Name it."

"Jesus. What is with you people? Why is a kid's game so much more important than my pro-ball career?"

"You got your start with the As, Charlie, and look where it's taken you. Why deny another kid that same opportunity?" Brian leans in, breaking the gap between them. "We live our lives through them. Don't you get it?"

"Can't say I do."

Brian relaxes back into his seat. Not one to give up without a fight, he asks Charlie, "Remember when you were a kid? Being out on that field, the crowd, the cheers… It means the world to them."

"Consider me a kid, then."

"Look, my wife's throwing you a 'welcome home' party next weekend. You stick around, I'll make it worth your while." Brian nods his head to the photo of him and the Dodgers' coach.

Charlie follows his gaze, his eyes landing on the framed image. Suddenly Charlie's face relaxes into an honest smile. It may very well be the first taste of relief he's had in years. Sure, he's been through enough beer to start up his own brewery, but he couldn't remember the last time he had just "chilled." Maybe that party wouldn't be so bad.

◊ ◊ ◊

Training wasn't reserved only for weekends. Serious teams like the As had midweek practice sessions. Just "winging it" during a game was a sure bet for disaster. Although T-ball was a tame precursor to the competitive nature of Youth Summer League, its players still learned the importance of practice and routine training. With Charlie in town, he found himself tagging along with Abe every now and then.

The Mustang pulls into the familiar parking lot until he's mere feet from where Abe leads his T-ball kids in their practice session of the day. Eight five-year-olds are on the field, each standing in the middle of a large plastic circle marking mock field positions. A few overbearing parents watch from the sidelines.

Abe stands in front of the kids and points to the circles. "These are called 'playing circles.' You go after the ball only if it enters your circle. Got it?" Most of the kids nod enthusiastically and chatter among themselves as Abe moves into position to hit the ball. He sends a gentle hit to second base. Kids from positions all over the field begin to run — but stop when they notice the circles on the ground. Shoeless Joe runs onto the field, joining in at right field. The kids cheer and disperse, distracted by the dog.

Charlie watches from afar. He approaches Abe on the field. "What are you teaching these kids?"

"How to play fair and have fun." Abe turns to face Charlie. "You know, the stuff we *never* learned." An awkward beat passes between the brothers.

Charlie speaks first. "I've been invited to another of those booster club parties… Want to tag along?"

Abe sighs. "I have to counsel troubled teens. Besides, I don't think I'd be welcome."

"Free food…"

"And man shall not live on bread alone," Abe replies. He chuckles when Charlie rolls his eyes. "Hey, want to hang around? Might learn a little something." Charlie scoffs dramatically but smiles. He settles in near the sidelines.

Back on the field, Abe hands out giant flashcards with the names of various field positions handwritten on them. Once everyone has a card, the kids sprint to their respective positions and then sprint back. Meanwhile, Abe has set up various training stations that the kids quickly move through.

Charlie watches as one of the kids hits three balls off a tee, followed by three throws and catches with a bounce-back. They all run the bases, flapping their arms like birds. The batter then runs five feet to pick up a ball that's waiting for him, and he throws it to no one. Afterward, Abe splits the kids into two groups and has them run a relay race around the bases. Each kid must run an extra five feet past first base and tag Abe's hand before moving on. Shoeless Joe reappears at home plate with a small bat in his mouth. He hits a ball off the tee. Charlie watches, intrigued by all of this free-spirited training, and soon enough, he joins in. He hits a fly ball, and Shoeless Joe runs to catch it. Joe brings the ball to second base and drops it for a double play. By then, all the kids are playing, chasing the dog around the bases. Leave it to Abe to remind everyone about the fun of the game.

On the other side of town, Herbert's elite baseball training camp is in session. The kids here, most from wealthy families, are used to having the *best* — nothing less than top-of-the-line. Thirty kids dressed in military-style uniforms run around one of the fields in a strict formation. This place could nearly pass as a Marine Corps boot camp. Fences topped with barbed wire surround the entire compound, making escape futile. One lone sentry stands in the guard tower, watching over the players as he regretfully daydreams about being a catcher for the MLB. The kids carry around bats like machine guns and run through obstacle courses as fake explosions go off around them. On one of the baseball fields, Billy Higgins slides into second base. The base explodes into a giant puff of smoke.

Sergeant Dick, a retired Marine, storms over to him. "Son, you are DOA! You are a disgrace to your unit! You failed to take that hill! What do you have to say for yourself?!"

Billy gets to his feet and stands at attention. "Sir, it won't happen again, sir."

"Drop and give me one hundred," the sergeant shouts at Billy. Just then, Herbert and his assistant coach, Guy, who is fresh out of college, walk past. Sergeant Dick falls into line behind them. Always chasing after Herbert's approval, the sergeant asks him, "What do you want to do about Privates Jefferson and Williams, Mr. Turner? Their performance is subpar."

"Yes… But how much disposable income do Jefferson's parents have?"

Coach Guy checks his phone. "According to their credit report, they live on the hill. Two Mercedes and an RV. Looks like they're up to their eyeballs in debt, but it surely doesn't show."

A group of twelve-year-olds in formation, led by a squad leader, runs by. The squad leader starts chanting, "Mama and Papa were layin' in bed!"

The kids respond, echoing, "Mama and Papa were layin' in bed!"

"Mama rolled over, and this is what she said!"

"Mama rolled over, and this is what she said," echo the kids.

Sergeant Dick watches the group go by and nods his approval before turning back to Herbert with his advice. "Second string both privates while you bleed their parents dry, sir. Then you make the privates miserable until they drop out. And finally, sir, the privates would be excellent candidates for special ops batting lessons."

CHAPTER NINE

C harlie and Shoeless Joe are in the middle of a walk around the neighborhood when they stumble onto a construction site. It's the new baseball fields, Charlie realizes, and they curiously stop to watch the goings-on. Charlie beams with excitement. He was enjoying the downtime more than he expected. It was nice being able to reacquaint himself with the landscape of his distant childhood. This was his hometown. He was born here, he grew up here, and yet, the only place he had wanted to be back then was anywhere *but* here. Maybe one day he would travel the world just like he had always dreamed — visit Japan, China, Korea, Puerto Rico, and the Caribbean, where baseball was also embraced. But for now, in this moment, he was content to be walking on familiar ground.

As Charlie and Shoeless Joe approach, they see Abe standing with his back to them, watching engineers and surveyors scope out the area. "What's going on here, Abe?"

Abe turns around, mildly surprised to hear Charlie's voice behind him. "Our new fields." Charlie and Joe step closer, observing Abe as he stares into the emptiness of the construction area, dreaming of what it might become. "It's the beginning of a new era, Charlie. This will become a main hub, and not just for baseball — for families."

Charlie nods his approval. "Where are you gonna plant the cornfields?" Abe laughs in response, amused. "But if you could? I mean, you have the Man upstairs in your back pocket..." Charlie chuckles to himself. "Why is the school district insisting on moving the fields?"

"Everything's a money grab. Must have something to do with the land. Plus, it's the league who pays me, so that's all I know. But just think about it... On these new fields here, there'd be more room for other kids to play too." Abe puts on his "preacher voice," the one that suggests anything is possible, and he points to the fields. "Imagine... Over there we'll have *two* T-ball fields. We won't have to turn away any more five-year-olds who don't make the initial cut."

"Won't that make playoffs harder for them? Diminish the value of the game?"

"Ah," Abe starts, "but the value of the game is *in* the game, is it not? Besides, we're doing away with playoffs for five-year-olds." He points to another area of the construction site. "And over there we'll have a challenger field where any special needs kids can play. We'll have a Sunday afternoon league too, where ex-minor league players will be invited to come down. Free hotdogs, lemonade, peanuts... Families will come from all around to watch baseball being played on a hot Sunday afternoon. Like I said, the beginning of a new era — all sponsored by the very shopping center forcing us out here."

"How do you plan to get all this past the 'Madam President'? Or the school district?"

"I'll have to wave some of that green under Judy's nose. Convince her that the more kids we bring in, the more money the league could make." Abe gets lost in thought, imagining what good the changes could bring.

Charlie nods his head, looking out over the empty fields. "See, that's what *you* need to do. Make it happen. You live here. You work on the grounds. Isn't that what the Bible says — if you see something, say something?"

"I don't think that's in the Bible, but sure, making a difference is important for all of us. I will try my best and see what's possible. Are you up for helping me campaign a bit?"

Charlie blurts, "Ahhh — no." Abe barely even blinks; that was the answer he expected. On one hand, Charlie admired his brother's faith, but he himself wasn't into all that asking and receiving stuff. He was happy to prod along Abe and his dreams, but Charlie had low hopes when it came to getting anything *he* asked for, whether in the realm of relationships, career, or otherwise. Hard work, he had learned, was what paid off. The longest relationship he'd ever had was with the idea of "hard work." *Work hard and play hard* — and boy, did he. Charlie's drinking had a way of winding him down after a long day of training. Understanding those around him was always a struggle. He found it tricky, navigating relationships with others, hence his closeness with Shoeless Joe. His dog was the only one who had continuously shown him selfless loyalty. He offers a delayed response to Abe. "But I don't get it. Community leaders... Coaches... Why do they all just stand by and watch the bigwigs tear down their fields?"

"Same reason our community's going to stand by and watch them tear down *our* fields... No one cares. And if they do, it's not enough for them to speak up."

"Well, I care... It just seems like the decision's already been made," Charlie counters.

"Nah, they fear the bigwigs and the school district more than they could ever love the game. They're even afraid of Judy. Though, she is quite a formidable woman."

"Formidable?" Charlie smirks. There's an awkward silence as he stares off into the distance. Just down the road lie the old fields that started it all. He turns to Abe. "Let's make it happen, then. Show Mr. G we care about the fields as much as he does."

"How?"

"Tell them. The community... The school district... Everyone. Tell them what you just told me. About all the possibilities — how every kid in the neighborhood would have a safe place to play. The Sunday afternoon league... Sponsorship opportunities... I know at least one of those parents is rich enough or smart enough to persuade the bigwigs to tap the brakes."

"Mmm," Abe begins, pondering. "You know, Mr. G would feel the same way if you decided to coach his team."

Charlie stifles a laugh. "Right..." The brothers contemplate the challenge that lies before them. Surely, it would take guts and a swift break out of their comfort zones. Life as they knew it seemed like enough to deal with as it was. "So, Brian Ragsdale invited me to a shindig tonight," Charlie says, managing to change the subject. "Wanna come?"

"An evening with the Ragsdale family? And you think watching grass grow is boring? Thanks, but I'll pass."

A security guard at the post of a private community opens up the front gate for Charlie, who drives through. He finally locates the entrance leading to the stunning Ragsdale mansion and for a moment feels the temptation to park his Mustang on their perfectly preened lawn. One of the uniformed valet boys stops him. With some effort, the confused teen drives the Mustang to a reserved parking section.

Charlie starts toward the grand front door of the mansion, trying not to look as stunned as he feels on the inside. He'd never before set foot in a home so huge. What was that word Abe had used earlier? "Formidable" — like a fortress. The mansion was complete with its own security gate, and the land spanned a good acre or so. All the place needed was a drawbridge and a moat. Charlie looks around at the massive property, with greenery in every direction as far as the eye could see. His Mustang, now parked, looks out of place with the modern cars on either side of it. Maybe he should have asked about a dress code, Charlie wonders, the thought only crossing his mind now. He supposed they would just have to be okay with his "come as you are" style. After all, the event was partially in his honor, while also acting as a networking fundraising night for Youth Summer League.

The Ragsdale family was a major supporter of Youth Summer League, wanting their son Casey to go all the way to the pros. Charlie had met a lot of parents over the years, and even more since returning to his hometown — but Brian Ragsdale was the first to come close to Charlie's old man in terms of the determination, grit, and pressure he placed on his son. Casey too was determined to make something of himself. Charlie instantly felt the heebie-jeebies whenever he heard Brian mention his son and had to mentally remind himself to chill; stop making comparisons to his own life. Casey didn't have any siblings, so the situation was completely different. Besides, the family could afford all the indulgences a kid could ever want or need — of course Brian would expect Casey to do great things. There was no backup plan.

Just inside the entryway and into the living space, Brian's wife Diane stuns in a bright magenta cocktail dress, accented with a feathered headpiece. A quartet plays classical music while no less than forty people mingle, each one dressed to the nines. Charlie looks a bit out of place with his combined getup of a suit jacket, shirt, and tie, along with his jeans and trainers. Nevertheless, Brian shows him around and makes introductions to various folks through the room, almost showing him off.

The two men stand by a grand piano. Brian breaks the ice. "Have you given any more thought to your predicament?"

Charlie gives a small laugh and briefly averts his eyes from Brian's. "I have no predicament, Brian. I'm finally trying out for the Dodgers next week. End of story."

Brian lets out a deep sigh and casually responds with, "I should've known you'd play hardball." He pulls out a sleek checkbook from inside his suit jacket. "How many zeroes will it take?"

"None. I don't want your cash." Charlie drains the last few sips of his drink.

"You know," Brian starts, inspecting Charlie, "I've never before met a man immune to money." Charlie shrugs and places his empty glass on the piano. "How about this? I buy out your contract with the Isotopes, and you stay here and coach. Problem solved."

Charlie begins to look impatient and tries breaking away from the conversation. Across the room, Teri stands in the corner, watching him. Her gaze is magnetic, and their eyes connect. Meanwhile, Brian suddenly looks through the crowd and waves someone over. A sporty-looking man approaches from behind, but Charlie doesn't notice him right away, turning back to Brian. "I told you, man. There is no problem. All I'm gonna do is hit one out of Dodger Stadium at the tryouts and get signed. There's even a new pitch I've been working on."

"Charlie, this is David Evans," Brian says. "He's a scout for the LA Dodgers. We were discussing your predicament earlier." The men shake hands. Charlie instinctively perks up as David begins to make small talk with him and Brian. They discuss the stamina and determination it took to reach the level of status held by the LA Dodgers. While "listening" to David, Charlie's eyes float back over to where Teri stands, his mind clearly elsewhere. He snaps out of it suddenly. *Stay focused. This could be a big break. Focus.*

Charlie cracks a smile, giving David his full attention. "Nice to meet you, David." Brian places a hand on Charlie's shoulder as though they were old friends. "Let me explain it like this... Local hero comes home to take his dad's team to the Youth Summer League World Series. After winning, he's invited by the LA Dodgers for a special tryout. What do you think?"

"And as a long-time scout, I can tell you with certainty," David explains to Charlie, "they're going to like what they see and be willing to sign you as a two-year contract playing Triple-A. Might even call you up to the show."

Brian smiles a toothy grin at Charlie, who simply stares back, taking it all in. "The press will eat it up," he adds.

David hands a stunned Charlie his business card. "Give me a call in three months — after you win."

◊ ◊ ◊

Now, Charlie sees the predicament... The feeling of overwhelm has hit all at once, and he breaks away from Brian in search of a stiff drink. He grabs himself a beer from the patio bar, and immediately a still calm pulses through his veins. On his way back through the house, Charlie passes the Ragsdales' giant sunken media room and spots some familiar faces. The A-Team kids sit piled onto a sizable, curved lounge piece that's in the shape of a baseball glove. They all take turns playing a virtual reality version of their own Major League Baseball teams, complete with headsets and all. Charlie stands in the doorway, beer in hand, and admires his players' form. Only a few of them could play at once, but the others cheered (and jeered) their teammates with laughter and smiles that were contagious. While virtual games could never beat the real thing for Charlie, the enthusiasm he saw in these kids was hard to knock.

Suddenly, Charlie gets swept out of the media room doorway by Judy, who wants to discuss the game — and get Charlie to volunteer his time for a one-off training session as a perk for the Youth Summer League's upcoming fundraiser. Judy has ushered him into the exquisitely lavish secondary living area where other baseball moms wine and dine themselves. They flock around him, each vying for his attention. Charlie couldn't be happier, completely in his element, surrounded by adoring fans. But one very special fan — Teri — stands off to the side. She fights the desire to step closer, not wanting to compete with the other women, and manages to steer clear of Charlie while he keeps trying to catch her eye. Soon enough, it's not only the moms desiring his attention; Charlie now also has the dads mesmerized as he talks baseball with utter enthusiasm and flair. But the joy of attention wears thin, and suddenly Charlie finds himself feeling like a paid entertainer rather than the night's honoree. He wishes to be in the media room, joining in on the virtual games, facing the world with nothing more than an avatar as his mask.

Finally, there is opportunity for an escape when Judy asks for a drink. "All this talk about baseball has really excited me. Charlie, can you get me a tall glass of ice water with at least two ice cubes — but no more than three — and a touch of lemon juice?" Charlie stares at her blankly but gives a nod in response and takes off toward the beverage station in the front room.

Charlie's in the process of fetching Judy's beverage when he overhears Brian's wife Diane offering her opinion of the Madam President to one of the guests. Diane is thirty-nine and convinced she's more attractive than she is while constantly trying to prove said attractiveness by spending her days shopping with Brian's money. "I heard she wants to do away with the whole A-Team."

The guest nods in agreement. "Mr. G's fields too."

"I'll tell you something else about our Madam President," Diane says to the guest, leaning in closer. "Her heart left baseball when that darling son of hers did."

"You mean when her 'darling son' was *forced* to leave?"

Diane sniffs daintily, appalled. "Mmm. And now, as far as she's concerned, our fields and the so-called 'new' fields... Might build collateral. Mark my words."

By now a few other women have joined the circle to quietly gossip. One of them chimes in with, "She couldn't— She wouldn't do that... She's the president of the league. The As are an institution around here and close to many hearts."

"And Casey is our only shot. He was born for that game. I couldn't bear to see her destroy the A-Team. It wouldn't be right." Just then, Charlie turns around from the beverage station, a clear drink in hand. He's barely taken a step when Diane locks her eyes on him. She gives him a huge smile of delight. "Charlie Maddox!" She gives his outfit a once-over. "Don't you look... Resplendent." Diane swoops Charlie's arm into hers and turns to her guests. "I need to have a word with Mr. Maddox in private."

As she leads Charlie into the luxury kitchen, Judy notices and sends a nasty glare his way. "Since Charlie seems to be busy..." She directs her attention to the other men around her. "Gentlemen, which one of you would like to pinch-hit?"

Meanwhile, Diane retrieves a bottle of wine and pours each of them a glass. Charlie watches, confused, as Diane then pulls on a pair of rubber gloves and begins to clean her oven. She looks anxious, and the wine only seems to make it worse. "Judy's heart has left the game. She doesn't care. And without a coach, she *will* do it. Without a real Maddox to stand up to her, the team will have no direction.

"So, what happens to the kids on the team?"

"What do you care?" Diane shoots Charlie an accusatory look. She's right... He doesn't care, really — or does he? Charlie takes a sip of his wine. "They get moved to other teams and their dreams of going to the World Series together get crushed. It's the end... Unless you *do* care." Diane has tears in her eyes. Charlie debates whether they're for real or if she's putting them on for him. Yes, certainly, baseball means the world to him. But Judy... She is *formidable*. Most often easily swayed by women and their desires, Charlie had never had an openly distressed woman confront him about something while wearing oven mitts. He appears to be listening, but inside, he's asking himself how much longer he needs to stay here in this room...

Life was again asking Charlie to step outside of his comfort zone. First, it was helping out Abe with his campaign for the new fields, and now, it was coaching the A-Team. He despised being put on the spot. Sure, he didn't mind being *in* the spotlight when it came to his playing ability, but this kind of attention put him on edge. His only desire was to be known as a star player — or better yet, a star pitcher. Playing any other roles in life, as dictated by others, had never been a part of his game plan.

CHAPTER TEN

C harlie has that "I haven't showered in days" look as he lies sprawled out on the living room couch, surrounded by empty food wrappers lining the coffee table and floor. Old video footage of young Abe plays on the TV as he hits a ball out of the park. Soon, it cuts to the tail end of the footage: Abe being hailed a 'hero.' The gangly teen sits high atop his dad's shoulders, with the entire team crowded behind them, cheering. All alone on the dugout bench sits a young Charlie, his head down, feet shuffling against the dirt floor, to the sound of cheers that were just about breaking his heart. Also caught on tape, the announcer's jubilant voice booms from the TV — *Abe Maddox is a hero today and the apple of his father's eyes as he takes the team to new heights.*

Charlie's head suddenly shifts to the side window adjacent to the front of the house. He notices a flying object careening through the sky. Is that... Is that what he thinks it is? No, it couldn't possibly... Has he been transported back to the past *for real*? While he stares at the window, he spots another object passing by. It's a roll of toilet paper, flying just outside, small sheets of white fluttering behind it like a tail as it soars through the air.

Charlie's eyes follow as several more toilet paper rolls fly past. "Those little—" Without stopping to turn off the video, he storms toward the front door, onto the porch, and into the front yard, where the A-Team kids take cover behind various trees and shrubs.

Amid the sudden silence, Charlie turns around to see the fruits of their labor. Both the garden and the house have been toilet papered — weakly, to Charlie's disdain. He hears laughter in the near distance and turns around to see Teri watching from her car. A smirk crosses his face before he returns to surveying the 'damage.'

"This is pathetic," Charlie shouts.

A voice calls from the bushes, "What?"

Charlie responds knowingly to the lone voice. "Get your sorry little butts out here, now!" The kids slowly emerge from their hiding places, each with different looks and levels of fear and anxiety regarding the prank they had just pulled. Seeing their faces is enough of a reward, so Charlie cracks a smile. "Who taught you kids how to toilet paper a house? You have to lay ground coverage first, then go for the trees." A cloud of relief washes over the kids as Charlie motions toward the bushes with vigor. "Look! You completely missed the bushes." An awkward silence permeates the night air as Charlie debates where to take this next. "No, this won't do. Get in the car, everybody. We're going shopping."

◊ ◊ ◊

Both Charlie and Teri push shopping carts down a grocery store aisle. The kids begin playing among themselves, tossing rolls of toilet paper around and eventually into the carts. Charlie pauses and looks at Teri. "So, this was your idea?" Teri looks up at him with a guilty smile in response. Charlie sucks in a surprised breath of air and shakes his head. "Their parents know where they are?"

"Permission slips from each of them," Teri answers.

Charlie laughs. "It's a sad world when kids need a permission slip to commit minor acts of vandalism, ain't it?"

"Tell me about it." Teri and Charlie lock eyes for a moment, right before Seth throws a package of toilet paper into one of the carts. "He shoots... He scores!" Except the aim isn't so good, and the package of toilet paper ends up hitting Charlie in the head. Seth runs but so does Charlie. Teri watches as Charlie and Seth race around the nearby aisles of the store.

A while later, they all prepare for their return to the house. Just as Charlie picks up the last bag from the checkout counter, Teri says to him, "Rumor has it that you're going to coach the As this season for your dad."

Charlie sets the bag into the cart with the rest and avoids making eye contact. "In your dreams." If only he could be privy to those dreams of hers.

Charlie, Teri, and the kids soon return to the scene of the crime — Gordon's house. Charlie instructs the kids to remove all evidence of prior toilet paper assault attempts. After a few minutes, there's nothing to see but a clean slate. Charlie has the honor of throwing the inaugural toilet paper roll, and the games begin. Teri giggles as she wraps toilet paper around a shrub and catches Charlie watching her while he shows the kids how to best wrap toilet paper around the bushes. With the groundwork set, they move onto covering the trees. It's easy to miss the target those first few times, but the kids quickly get the hang of it. Even Shoeless Joe gets into the shenanigans and runs around with a roll of toilet paper in his mouth, the unraveling roll flapping behind him in the wind. The kids busy themselves with toilet papering the remainder of trees in the yard. Soon enough, they move on and begin wrapping up Charlie in toilet paper. Charlie jokingly stumbles through the yard, arms outstretched like a cartoon mummy. He falls to the ground, laughing, as the kids pile on top of him.

After a little while, Charlie and the kids stand out on the sidewalk, admiring their work. The house and entire front lawn are completely covered. A police siren sounds in the distance, and moments later, a patrol car's spotlight illuminates the lawn. The kids, along with Charlie and Teri, scatter and take cover behind various bushes and trees. The two adults find themselves behind the same bush.

Teri looks at Charlie and whispers, "Why did *you* run? It's your house."

"Force of habit," he quips, validating his trademark move to run at the slightest provocation, before stepping out into the flood of light. "Can I help you, officer?" Charlie asks, shielding his eyes. He resembles a deer in headlights. Officer Tom White stands there — the bearer of the torch. Recognition flashes in

Charlie's eyes, but he can't quite place the name.

Tom steps forward. "We received a report of a five-seven-two in progress."

"Not here. This is my house," Charlie answers. "We're just decorating it for National Toilet Paper Day. No crime in that." Tom stares at Charlie, his head cocked to one side. Charlie decides to smarten up. "Sorry to inconvenience you, officer."

Tom closes in on Charlie, shining his flashlight into the familiar face. "Charlie Maddox, is that you?"

Then Charlie remembers. It all comes rushing back to him. "Tom White?" The two men embrace.

"You hippie punk," Tom says, slapping Charlie on the back as they pull away from each other. "Where's Teri?" Tom shines his flashlight across the yard.

"Over here," Teri shouts from behind the bushes before awkwardly stepping out into the light. She shields her eyes and walks toward the officer. "Your wife wants you to pick up a gallon of milk when you get off work."

Tom chuckles. "Thanks. Hey, is Michelle here?" Tom's daughter Michelle, with long dark brown hair, sheepishly steps out from behind another bush across the yard. The other kids follow her lead, their hands lifted high in the air as they emerge from the greenery.

Teri joins in, placing her hands in the air to accept responsibility for the night's mayhem. "Guilty as charged."

Tom addresses Charlie with suspicion. "So, you *are* their coach?"

"No, sorry, mate." Charlie takes a step back. "We were just having a bit of fun. You remember what it's like," he says, appealing to Tom's sense of the past.

But things don't go as planned when Tom whips out his handcuffs and spins Charlie around. "Charles Maddox..."

Charlie panics and shouts, "Hey! What are you doing?!" Tom pushes him toward the patrol car. "You can't arrest me for vandalizing my own house!"

"I'm charging you," Tom begins, "for contributing to the

delinquency of minors."

"I have permission slips from all the parents! Teri," Charlie spews dramatically. "Show him the slips!"

"I'm aware. I signed one for Michelle." Tom tries to hide the trace of a smile.

Teri yells out teasingly, "Sorry, Charlie, but I think you'd do good to spend a night in the big house. Maybe it'll help you see the error of your ways…" Teri turns her head dismissively. "Cuff him, Tom."

Tom shoves Charlie's face against the hood of the patrol car. "Charlie Maddox, you have the right to remain silent—"

"This is ridiculous," Charlie says with a growl.

"You also have the right to make this all go away…" Tom spins Charlie around to face him. "By agreeing to coach the As." Tom smiles wide.

Charlie breathes a sigh of relief and looks past Tom to see Teri and the kids all standing by with hopeful looks on their faces. "Alright, alright! I'll do it. I'll coach the team."

Tom takes out his bullhorn from the patrol car and speaks into it. "Kids, come on down and meet your new head coach." The kids cheer and rush Charlie. He falls to the ground as they pile on. Shoeless Joe barks happily, while Teri and Tom exchange a smile and a nod.

The atmosphere turns electric, with the kids running around, throwing toilet paper in celebration of being an official team once again. The combined haze of excitement and whoops of laughter remind Charlie of the joy he felt while toilet papering someone's home back in the day with his own crew.

His mind wanders to when he and Teri were fifteen years old. She was gorgeous to him, although quite typical at the time, dressed in acid-washed jeans, a crop top, and Converse sneakers, with long, straight hair. Young Charlie wears Levi 501s and his Letterman jacket. The two teens stand amid the aftermath of a freshly toilet papered yard. Suddenly a patrol car cruises down the street. A headlight lands on them.

Charlie screams to Teri, "Let's make a run for it!" He grabs her hand, and they run through the streets, cutting through Mr. G's fields. They clumsily ascend the ladder leading up to the scoreboard, nestled safely away and out of sight from anyone who might want to question them. They cozy up in the cluttered space amid giant scoreboard numbers and peer up at the nighttime sky. Teri holds the edges of Charlie's jacket, smiling coyly at him. Charlie stares back at her a bit awkwardly, holding her tightly across her exposed back. The two teens make out awkwardly but passionately.

Charlie abruptly snaps out of his daydream memory at the sound of Tom's voice asking, "Got any beers?"

"Sure. Shift over for the night?" Tom nods in reply. Charlie looks over at Teri, concealing his desire to kiss those luscious lips once more. "You want a beer?"

"Why not," Teri answers.

Minutes later, Charlie, Teri, and Tom drink beer from a six-pack, just like old pals, sitting on the front porch's rattan couches. Trisha Yearwood's song, 'She's in Love with a Boy,' plays softly in the background from a vintage radio. On the front lawn, the kids occupy themselves with a tame round of baseball under the light of just a few street lamps and some candles sitting atop the porch railings.

Charlie breaks the silence among the adults. "You weren't really gonna arrest me, were you, Tom?" The officer shakes his head as he swallows a sip of beer.

Teri gives Charlie a playful slap on the arm, turning to him excitedly. "Remember that time you got busted for stealing all of Mrs. Reilly's prize-winning roses? Tell us… How'd you get caught again?"

"This story does not need to be told," Charlie begins until Teri cuts in.

"He forgot to zip up the bag," she says to Tom. "So, he's running along, and all these roses are falling out behind him. Left a trail all the way back here to the house." Teri looks back at Charlie. "How many hours did you get for that?"

Charlie averts his eyes, embarrassed. "One for each rose."

He takes a swig of beer before turning boldly to Teri, their eyes locking. "The worst punishment was that I never got to give them to you." A shy smile crosses Teri's face, and she looks away. Charlie casually refocuses on the baseball game happening a short distance away, where Seth delivers a solid pitch. "He's got a good arm," he comments. "Where'd he learn to pitch like that?"

Teri avoids eye contact with Charlie as his gaze makes its way back to her. "Probably from watching you," she says, looking at Seth. "You really are his hero, ya know." Teri chuckles to herself as she reflects briefly.

Tom silently observes the two of them. Something electric buzzes between them — and it isn't just the adrenaline from reliving their toilet papering days. "So, you two still an item?"

Charlie looks at Teri, hopeful. She returns the look casually. "No. Just friends."

Later that night, Teri and Tom watch an exchange between Charlie and Seth as he gives pointers to the young pitcher in the making. Teri speaks under her breath so only Tom can hear. "It's in his blood."

Tom leans in and asks quietly, "You going to tell him?"

"No. He had his chance."

◊ ◊ ◊

Charlie gives Earl a call in the middle of the night. He had just finished TPing Gordon's room while the old man was asleep and couldn't manage to settle down himself. Earl had been fast asleep as well, busy dreaming of the money he would make from all his star players. He didn't want to hear what Charlie was in the middle of telling him... That it would be a while before he returned to play ball. Charlie was committed to seeing out the season in his hometown and simply 'hoped' that the Dodgers would get back to him. It was a long shot...

Always the optimist, Earl spews, "What if you don't get a call back?"

"Well, then, I'll just wait until next year," replies Charlie.

"You got a sure thing right here," Earl reminds him.

"But there's a girl *here*."

Earl scoffs. Charlie can almost see him rolling his eyes through the phone. "There are girls everywhere."

"This one's different." Charlie paces the room.

"How? She got a brain?" Earl chuckles.

"As a matter of fact, she does."

"Anything I can say to change your mind? Could be the end of your career as you know it."

"Just keep me posted, okay? Let me know if the Dodgers call," Charlie answers. Earl doesn't respond right away. "Okay?"

Earl sighs deeply into the phone. "I don't have a great feeling about this. Maybe I'll come pay you a visit soon and convince you to come back."

Charlie laughs. "Sure, anytime. I'm coaching Gordon's team—"

"You're *what*?"

"I know, Earl. I know. But hey, never say never, I guess."

"Righty-o," Earl replies, unimpressed. "I'll catch you later." Charlie looks down at his phone thoughtfully. Earl had indeed ended their call. Amid the silence, Charlie reevaluates his decision. Were there any doubts? Tom had pressured him into it, after all, just like the rest of them had tried to do. But on the other hand, it was something Charlie felt needed to be done. He was determined to show Gordon for once and for all the true extent of his competence and that his whole life wasn't solely built on his own selfish need to make something of himself. Perhaps it was time to give back to the community that birthed his own love of the game way back when.

That morning, a nurse delivers breakfast to Gordon, who lies propped up in his bed, reading a baseball magazine. She sets foot into the room and looks taken aback by the mess. Toilet paper decorations cover the entire room. The nurse smiles when she sees Gordon. He looks better than on previous days and seems unbothered by the room's current state of decor.

"Good feng shui," the nurse jokes, with a smile, nodding her head toward the hanging toilet paper. Gordon smiles back but remains quiet. The nurse sets down the breakfast tray onto the side table and hands him a photo. "Your son asked me to give you this." Gordon looks down at the photo. It's a polaroid of Charlie and the As with a sticky note taped to the bottom corner: *For you and your team. —Coach Charlie*

CHAPTER ELEVEN

I t's Opening Day, and Mr. G's fields are abuzz with undeniable excitement. Local firefighters grill up hamburgers for the line of people that winds around into the parking lot. On the Minor A Field, various teams get their group photos taken by an overly enthusiastic photographer. A bounce house, a ring toss game, a can knockdown game, and a dunk tank grace the green of the T-ball field across the way. All along the rest of the fields, families gather for a communal picnic of sorts. The younger kids sprawl out on blankets, occupied by their toys, while most of the adults sit in folding lawn chairs, eating and soaking up the sun on the lazy afternoon. Some of the dads stand around together, chatting.

Charlie and the A-Team kids wait in line to have their photo taken. Abe walks up to the group, all decked out in the team uniform. "Hi there," he says, reaching toward Charlie for a mock handshake. "Abe Maddox, your new assistant coach."

"Oh, yeah? You gonna put on a wig and be the team mom too?" Charlie jokes, with a smile.

Teri joins the group, coming up behind Abe. "Hey, that's my job — and it's 'team administrator' to you," she says, sidling up to Charlie and jabbing him in the ribs. "'Team Mom' sounds so chauvinistic."

Charlie's gaze darts between the two. "And I have no say in this?"

"That's what happens when you miss team meetings," Teri points out. Finally, the As have reached the front of the line. Everyone gets into position for the group photo.

The photographer prepares to snap away. "Everybody, smile!"

◊ ◊ ◊

Charlie, Abe, and Teri wander the fields while the rest of the team scatters to show off for their families. Things sure have changed since the last time Charlie played here. He turns Teri's way and asks, "What happened to the pancake breakfast?"

She snickers in response. "Everyone but Judy hated it, so I changed it to an all-day barbecue with carnival games the first chance I had."

Later on, Charlie finds himself in line with Nicky for the dunk tank, at which Abe sits as the designated dunkee waiting to plunge down into the cold water. As soon as it's Nicky's turn, Charlie crouches to face her at eye level, offering up some 'coveted' pitching advice (so he thinks).

"It's harder to hit the target than it looks," Charlie says as he sets the ball into Nicky's open palm. "Take your time, and focus." Without a word of acknowledgement, Nicky lets the ball roll off her hand. It lands with a plop at Charlie's feet. The girl runs over to the tank and pushes the 'dunk' lever with vigor. Abe drops down into the water and almost immediately comes up sputtering for air.

Nicky leans up against the lever and turns to Charlie, who tries to cover up a laugh. "You need to think outside the box, Uncle Charlie." Abe, ever the good sport, returns to his perch within the tank. Once he settles in, Charlie steps forward to take his turn. He picks up the ball and winds up, his eyes locking on Abe — then, he freezes. The ball drops to the ground as Charlie walks away, leaving Abe confused in the dunk tank.

He yells at Charlie, "Come back." But Charlie keeps on going until he's out of sight.

◊ ◊ ◊

Herbert's arms nearly overflow with plates as he struggles to put ketchup on a burger at one of the food stations. "Here, Herb, let me help," says a voice behind him. Charlie manages to walk up in the knick of time and seizes the opportunity presented. He takes the ketchup bottle and proceeds to squirt splatters of red all over Herbert's crisp white shirt. "Oops,"

Charlie says, not even trying to cover his laughter. With a blatant smile, he slams the bottle down onto the table, causing more red goop to spurt out all over the place, and walks away.

Herbert stands there, shaking with rage, fists clenched at his sides. "Do your dad a favor and quit, Charlie. Let his team get a *real* coach. Maybe then those As of yours would have a fighting chance at beating my army." Charlie doesn't slow down in the least — not even when Judy shoves past, gasping at the crime scene that is now Herbert's shirt. She grabs a napkin off one of the tables and attempts to dab at the stain while glaring at Charlie and cooing to Herbert. Unfortunately any attempts to fix the situation only makes it worse.

Across the way, several sets of large folding tables and metal chairs occupy one of the fields where a mobile stage has been set up. Each table wears a plastic covering in select primary 'Americana' colors. Families fill the tables. Charlie and Teri settle into their seats, both facing the stage, with Gordon beside them in his wheelchair. The old man keeps nodding off. Charlie watches thoughtfully as Abe, Nicky, and Shoeless Joe walk toward them from the gaming area.

He nudges Teri and nods their way to direct her attention. "How'd that come about, anyway?"

Teri looks over. "Nicky?" Charlie nods. "It was her mom's dying wish," she answers. "Poor girl's family disowned her after she became pregnant out of wedlock. She had nowhere else to go."

Charlie shakes his head. "That's my brother... Guardian of lost souls."

"Well, you wouldn't let Abe look out for you," Teri explains. Charlie barely has time to process before the trio joins them. Abe takes a seat next to his brother while Nicky and Joe stretch out in the grass beside them. Charlie turns to Abe with an unusual sense of pride and even debates giving him a pat on the shoulder. But then Judy steps onto the stage.

She loudly clears her throat into the microphone and directs a sharp gaze in Charlie's direction. "We'll be doing things a little differently this year, folks." Herbert sends one of his signature smile-smirks to Charlie from his spot at the food station, lagging behind as usual.

"The board has decided that *all* teams — not just the A-Team — should have a shot at the wildcard for this season's World Series." Gordon perks up at that, and he and Charlie exchange incredulous looks. "What this means is that," Judy explains, maybe a bit too excitedly, "the winner of this tournament will be the team progressing into the championship!" She stares out at the crowd with high expectations of a standing ovation. Her expression turns sour when all she gets is a mixture of cheers and jeers from the few actually listening below. Judy manages to shake it off and continues her speech. "And now, what Opening Day ceremony would be complete without Mr. G himself throwing the opening pitch?" More cheers come from the crowd for Gordon than for Judy's announcement, to which she turns *doubly* sour.

Teri pushes Gordon's wheelchair onto the field and finally the pitcher's mound, where he makes his own announcement, calling for a stand-in pitcher. "Charlie Maddox, the field," Gordon booms from the mound. This time, the crowd jumps to their feet, clapping, hooting, and going wild. Judy walks off the stage in disgust.

◊ ◊ ◊

The first day of practice begins at six o'clock the next morning, with the determined A-Team kids showing up at the Maddox home. They wind around to the back of the house where they climb through an open window, one following after the other, like in 'The Pied Piper.' Soon, the kids surround Charlie, who's still sound asleep in bed. Shoeless Joe lies curled up in the corner of the room but raises his head in question the moment he detects the intruders. The As watch Charlie expectantly; surely his eyes will crack open at any second...

Casey breaks the silence and whispers to the group, "Is he dead?"

Michelle takes a whiff of the room and covers her nose.

"Sure smells like it." Shoeless Joe still watches curiously from his corner but doesn't make a peep, content to observe. Taking a few careful steps forward, Seth picks up a glass of water from the nightstand beside Charlie's bed and slowly drizzles it onto the sleeping man's forehead. Moment later, Charlie awakens. He looks around, confused, squinting up at the kids.

"See? He's just drunk," Seth tells the others. "Get up, Mr. Maddox. It's time to train," the boy calls loudly. Charlie fights the unwanted wake-up call for as long as he can, doing his best to keep the covers pulled high over his head, but quantity manages to beat out strength in this case. After dragging their new coach to the bathroom, encouraging a shower, the kids decide to check in on their old one, Mr. G, in the room down the hall. They enter Gordon's room, still filled with various balloons, flowers, and other get-well-soon wishes from countless parents. By now, the toilet paper has been dismantled throughout the room.

Gordon greets the kids cheerfully, and they take turns sitting on the edge of his bed, spewing all the latest town gossip. For once the old man lets them do all the talking, and he can't help but feel a sense of pride when taking in their attire. Each one of them is ready for action, complete with baseball gloves, team caps, and all. One of the kids standing off to the side anxiously tosses a ball between both hands as they wait to get a move on.

Finally, Charlie appears in the doorway of Gordon's room, ready for the team's first official training session — or at least as ready as he'll ever be. And so it begins… Charlie and Shoeless Joe lead the pack of As as they jog up a hill. Joe takes over at the front of the line as Charlie's speed dwindles, the kids passing him one by one. They run down the hill, which leads to the little-known back entrance of the fields. Neither the kids nor Joe stop until they reach the outfield. They turn around and watch, patiently waiting on Charlie, who lags behind. His arrival is met with cheers from the kids, along with a few barks from Joe, who goes straight to the dugout for a nap.

Charlie leads the team in various exercises on the practice

field. They start with jumping jacks, followed by running in place, and lastly, stretching. By the time 10 a.m. rolls around, Charlie and the kids are in a heated game of defense on the field. The kids stand spread across the entire outfield, while Charlie hits pop flys for them to catch.

Soon, Abe and Nicky walk onto the field. They couldn't help but check in on Charlie out of curiosity, and they had expected to assist with the day's practice, anyway. Abe pulls aside Seth and Casey to work on their pitching, while the rest continue their catching drill. Nicky watches the team from the dugout with Shoeless Joe by her side. She stands by during breaks, ready to top off water bottles and hand out orange halves. For lunch, Teri swings by and picks up Nicky for a drive to the pizza parlor while everyone else hangs back, still hard at work.

Charlie has the team run a few drills, starting with a few of the kids lining up next to first base, along with a few others playing various positions on the field. The player at the front of the line makes a break from first to second base. Charlie rockets the ball over to to the shortstop. The shortstop throws to the second baseman, who hurries to tag out the runner. But the runner thinks fast and slides, escaping the out. For the second drill, the pitcher throws to the catcher, who purposely misses the ball. Charlie signals the next runner on first to steal second. The catcher scrambles for the ball and fires it to the second baseman as the pitcher ducks in the nick of time, much like a choreographed dance. Managing to catch the ball, the second baseman tags the runner as he slides for safety — he's out. For the final drill, Charlie stands behind a net on the pitcher's mound. He drops a ball into the pitching machine in front of him, and the machine spits it out, sending the ball speeding toward the batter at sixty miles per hour.

◊ ◊ ◊

It's almost time for lunch, and the As surround Charlie while he tests their knowledge of coaching hand signals. Charlie does a hand signal and squints down at the group. "Okay. What's this one?"

The kids all shout out simultaneously, "Steal second." Charlie does another signal. Again comes a resounding answer. "Steal home if the batter hits to left field." Each time, Charlie's hand signals get longer and more complicated. "The runner on first does a fake steal to second. Wait for the pitcher to throw it to second base. Then the runner on first gets caught in a rundown between first and second — and if the first baseman overthrows it to the second baseman, the runner on third steals home." A few of the kids breathe sighs of relief after getting out that mouthful. Next, Charlie does several single gestures, and the kids respond unanimously. "You're ugly... Your mother dresses you funny... This is a test of the Emergency Broadcast System." Everyone, including Charlie, laughs. Abe walks over from the dugout while Charlie rubs his own stomach. Casey and a few others echo the last message. "Lunch is here!"

The kids, plus Shoeless Joe, race up to Teri and Nicky, who walk onto the field carrying a feast of pizza and sports drinks. Abe dashes over to help with the food.

No more than five minutes later, empty pizza boxes litter the field. Man, were they hungry... Everyone lounges around on the luscious green grass, relaxing and digesting. The kids joke around for the last few minutes of a great first practice until their parents get there to pick them up. A few of the kids who live just down the block would walk home under Abe's watchful eye. But for now, Charlie and Teri sit on the grass and watch as Abe helps Nicky hit balls off a tee, with Shoeless Joe chasing closely behind each one as they come.

A confused look comes across Charlie's face. He asks Teri, "Where do you suppose he got those fathering skills from?"

Teri shrugs. "Where does every man get them from? Their father, I guess."

"Have you gone mad?" A hint of anger creeps into Charlie's voice.

"Oh, come now, Mr. G has a soft spot," Teri says, chuckling. "You're just blind to it because you're his son."

Charlie shakes his head. "I'm blind to it because I never saw it." An awkward pause lands between the two. Charlie finally breaks the silence. He turns to look Teri in the eyes and asks, "How about Seth's dad? What's he like?"

Teri calmly picks a few blades of grass, twirling them between her fingers while she debates how to answer such a question. "Couldn't tell you. It was a one-night stand."

Charlie cocks his head in surprise. "That doesn't sound like you at all."

Teri looks a bit caught off guard by his reaction. She swallows a sip of water, buying herself a few extra seconds. Now is definitely not the time to drop that truth bomb. "He was just passing through," Teri says, shrugging, overly casual. "It was one of those unexpected turns, Charlie." Their eyes meet, and Charlie nods, letting the subject go for the time being. It had been such a long time ago... When she made the decision not to contact him about the news, she had been resentful, yet proud in some way. This time Teri's the bearer of the uncomfortable silence between the two. She considers telling him right then — but she can't. Not right here, and not right now.

Charlie clears his throat. "Seth's a good kid. You're lucky." Teri smiles somberly. If only she could let him know that, in fact, he were 'lucky' too. But it didn't feel right to suddenly give that privilege to him after so many years had already been lost. It wasn't time. Charlie continues. "He has a good shot at playing college ball. You don't see many left-handed pitchers these days."

"Thanks," Teri says, smiling for real this time. "And thanks for sticking around a bit." Charlie smiles back — but certainly she must know she doesn't have to thank him for anything. As far as he's concerned, the feeling of contentment has never been more prominent than while sitting in this moment with her.

Later that week, Charlie and Abe have the opportunity to attend a Dodgers game. They hand over a pair of tickets to the unenthused ticket agent slouching behind the glass. The ticket agent examines them and then pushes them back at Charlie through the slot. "Excuse me, sirs, but there seems to be a mix-up," the ticket agent says.

Charlie steps forward, confused and ready to rumble. "Brian Ragsdale gave me these tickets. He assured me there wouldn't be any problems."

The ticket agent looks taken aback for a second. "Oh, no, sir, no problem with the tickets. You're at the wrong gate. The VIP entrance is right over there." He points to a secluded area behind them. *VIP?!* Charlie and Abe exchange an impressed look. "Tell the gate attendee you're looking for the dugout suites," the ticket agent adds with a smile and a nod toward the exclusive seating.

As they walk through the tunnel, Charlie starts to envision himself not as a VIP *in* here, only able to watch from afar, but instead as a VIP *out there* on the field — for real. Although he was indeed a professional player in his own right, somehow it still felt as if he'd been living life by experiencing it via secondhand memories, rather than actually being there in the moment himself. The brothers step out of the tunnel and up the steps leading to the dugout suites. Charlie looks up at the bright lights and all the people filling the stands. He daydreams... *Now pitching for the LA Dodgers, Charlie Maddox...*

But the daydream comes to an abrupt halt when Abe nudges him with an elbow. "Mr. Maddox, can you take your seat, please?"

"This time next year, it'll be me pitching for the Dodgers."

"Well, with God, anything is possible," Abe offers.

"No, it's not God," Charlie says, rolling his eyes. "Brian's got me a second tryout. A VIP meeting... After the A-Team wins the World Series."

Abe nods. "I see. I thought you wanted to stay. Just hang out. Be with Gordon for a bit?"

"Maybe. But you're here. He doesn't need me." Charlie remarks before heading for the suite's complimentary buffet to load up on hotdogs and drinks. After the brothers pile their plates high, they settle in to watch the game from the privileged suite. Life was pretty great. Hey, maybe Charlie would end up sticking around for a bit longer. Who knew what was next in the game of life?

◊ ◊ ◊

The team pool party takes place every year before the first game, and today was that day. An overhead banner sways happily in the warm breeze: 'Welcome to the Annual A-Team Pool Party.' The A-Team kids, plus Shoeless Joe, line up along the pool's longer edge. Charlie faces the group. Michelle, standing tall, is first in line. Her dream is to become a female playing in the major leagues.

Charlie approaches. "Michelle, you're officially a member of the A-Team," he says as he pushes the girl into the pool. She lands with a splash, laughing. Charlie continues down the line. Next up is Shoeless Joe, who stares up at him. "Of course you too, Joe." The dog wags his tail and jumps into the pool, doing the doggy-paddle. Charlie steps forward to find Seth next in line. "Seth, you're off—" As Charlie moves to push him into the pool, Seth ducks behind Charlie and pushes him instead. Seth jumps in after, and the rest of the kids follow his lead, jumping into the pool. Everyone laughs, splashing around, and having a blast.

Across the way, Abe cooks up steaks on a grill while Teri watches, bored. Brian and several other parents walk up and join the non-existent conversation.

"Here you go, Abe," Brian says, holding out a baseball cap to Abe. "We thought we'd make it official." The man shoves the cap down onto Abe's head before walking away. Abe quickly takes it off to get a closer look. Embroidered on the hat: 'Coach Abe.' He stares at the gift, speechless, and then puts it back on his head, smiling from ear to ear. The other parents shake Abe's hand in acceptance. Most of them had been reticent about letting him be a part of the Youth Summer League lineup due to his involvement in the church and the teen youth group. Abe also had reservations about joining forces with those who had their hearts set on the World Series, no matter the cost. That singular goal had become much like an idol to not only the coaches but to many of the youngsters too. It was as though their whole sense of self and belonging was based only on whether or not they made the cut. In lieu of losing the chance completely, Abe decided to consider the thought of perhaps changing the game from within — much like Joseph did in the Old Testament by helping his family when working with the Egyptians.

As the newcomers leave, Teri looks at Abe with excitement. "See? You were wrong about the parents not accepting you."

Abe tries not to look as thrilled as he feels and replies, "I guess so." His eyes shift to the swimming pool where Charlie and the rest of the team horse around. "And maybe you were wrong about him." Teri follows Abe's eyes. Charlie looks at exactly the right moment, and they lock eyes. He waves before jumping into the pool, knees hoisted up to his chest. Teri giggles at the show. Abe just watches. The two of them stare at Charlie. Abe flips the steaks over on the grill — loud sizzles break the silence.

Charlie walks over, still dripping from the pool. He nods his head toward his brother's new baseball cap. "'Coach Abe,' huh? What's that all about? You told me the parents would never accept you as an assistant coach."

Abe takes a deep breath before switching on his pastor voice and explains, "You have more than seven hundred kids in a league. I felt the only ones getting any attention were the all-stars. We had kids sitting on the bench for the entire season. They would rather play for a losing team than sit out on a winning team.

"What do you care?" Charlie asks pointedly. "That never happened to you. Not once. Growing up, you always thrived on the competition of it all."

"I care..." Abe hesitates. "I care because that was you, Charlie. You sat there, game after game, and I begged to switch places with you so many times but Gordon wouldn't let me. I wanted you to play. I would have given anything. My prayers weren't answered until you got older, but still, they *were*."

"You prayed for Gordon too?" Charlie scoffs.

"Yeah, and it worked."

Teri chimes in and slaps Abe on the back. She explains, "Abe's always been a staunch supporter of *cooperative*, rather than *competitive*, sports." Abe had become the safe haven for kids like Charlie. He had seen one too many militant coaches cram their disastrous rhetoric down kids' necks, hoping that the useless cycle would somehow create stronger ballplayers.

Charlie nods his approval. "Congrats," he says to Abe before taking a running start and jumping into the pool, knees again hoisted up to his chest. The splash his body creates is larger than ever this time, traveling far enough to splash Teri and Abe. Teri barely even notices. She's too busy staring at Charlie, who's back to goofing around with the team. His energy is infectious. Teri laughs under her breath. She's fallen in love with him all over again...

◊ ◊ ◊

When Charlie gets home, he's thoroughly exhausted. He can't remember the last time he'd been surrounded by so much infectious laughter and joy. Before settling into his room for the night, Charlie stops to check in on Gordon. The old man grumbles in his sleep.

"He doesn't deserve to play," Gordon booms in a slurred demonic-like voice. Charlie can't help but wonder if Gordon was dreaming about him as a child. Or another child... *Is there any kid out there who deserves not to play a game?* Charlie stands in the doorway and listens to the babbling of Mr. G. "The commie minister thinks all kids should play — even in the upper divisions. I say, if the kids can't cut it in T-ball, kick 'em out."

Charlie smiles selfishly for a moment. Phew, he's off the hook this time, but poor Abe... His brother has to be here in this house, constantly getting nothing but wrath from the man who is supposed to love him unconditionally. Charlie felt torn. He could see both perspectives — Abe's and Gordon's. Charlie himself had been one of those kids, forever sitting on the dugout bench, and now, he was the one with the power to deem who sat and who played.

CHAPTER TWELVE

It's the first game of the season. The A-Team is in the midst of facing their opponents, the Royals. By the bottom of the fifth inning, the As are in the lead at seven versus zero for the opposing. The A-Team is at bat with Seth on third. On the mound for the Royals, Kurt Jr. releases a wild pitch, kicking himself the moment the ball leaves his fingers. With the slip-up, he forgets to cover home plate. The catcher, Jose, scrambles for the ball. With the ball clutched tightly in his hand, Jose spins around, ready to throw to Kurt Jr. at home — but he's still up on the mound. Seth barrels down the line from third and jumps into the air, landing square on the plate. Charlie's Uncle Hank, acting umpire on the field, makes the call: "SAFE!"

One announcer, a bald guy who likes to talk too much, follows the game's movement closely. He recounts details of the last play to the cheering crowd of families sitting in the bleachers and behind the sideline fence on either side. "And another runner scores. A crucial error made by the Royals' pitcher there. It's a hard thing to remember, but whenever the ball gets past the catcher, the pitcher becomes a fielder."

Back on the field, Kurt Sr., coach of the Royals, with the build of a major league power hitter signals Hank the umpire, who takes off his mask and shouts, "Time!" Kurt Sr., Jose, and Kurt Jr. meet halfway down the third baseline.

The coach begins his pep talk, staring directly at Kurt Jr. "It's just an error, son. Don't beat yourself up. I believe in you," Kurt Sr. says before turning to Jose. "Jose, you have to cover those off-speed pitches, buddy. I know you can do this." He leans in closer to the boys. "Now, both of you, take a breath, and come back and fight." Kurt Jr. and Jose nod in unison.

The announcer sits at a makeshift booth behind the sidelines, observing, and gives his own take on what's happening out there on the field. "The Royals' coach is doing everything he can to right this ship as things begin to sway…"

Hank steps up to Kurt Sr. and the boys. "Time's up, coach."

"Now, come on. Shake it off and fight. You can do this," Kurt Sr.'s voice echoes loudly through the field as he wraps up his speech. He claps his hands, and the two return to their positions on the field.

◊ ◊ ◊

It's the top of the sixth when Casey steps up to the plate. The pitch comes speeding down, fast and inside. Casey swings and connects — CRACK! The ball sails over the fence.

"It's going deep! It's gone," the announcer says excitedly, calling the play. "It's outta here, folks. Another home run for the A-Team's mighty Casey. Now, that was a great hit. He keeps his front shoulder in there and drives it over the right field fence. The As are still in the lead. Nine to zero. Just one more run, and the umpire will have no choice but to invoke the mercy rule and call the game." The A-Team kids pile out of the dugout and line up along the foul line between third plate and home. Casey slaps their hands as he rounds third and bounds home. Charlie stands in the dugout, applauding the solid hit. He turns excitedly to Abe, who watches him with a careful eye.

"Time to ease up on the throttle, Charlie."

"What— Why? We're on a winning streak. Mr. G's going to have the biggest smile on his face when we get home and tell him the news."

"Kurt's an outstanding coach, and I'm not saying we should let his team score on purpose, but let's move some players around. Maybe try putting Seth and Casey in the outfield."

"Alright, but if Gordon finds out," Charlie starts, "he will give me nothing but hell, so this one's on you, man."

Abe swallows down a laugh as Charlie gives a signal to the A-Team's on-deck batter, who nods, confirming receipt of the message. When the batter steps up to the plate, he takes a few practice swings, cool and calm. The ball whizzes down from the mound. The batter swings and misses the first pitch... Then the second pitch... And finally, the third.

Hank makes the call on the field. "Strike three!"

The announcer's voice booms over the field speakers. "This is one of the great things about sports, folks, especially the Youth Summer League. These kids, whether they win or lose, will end up learning a lot about themselves."

Meanwhile, the A-Team kids gather around Charlie in the dugout as they receive their positions for the field from their new coach. "Seth, you're playing left field. Casey, you're in right. Michelle, you'll be pitching." Michelle stares up at Charlie, barely able to contain her excitement. Charlie gives her an encouraging nod, and she runs out of the dugout and heads straight for the mound. Seth's far from happy about the position switch-up, but he walks out to left field without a word of disappointment.

From the announcer's booth... "And it's a pitching change for the A-Team, with Michelle relieving Seth, who's pitched one heck of a game here today. Give him a round of applause, everyone." The crowd goes wild in the bleachers.

On the mound, Michelle winds up. She releases the pitch. It's a fastball, but the Royals' batter manages to connect, hitting the ball out to right field.

"The Royals' own Danny smashes a grounder hard into right field. The first baseman dives—" The crowd, along with the announcer, lets out a sigh of defeat. "Oh, he misses it. Casey, this time out in right field, scoops it up and fires the ball to first... Except no one is covering the base. A rare error by the A-Team here allows the Royals a solid base hit.

Charlie stands in the doorway to the dugout, clapping like the good sport he's trying to be. "Good hit, Danny," he says, acknowledging the successful play for the opposing team. On the mound, Michelle winds up again, this time releasing a wild pitch.

"Ooh, that's a wild one," says the announcer.

Hank calls it. "Ball!"

The announcer continues. "Danny advances to second." Michelle's next pitch comes in high and outside. The Royals' batter swings and hits the ball — it goes foul just outside of right field. Casey makes the play, snagging the ball in the air. "Beautiful play by Casey for the first out. This kid can't put a foot wrong today." It's Kurt Jr.'s turn at bat once again. He bunts and makes it to first base. Danny gets to third. "And it's one out for the Royals with a runner in scoring position." Jose steps up next. Michelle throws the ball.

"Ball," yells Hank, his voice echoing through the field. Jose steps out to take a practice swing. Once he's back into position, Michelle releases her second pitch. Jose hits a high fly ball to left field. Seth catches it seamlessly. Meanwhile, the runner on third tags back and runs home. Seth rockets the ball to the catcher waiting on the plate. The runner slides in the nick of time.

When the dust clears... "Safe," booms Hank. Michelle strikes out the next batter for an easy third out, and the A-Team wins the game.

The announcer makes his final call. "And that wraps things up. An easy victory for the A-Team." The crowd in the bleachers goes wild. Both teams gather on the field and cordially shake hands with one another. As the crowd disperses and the A-Team kids return to their parents, Charlie clears the dugout of any trash and equipment left behind.

From the bleachers, Teri comes storming over to Charlie just as he steps out of the dugout. She jabs her pointy finger into his chest. "What was that? Why'd you move him to left field?" A look of panic flashes across Charlie's face. Then Teri grabs him by the shoulders. "I'm kidding. It's good for him." She flashes those pearly whites at him, and Charlie nearly melts at the view. He just about gets up the courage to embrace her, but Teri pulls away and reaches out to hug Seth, who approaches right then.

The sun sets over the field, and by now, the stands are clear of people but covered in trash. Abe hoses down the pitcher's mound while Charlie rakes the infield. Hank approaches with a handful of beers. He passes one to Charlie. "Congratulations.

Great game."

Charlie accepts the drink from his uncle and proudly spews, "One game down, six to go, and then we're championship bound!" Shoeless Joe wanders over to the gang, his water dish in his mouth. Abe finishes his task at the mound and walks over just as Hank pours a little beer into Joe's dish.

"I'm not talking about the win. I'm talking about the *way* you won," Hank says. Abe collects his beer and takes a long guzzle as Hank continues. "Letting the Royals score like that. You're a good man, Charlie." Abe's eyes sweep over to Charlie, who shows minimal recognition.

◊ ◊ ◊

As the season goes on, Herbert's Giants obliterate the A-Team in a sweep of ten to zero by the second inning. The standings board shows that the two teams are currently tied for first with two wins, followed by Kansas City with one win, and the Dodgers in last place with zero wins. The Giants secure a third win — twenty to two — followed by a close win for the A-Team. The battle rages on, and the standings board shows the Giants and the A-Team are still tied for first place, now holding four wins each.

Charlie finishes raking the infield after a game and makes his way over to the bleachers, where he spots Jack picking up trash. Abe follows him closely with a bell, which he rings at regular intervals. "Shame," he says, ringing the bell toward Jack as the teen puts some trash into a garbage bag. Abe rings the bell. "Shame." Jack adds more trash to the bag.

"What's this all about?" Charlie interrupts just as Abe is about to ring the bell again.

His brother replies, "Young Jack here was caught operating a black market candy bar and fireworks racket right here on the field." Abe goes back to ringing the bell. "Shame," he says to Jack before turning back to Charlie. "He was trading fireworks for snack bar tickets, which he then sold to parents for half their face value. Picking up trash is his punishment."

Charlie watches Abe ring the bell, amused. "The bell and

the shaming is a bit much, isn't it?"

"Shame," repeats Abe.

"Oh, that was my idea," Jack chimes in. He dumps his trash bag into a nearby garbage can and then turns to Abe. "That was so cool, man."

Abe gives the teen a look. "Punishment isn't supposed to be fun, Jack."

Jack shrugs. "Not my problem, preacher."

"Might I suggest something else?" Charlie says and sprints to the dugout. He comes out holding Abe's embroidered 'Coach Abe' cap and returns to the group. "We could have one of these made up for you." Charlie tosses the cap over to the teen. "Coach Jack's got a nice ring."

Jack looks down at the cap. "Nah, that was a one-off." He shoves the cap back at Charlie. "I don't do baseball anymore."

Charlie shrugs, a serious look on his face. "Should've thought of that before you turned to a life of crime." Jack looks to Abe for an escape but is instead met with a pokerfaced look that only reinforces Charlie's.

◇ ◇ ◇

Charlie sprawls out on the living room in front of the media center at Gordon's house. Doing so has become a bit more challenging, with Gordon's nurses and various well-wishers stopping by at all hours, and now the A-Team kids popping in every now and then, hoping to inspire more training sessions. There's a knock at the front door. *What now?*

Abe comes down the stairs just as Charlie opens the door, revealing Jack carrying an Xbox gaming console. Charlie stands by as the teen invites himself in and begins to set up shop in the living room. "What's with the Xbox?" Charlie asks, shutting the door before he and Abe join Jack in the room moments later.

Jack mimics Charlie's voice. "'What's with the Xbox?'" He laughs and continues in his regular voice. "Dude, you're so out of touch. It's an Xbox Series X." The brothers take a seat on the couch and exchange a confused look as Jack connects the console to the TV.

Moments later, Jack stands tall before Charlie and Abe. "Gentlemen, let's start with the highlight clips from Herbert's past games." Jack uses the Xbox controller to open YouTube. He navigates to a playlist featuring various baseball related videos and selects one of them. It begins to play quietly in the background, with Jack narrating the footage for Charlie and Abe, crouched down next to the TV.

Jack points to something on the screen. "This is Herbert signaling his outfielders to reposition themselves, see?" The video cuts to a closeup of Coach Guy. "Here's his assistant, Coach Guy, recording the batter. A program on the laptop then analyzes the footage and determines, based on the batter's stance and history, where the ball is most likely to go." Charlie and Abe take it all in, eyes wide.

Grabbing the controller, Jack fast-forwards through the video and resumes it a few seconds in. "Here we can see, Herbert goes for broke in the first inning. He not only demoralizes the other team, but also, it gives him a shot at the plate, with the umpire forced to invoke the mercy rule."

The three guys watch as the Giants' batter on-screen hits a foul ball. "And finally, one of Herbert's favorite tricks — he has his players hit several foul balls in a row. This really wears down a pitcher." Jack exits the YouTube app and navigates to the main screen, where he selects a baseball game. He hands both Charlie and Abe a controller. "Now, we're gonna play some 'Fantasy League Baseball.'"

Abe looks excited. "I love this game! One time I picked all three Molina brothers," he jokes.

"This is different. I loaded Herbert's players and the A-Team kids onto the game. Charlie, you're playing for Herbert's team, and Abe, you'll be playing for the As."

"Cool," Abe exclaims. "How do I get virtual Charlie drunk? You know, so it's more realistic."

Jack laughs, but Charlie ignores Abe's quip and instead asks, "Shouldn't I play on my own team?"

With perhaps the worst impression of an Asian accent to

ever exist, Jack replies, "Grasshopper, to defeat your enemy, you must learn to act and think like him."

"Act like Herbert?" Charlie asks. "You mean you want me to pick my nose?" He laughs at his own joke while Abe just rolls his eyes.

Within two hours, empty water bottles litter the room as Charlie and Abe sit in the living room, playing game after game. Abe tosses his controller onto the couch. Jack stands by, nodding approvingly at the brothers. "Not bad, Charlie. You beat your own team eight games to one," he comments.

"It was easy. I could predict everything Abe was going to do." Charlie's eyes light up in realization. "I know how to beat Herbert."

"Remember, grasshopper," Abe says, looking at Charlie, "you can lose the game and still win."

Charlie scoffs. "On what planet?" He couldn't understand where Abe's head was. Charlie wanted to win — because on his turf, winning was *everything*.

◊ ◊ ◊

Later that week, Jack works on the Youth Summer League fields as another tier to his original punishment. He was supposed to be helping Abe, but the pastor is nowhere in sight for the moment. Jack glances over his shoulder before pouring liquid down several fake gopher holes. Casey walks up just then, and Jack decides to test out his theories on the unsuspecting.

"Want to see something really cool?" Jack asks. He lights a match and throws it down one of the holes. Almost immediately, several huge fireballs erupt from the holes in the ground.

"What the crap?!" Casey exclaims, his eyes wide.

With a big grin, Jack replies nonchalantly, "It's mostly Diet Coke and Mentos, but I also added a little soap and liquid methane. I saw it on an old episode of *MythBusters*."

"*MythBusters*?" Casey looks a bit worried. "Well, that's something. You looking for more community service?" Despite the age difference, even as the younger one of the two, Casey's maturity level was worlds above Jack's. The rambunctious teen constantly acted like a kid let loose in a candy store, never once stopping to think about the consequences of his actions.

"Lighten up, goody two shoes, you don't *have* to be so perfect all the time." Another fireball erupts from one of the fake gopher holes, nearly cutting off Jack, who smiles with satisfaction. "Ah, the smell of napalm in the morning... Smells like victory to me."

Abe returns to the main field from the direction of the outfield and quickly spies the small explosions taking place on the field. He smiles at the explosions with approval. The exploration of scientific nature was something he always encouraged the teens to take part in. Although, he often combined the science lessons with messages from the Bible, so it was nice to see that something had registered Maybe he was finally getting through, breaking down each teen's internal barrier. Maybe they had actually started listening to the messages of grace, hope, and love he tried to convey each and every week.

The work done as acting groundskeeper was not a high-paying position, but Abe chose to do it for his love of the place. The fields had been named after his own father, and the idea of this place potentially turning into another shopping complex stirred up ill feelings within. Something would need to be done — and soon. Tonight he'd work on sending off a letter to the school district, along with the council, asking them to reconsider the decision on the fields, spelling out the historical importance and traditions of the game... The community spirit. He could enlist Jack to begin a campaign via social media. Surely the board would understand. Surely they'd encourage a petition. Surely they'd do something...

CHAPTER THIRTEEN

I t's the day of the big game between the A-Team and the Giants. Les, one of the other groundskeepers, is the first to arrive. He pulls into the empty parking lot at precisely six-thirty that morning. While Les rakes the leaves around the snack bar, Teri arrives, her arms piled with boxes of donuts. She manages to balance a large cup of coffee in one hand, plus a bagel wrapped in parchment paper on top of the slim donut boxes. Seeing her approach, Les airlifts the coffee from her hand and catches the bagel just as it begins to slide off the box top.

"Thanks, Les," Teri says.

Les sips on the coffee. "And thank you," he responds, eagerly taking a bite of his bagel. Teri continues to the snack bar, unlocks the door, and begins to set up shop. She preps the coffee and hot chocolate machines, wraps hotdogs in yellow paper and puts them in the steamer, and fully restocks the churro warmer.

Abe and Nicky arrive to the fields soon after. A hot chocolate sits next to a chocolate donut, waiting patiently on the snack bar counter for Nicky. Abe grabs a maple bar from one of the donut boxes and a sports drink before he goes to water the grass for the upcoming game.

The rest of the early morning prep goes on without a hitch. Les pulls out the bases and umpire gear, doing an equipment inspection. From the outfield, Abe returns with a golf cart. Nicky runs over and takes the wheel while Abe piles the bases into the cart. They drive between various fields, Abe installing the bases one by one.

By now, it's nine o'clock. Hank, Charlie, Jack, and the A-Team kids have already arrived. Families begin to trickle in and settle around the fields. The snack bar opens for business, and

Teri finds several people already lined up to buy the breakfast of champions — dogs and donuts. Judy finally makes her appearance, bringing the American flag to the flag post so Abe can raise it as the National Anthem plays over the loudspeakers during the opening ceremony of the day.

Charlie makes his final pre-game run to the snack bar, where he talks with Teri. "Well, it's time for the big game. Wish me luck."

Teri gives him a look of assurance. "You don't need luck; not with baseball." Off in the distance, Wagner's 'Ride of the Valkyries' blares, getting closer by the second. He and Teri look to find three Hummers storming their way into the parking lot.

Charlie uses his Poltergeist girl's voice and says, "They're here…" A look of excitement comes over his face, suddenly giddy as a kid. He runs out to the parking lot to greet the competition. The Hummers pull up to the main gate, and the Giants players disembark with their pristine matching gear bags. They march in formation to the gate, with Herbert, Coach Guy, and Sergeant Dick bringing up the rear.

Charlie watches from a few feet away before walking up to Herbert. "Coach Herbie, may I park your Hummers for you? Our valet is on break."

"Maddox, when we are on the field of battle, I expect you to call me 'Coach Herbert,'" he demands. Charlie just laughs, which pisses off Herbert even more. The *true* game has begun… As they continue on their way, Charlie stares, a bit concerned, his stomach doing flips.

Meanwhile, on the field, Abe helps to warm up Seth and Casey. The Giants march onto the field and pile into the visitor's dugout, generating much more fanfare than expected. Abe turns to watch. "What the f—" Casey cuts off the pastor with a cough. Charlie anxiously runs to the A-Team's dugout and corrals Jack to play their own 'theme' music over the field speakers. Moments later, the theme song from 'Mortal Kombat' blasts across the field. Abe, Seth, and Casey dance their way to the dugout where the rest of the A-Team gathers. It's almost time.

Breathlessly, Charlie beckons to his players. "Seth and Michelle, come with me." The two kids nod and follow Charlie. He leads them behind the dugout. "You want to win this game, don't you?"

"Is this a trick question?" Michelle asks.

"There are things I'm going to ask you to do. They won't make any sense. But I need you to do them without question, okay?"

Seth shrugs. "You won't have to ask me twice."

"Good," Charlie says, nodding. "First thing — don't throw the new pitch until I give you the signal."

"But I've been practicing, and they won't even see it coming," argues Seth.

Charlie holds up two fingers in a request for silence. Turns out that Judy's technique works. "Not until the signal. Okay?"

Seth hangs his head slightly in defeat and answers, "Okay." Charlie shows Seth and Michelle the new signal, rotating his arm.

Now, there's only thirty minutes left before the big game. The A-Team practices haphazardly on one side of the field, while the Giants warm up on the other side, their practice well-drilled and synchronized.

In his umpire garb, Hank stands with Charlie and Herbert, both coaches keeping a watchful eye on their respective teams. "I want a nice, clean game this time," Hank says. "Understand?" Charlie and Herbert give each other a snide look. Hank prompts them. "None of the little kids can lead-off until the ball passes home plate. Got it?" Charlie and Herbert slowly nod in unison. "And try to remember, fellas — it's a baseball *game*. Let the kids have some fun for a change."

◊ ◊ ◊

The usual announcer sits in the booth. "Look who we have here with us today... Rainbow Man!" The local character 'Rainbow Man,' wearing a rainbow-colored afro wig, stands on the uppermost row of the bleachers, mingling with the crowd. "You might remember him as the guy who held up Bible passages

120

during pro baseball games," the announcer continues. "My favorite was Luke, chapter eight, verse seventeen."

Jack and Abe stand around outside the A-Team's dugout. The teen turns to his older counterpart. "Bet you don't know that verse by heart, preacher."

"All work and no play makes Jack a dull boy," Abe answers without missing a beat.

Jack shakes his head in disbelief. "Smart a—"

"Nothing is secret but what will be known,'" Abe says, quoting the verse by heart. "'Anything that is hidden will be brought into the light.'" Jack doesn't look impressed.

The announcer's voice blares through the speakers again. "So, Rainbow Man, what do you think is going through Coach Herbert's head right now?" Rainbow Man holds up a sign with 'Jeremiah 51:4' printed on it, along with the verse. With a Godlike voice, the announcer reads the verse. "'I will bring them down like lambs to the slaughter, like rams with the goats.'" The announcer nods and comments in his regular voice, "I was thinking the same thing too, Rainbow Man."

On the field, Hank brushes off home plate. The crowd in the bleachers goes wild with excitement; the game is about to begin. Teri takes a well-earned break and claims a spot on the bleachers from where she can simultaneously keep an eye on the snack bar. She holds a 'Go A-Team' sign and cheers along with the rest. This particular season has proved to be more exciting than ever before with her childhood sweetheart coaching the kids. Until Charlie's reappearance, Teri had always been the sort of mom to put her child's needs before everything and everyone else; it had defined her life for so long. But with Charlie's influence as of late, she no longer felt the pressure to be a 'my kid is the center of my universe' sort of mom but instead now felt free to be a mom who can enjoy watching her kid play his favorite sport while having just a little bit of time for herself too. It was an unfamiliar but enjoyable feeling.

Behind the back fence of the field, Brian and Diane sit on a picnic bench. Brian looks busy, maintaining the A-Team's stat book. In the distance, Judy paces, her cell phone glued to her ear. Shoeless Joe crosses the field and lifts his leg on the Giants' dugout entrance before disappearing into the A-Team's dugout.

Finally, it's time. Charlie, Abe, Jack, and the A-Team kids line up on the third baseline, while Herbert, Coach Guy, Sergeant Dick, and the Giants line up on the first baseline. Nicky stands at home plate, with Hank holding a microphone for her.

The little girl's voice is the epitome of innocence and joy as she recites the well-known pledge. "I trust in God. I love my country and will respect its laws. I will play fair and strive to win. But win or lose, I will always do my best." Nicky nods to Hank and then moves to the side.

Hank takes his spot behind home plate and yells, "Play ball!" The crowd goes even more wild than before. On the scoreboard:

INNING #1
A-TEAM — 0
GIANTS — 0

The Giants take the starting at-bat. Seth pitches. The batter swings and misses the first pitch.

"Strike," calls Hank. Seth sends two more pitches over the plate and strikes out the batter. From the A-Team dugout, Charlie signals Casey, the catcher — but then spots Herbert watching from across the way. Charlie switches up the signal.

From the Giants dugout, Herbert reads Charlie's signal aloud. "One down, two to go, Snot Nose." He scoffs in annoyance.

Meanwhile, on the field, Seth strikes out the second and third batters. The Giants repay the favor, striking out all three batters on the A-Team.

INNING #2
A-TEAM — 0
GIANTS — 0

Twice more, Seth manages to strike out the Giants batters.

Once again, the Giants repay the favor. No hits for either team yet. The tension, both on the field and in the audience, is palpable.

Even the announcer's pep has come to a standstill. He drones on. "It's the top of the fourth. So far it's been a pitcher's duel. But we have new pitchers coming on board. Rainbow Man, how's the game looking to you?" Rainbow Man holds up another sign from the bleachers. This time 'Samuel 4:1' is printed on it, along with the verse. The announcer dons his Godlike voice. "'Now Israel went out against the Philistines to battle and pitched beside Ebenezer: and the Philistines pitched in Aphek.'" He continues in his normal voice. "Couldn't have said it better myself."

Back on the field, Seth stands on the mound and releases a fastball to the plate. The batter misses it. Hank does a pounding motion signal with his fist as if knocking on a door. "Strike!" The batter eases in closer to the plate. Seth pitches another fastball, and this time the batter foul tips it. From the dugout, Charlie signals Casey, who relays the signal to Seth: *Trust me; throw it slower.* Seth gives Casey a begrudging nod. He winds up and releases the pitch — a slow one. The batter swings at the ball too early and misses, striking out.

Hank signals a clenched fist. "Out!" Back on the mound, Seth turns to the dugout and smiles at Charlie, who nods in return. He gives the kid a thumbs up.

When Seth looks away, Charlie talks aloud to no one in particular and says, "Step one to beating Herbert... Don't let him wear down my pitcher." He looks over at Herbert in the Giants dugout and catches his eye. Herbert sends a signal across the way, and Charlie reads it aloud. "I hope you like the taste of blood." Charlie shakes his head for a moment, unfazed.

Sergeant Dick stomps out of the Giants dugout and gets in the batter's face as the kid walks back to the dugout, head digging into his chest. "What's the matter with you, soldier? When I give you instructions, I expect you to follow them. You understand me, private?" The batter weakly nods in response.

"Now, drop and give me twenty," growls Sergeant Dick.

The next batter for the Giants steps up to the plate. Seth winds up and releases the pitch. The batter swings and drives a ground ball right between first and second base. The second baseman runs to make the play and sends an underhand throw to the first baseman, who has a foot planted firmly on the base. Knowing he's already out, the batter stops short of first and walks back toward the dugout.

The announcer calls it. "He tried to beat it out but came up short."

Fuming, Sergeant Dick's voice booms as the batter enters the dugout. "Private, you are never, under any circumstances, to stop short of the base. Do you understand?" The batter nods, intimidated by the sergeant. "Now, drop and give me a hundred."

The next batter up swings short and hits the first pitch hard, sending it straight into Seth's direction. He quickly ducks, and the ball just barely misses him. The second baseman makes the catch, giving the batter an immediate out. As the As run off the field, they pass by the second of the two reprimanded Giants batters, who still does push-ups outside the dugout. Charlie stands to the side of the A-Team dugout and talks aloud to himself, eyes focused on Herbert's side of the field. "Step two... Make sure your pitcher can duck."

◊ ◊ ◊

It's the A-Team's turn at bat. Michelle has already reached first base, and Casey is up next. He's ready, with a bat in hand, practicing his swing.

In the Giants dugout, Coach Guy analyzes a video of Casey's practice swings on the laptop. He enters a few keystrokes before turning to Herbert. "He's swinging high and down." Coach Guy looks back at the screen. "Looks like he'll hit deep into right field," he adds.

Herbert turns to signal his outfielders. The centerfielder moves to the right, while the right fielder goes deep, and the left fielder moves toward the infield. With Casey now at the plate, the Giants' pitcher throws a fastball that comes in low and outside. Casey swings high and down and misses.

"Strike," shouts Hank.

The pitcher winds up again. Casey takes a small step back, repositions his feet, and swings low, sending a rocketing homer over the left field fence. The announcer goes crazy in the booth. "And there it goes. It's out of here! Casey Ragsdale has done it again. That's his nineteenth home run of the season."

The crowd goes wild. Everyone in the bleachers hops to their feet, cheering excitedly as Casey jogs around, hitting all the bases. Beyond the back fence, Brian still sits at his picnic table post. He marks down Casey's latest stats in his little book. The As come out of the dugout and form a line, giving their teammate high-fives as he rounds third.

Charlie smirks from the dugout. "Step three… If Herbert is going to throw low and outside, they're going out of the park."

Herbert rips off his cap and throws it to the ground in disgust. Following his lead, Sergeant Dick picks up the laptop and violently throws it against the dugout wall. It smashes to pieces, bits of plastic and metal going everywhere.

Herbert whirls around in shock and spews, "That's coming out of your salary, sergeant!" He turns back around and peers over at Charlie's side of the field. Charlie sends a signal to Herbert, which he reads aloud. "That new signal is simply smashing." Herbert flashes Charlie a single-finger signal in response, then storms out of the dugout and onto the field, calling a time-out. He stomps over to the pitcher and says quietly in his ear, "From here on out, I want nothing but fastballs."

In a timid voice, the pitcher attempts to counter the demand. "Sir, permission to speak. I don't know if I can pitch two innings like that."

"Deal with the pain on your own time. And watch for my signals." Herbert dismisses himself and walks back to the dugout. The Giants' pitcher manages to strike out the next two A-Team batters, closing out the inning.

INNING #6

A-TEAM — 1
GIANTS — 1

The Giants are at the plate, with Seth back on the mound. Curtis, the first batter, hits a single to left field. Reporting the play, the announcer says, "Curtis makes a terrific lead play on a one-hop, driving that ball straight out to left field. Folks, this is the last inning, so the Giants need to load the bases in order to win."

In the A-Team dugout, Charlie nudges Jack with his elbow. "Get Michelle warmed up." Jack stares back in shock for a moment. When Charlie doesn't change his request, Jack gets up and handles the assignment.

Abe sits on the dugout bench, looking up at Charlie in disbelief. "You're not going to let Seth finish the inning?" Charlie shrugs, watching Seth wind up on the mound. Seth throws the ball. The batter hits a grounder straight to the shortstop, who smoothly fields it and throws to second, forcing the runner out. The second baseman throws a rocket to first.

"Out," cries Hank.

"A double play," the announcer booms. Over in the bleachers, Teri looks down and covers her eyes, barely able to contain her excitement. The announcer calls her out. "And mom can't believer her eyes. The As are one out away from taking first place in the standings."

Back on the mound, Seth pitches to the next Giants batter, Devin. He hits it foul. The announcer adds, "The Giants are fighting to stay alive here, folks." Seth winds up and throws another pitch.

Hank calls out, "Ball!"

"Seth pitches with such gusto," says the announcer, "his hat falls off in the process." Another pitch from Seth. "Two-two pitch... Another foul." Hank tosses a new ball to Seth. The kid winds up and releases the next pitch, and this time the batter drills it down the left field line, all the way to the fence. "And Devin keeps things going," the announcer exclaims. As Devin rounds third, Coach Guy windmills his arm. "The Giants are going to try to score on this one…"

A hush falls over the crowd, and the announcer stands up for a better look. The left fielder whips the ball to the third baseman, who throws it high to Casey, waiting on the plate. Casey throws to third as Devin turns back from his race for home. Suddenly he's caught in a rundown.

The announcer continues. "Now, they're trying to get Devin out on third." Devin slides into the base. "And he is…" The announcer looks for Hank's cue. "Safe! The Giants now have the tying run on third." After the intense play, Charlie steps out of the dugout and signals for a pitching change. Abe watches him, skeptical.

Hank yells over to the announcer, "Switching out Seth for Michelle." The crowd responds with a loud swarm of 'boos.'

Hearing this, Seth rips his cap from his head and angrily storms toward Charlie. "What?! You're taking me out again? You're gonna cost us the game, coach!"

Charlie rests his hands on Seth's shoulders, trying to calm him down. "You're our starting pitcher, bud. Michelle's our relief. Now, go take a seat, and let her pitch."

Seth storms into the dugout. On his way, he passes Michelle, who looks terrified. "Better not lose us the game, *girl*," Seth hisses to her. Michelle looks over her shoulder at him, but Charlie's voice interrupts her thoughts.

He pokes his head into the dugout. "C'mon, Michelle!" The girl exits the dugout and follows Charlie to the mound, where he gives her a mini pep talk. He smiles down at her as she situates herself. "Just give it your best, hon." He leaves her and returns to the dugout.

From the bleachers, Tom stands and cheers on his daughter. "Come on, honey! You can do it!" The crowd quickly joins in. Michelle winds up on the field. The batter swings and misses.

"Strike one," calls Hank. Michelle smiles, her confidence growing. She faces the Giants' third batter again and winds up.

Hank signals a ball as the pitch sails anywhere but over the plate. Same goes for the next pitch. One strike, two balls. Michelle kicks the mound, frustrated at her performance. She readies herself for the next, but the pitch doesn't work as planned this time either. "Ball three!" Michelle releases yet another pitch. The batter finally manages to get a piece of it but it sails foul.

The announcer's voice cuts through the tension. "And the count is full. You really gotta feel for little Michelle out there on the mound. Must seem like it's her against the world."

In the bleachers, Tom jumps to his feet again and leads the crowd into a slow clap. "Mi-chelle! Mi-chelle! Mi-chelle," he chants. Several others join in, and pretty soon, the whole crowd is chanting along with him.

Michelle looks over at Charlie from the mound. He stands near the dugout, nodding his head. Then he signals — rotating his arm. Michelle nods in acknowledgement and winds up. She releases Charlie's 'slushie' pitch. It barely makes it over the plate. When it reaches the batter, he doesn't swing, confused as the ball manages to find a piece of the plate.

The announcer scrambles to his feet and yells into his microphone, "Look at that pitch! I couldn't tell if it was a slider or a curveball."

Hank perks up once more. "Strike three," he calls to the batter. "You're out!"

The announcer continues. "And the A-Team has won the game! One more, and they'll be on their way to the Youth Summer League Baseball World Series! Rainbow Man, any final words?" In the bleachers, Rainbow Man holds up a sign that says: 'Apocalypse Now.' The announcer channels Jim Morrison and starts singing. "This is the end. My only friend, the end." The crowd is still busy going wild. Tom races down from the bleachers, onto the field, and hugs his daughter. The rest of the A-Team clears the dugout, running onto the field to join in on the celebration. Seth is the last to exit, but he pushes his way through the throng of his peers and hugs Michelle.

Suddenly, Herbert charges up to Hank. "That was a ball,"

he argues snootily.

"It was a strike. You're just blind, dumbass," responds the umpire. Inside the dugout, only Casey and Abe remain. Abe sits there, petting Shoeless Joe, but the young player was fuming inside. *That coach doesn't know what he's doing, and his own dad was the one to coerce him into coaching the team; how pathetic.*

INNING #6
A-TEAM — 2
GIANTS — 1

Teri rushes onto the field to swoop up Seth and Charlie into a hug. Charlie thinks to himself... *Step four: win the game — win the girl?*

CHAPTER FOURTEEN

Charlie, Abe, Teri, Jack, and the A-Team kids — all except for one — celebrate their latest win down at the local pizza joint. "Where's Casey?" Charlie whispers to Seth, nudging his arm gently.

"He had to go home early," Seth replies with a shrug. Charlie nods but furrows his brows. His attention gets drawn to Abe, who stands at the head of the table, looking primed and ready to express a big congratulations.

"Well done today, everybody," Abe says, breaking out into a huge smile. "Mr. G is so proud of you." The other adults nod in unison.

Teri chimes in with, "We all are." Her gaze lands on Charlie, who grins.

"Really," Charlie says, more to himself than to anyone else, taking in the revelation. For so many years, he'd felt that Teri didn't truly understand his passion for the game — didn't truly 'get it' — despite her being no stranger to the fields. The failure to understand his passion was the reason why she chose to stay behind when he left for New Mexico all those years ago… *Wasn't it?* Charlie snaps out of it, realizing he'd better say something nice too. He stands up to address the team, raising his glass of beer high in the air. "Just echoing what Abe said. I am so proud of you all, going out there and playing a great game." Everyone else holds up their glasses. "Cheers, everyone."

"Cheers," everyone says, echoing their coach's sentiments. Charlie settles back into his seat, smiling at Teri like the Cheshire Cat. Nothing could squash this feeling of pure joy, and in some ways, he thinks it superior to the adulation he experienced back on the field in New Mexico. Maybe it wasn't so bad, getting to spend some time on his home turf. But just when he thought things were looking up, the front door to the restaurant opens wide and in marches Sergeant Dick, with the Giants bringing up the rear. They come to a halt at the A-Team's table, standing in an organized row.

The sergeant addresses his troops. "This is what happens when you win a big battle! But you pathetic losers—" Sergeant Dick walks down the line of Giants, shoving a finger into each one of their faces. "You *lost*. So, now, you will stand here and watch your sworn enemies celebrate."

Charlie keeps his cool but swiftly gets up from his seat and approaches the sergeant. "Uh, no, you guys need to leave."

If it were up to him, Sergeant Dick wouldn't have wasted the breath it took to argue with the lowly opposition, but he'd sworn to follow his own set of orders. "You are not my commanding officer. I do not take orders from you."

Teri stands up and clears her throat, trying to reel in the kids' attention and possibly defuse the hint of an impending confrontation. She pulls out a tote bag from under the table and sets it on top, pulling out mini handmade scrapbooks and goodie bags. "I made one for each of us."

Sergeant Dick snaps up one of the books and gives it a once-over. "Look, the sissies are getting cute little books to remember each other by. Isn't that sweet?" His voice drips with condescension as his fingertips clutch the very edge of the book in disgust.

Charlie makes another attempt to control the situation. "Really, you guys need to leave. This party is ours… Just like that championship."

The sergeant ignores Charlie as he flips through the book with increasing rage. Finally, he stops. Tension wafts through the still air. "I said, I don't take orders from you," growls the sergeant. He makes a move as though going to tear out one of the photos — now, it's personal. Charlie goes ballistic and lunges at Sergeant Dick, trying his best to wrangle away the scrapbook.

Ever the troublemaker, Jack picks up a half-eaten slice of

pizza and releases his battle cry. "Food fight!" He flings the slice at one of the Giants players, Private Jefferson. The pizza sticks to the side of the kid's head. He makes a move to retaliate, but Sergeant Dick confronts the private, giving Charlie an opening to rescue the special book for Teri.

"Don't you dare break formation, Private Jefferson," the sergeant threatens. Jefferson freezes for a moment before launching the pizza slice into the air, sending it hurtling toward Sergeant Dick's face. "You're already on thin—" Complete silence except for the pizza connecting with the sergeant's skin. *Game on.*

Suddenly, both teams are at war, flinging pizza around the room at each other. Meanwhile, Shoeless Joe happily gobbles up a slice that lands on the floor. Teri and Abe take cover, huddling underneath a table in the corner. Abe is just about to take a bite from the emergency slice he brought with him when another slice flies through the air and slams into his head.

He pokes out from hiding in search of the culprit and finds none other than Seth in joyful hysterics. "Seth!"

Right at that moment, Teri's goodie bags soar across the room, one by one. She sighs in defeat and turns to Abe. "And there go the goodie bags..."

Abe returns fire on Seth with the emergency slice he was in the middle of eating. "When are you going to tell Charlie?" He looks back at Teri, who gives him a look of disdain. "Teri, the boy's about to become a man. He needs that male guidance." Suddenly the restaurant manager comes barreling into the front room and chases everybody out.

◊ ◊ ◊

Abe stands in front of the door to Gordon's house and knocks. Moments later, Charlie opens the door for his brother, a beer in hand. "Hey."

"Hey. Got another one of those?" Abe asks, nodding toward Charlie's beer as he shuffles into the living room. Charlie pops open the cooler he's temporarily parked beside the couch and retrieves a beer for Abe. They sink into their chosen seats with their drinks, mindlessly watching the baseball game that quietly plays on the TV. Charlie looks off in thought, his mind elsewhere.

Abe takes a sip. "You know, it was a stroke of genius to get Jack onboard. He's a good kid. A bit off the rails, maybe… But he'll find his feet."

Charlie nods, still distant. "And clearly, he knows his stuff."

"He was a star pitcher. Lived and breathed the game. Could've been the next you." That snaps Charlie back to reality.

He turns to Abe, confused. "Why'd he stop playing?"

"His parents got divorced. Dad left town," explains Abe. Charlie nods solemnly. Abe continues. "You know, I feel for these kids. They cop so much pressure from their parents, teachers, coaches…" Charlie thoughtfully turns back to the TV while Abe takes a sip of his beer. "I spoke up about it at a parents' meeting once. Said we should be letting them play and have fun."

Charlie looks amused. "How'd that go down?"

"Like a Giants batter in the bottom of the sixth." Charlie laughs at his brother's response, but Abe just shakes his head. "It's a shame what can happen to a kid when his dad isn't there."

"Don't we know it," Charlie says. "If I had a son…" He takes a swig of his beer and shakes his head.

Abe stares, impatiently waiting for Charlie to finish. For a moment, he wants to whack him upside the head with his baseball cap. "Yeah?"

"I'd wanna be there for it all." Charlie pauses and then asks, "How do you know all this?"

Abe shrugs, trying not to look too pleased with himself. "The teens at the youth group do open up to me now and again. Usually about the pressures they feel from coaches, parents, and their peers. I went to bat for them in the community, and they respect that."

Charlie turns to his brother. "You're a good man, Abe."

"I try." Abe shrugs, avoiding eye contact. "We had a teen commit suicide over the pressure not too long ago. A few of the kids turned to drugs to help cope after the death of their friend. Some of them have been on the streets, kicked out by their folks. Some have settled back at home out of necessity despite their poor relationship with their parents. I didn't have a great relationship with their parents back then either."

Charlie smirks and lets out a chuckle. "Yeah, you told me."

Abe continues without missing a beat. "Gordon hated the position I took on baseball. It is a *national* sport! Anyone who wants should be allowed access to the game and welcomed to become a part of it. The competition certainly isn't worth the price of a young man's death."

Charlie nods, choosing to remain silent for a few long moments. Finally, he asks, "You do anything about the new fields?"

"Actually, yeah, I wrote a letter to the council and the school board. Yet to hear back," Abe replied. Charlie ponders whether a letter would make any difference. *'The pen is mightier than the sword,'* said someone famous. But he couldn't recall anyone ever winning a war with words.

◊ ◊ ◊

That night Charlie dreams of Gordon shouting and stumbling over his words, and for once, Abe is the target of his rage. When Gordon finally takes a breath, he turns to Charlie, slurring. "Nonsense. Only the best kids should play. They *earn* it. And that's why myself and the parents put a fork in Abe and told him he was done."

Then suddenly, the gears shift in his dream, and Charlie's mind journeys its way back to the *infamous* flashback. Such an indiscriminate memory yet one that would never leave him, much like a recurring nightmare — except it visits him not only while he sleeps but also when he's wide awake, assaulting him with no warning, issuing a swift kick to the gut each and every time. *Why now?* Was it because he had finally returned to the place where reminders of the past were all around him like some sort of a shrine? This time the horrid memory presents itself in the dead of night, replaying in Charlie's head for what felt like the millionth time.

He was twelve, competing in the Youth Summer League World Series for the first time. Abe stands on second base and another player stands on first. A much younger Gordon talks strategy with Charlie in the dugout. "We don't need heroics, Charlie. Abe's gonna steal third, and you're gonna bunt."

"But Dad, I want to knock one out of the park," whines twelve-year-old Charlie.

Gordon screams in his face. "I said you're gonna bunt, you idiot! Bunt!"

Back to reality, Charlie wakes up, sweating profusely and chanting, "I want… I want…" He wishes for the answer to making this memory go away for good. Was there something that Charlie needed to realize or perhaps accept before he could move on? Only now could he see that memory from a coach's perspective. What Charlie wanted back then had been fueled by selfishness and not at all what the coach ordered. He'd had no sense of what it meant to play for the team and only desired to seize any chance he could get to show off, a trait that still lingered even in his adult life. Such a mentality wouldn't get him far, and Charlie knew that. The irony here was that he'd never before noticed the detriment of that quality up until this moment, after getting the experience of working with a team where personality clashes are rife. He could see Casey as someone who wanted all the glory for himself. With his own parents encouraging that type of mindset, how would the kid ever learn? Maybe not until he was nearly thirty years of age and coaching his own team.

It had taken Charlie just as long to uncover the selfish nature he had when it came to playing the game he claimed to love wholeheartedly. He peers around at the walls of his childhood bedroom where nothing had been changed in years; it was time for the posters of his youth to come down. When it came to coaching, Herbert wanted his players to shine in their own right, never hesitating to pit one against another. But as a coach, Charlie wanted something different from the kids — he wanted the *entire* team to shine as a well-oiled machine, each piece moving in mesmerizing synchronicity. Boy, he sure had come a long way from his choices at twelve years old. Charlie jumps out of bed and tears the old band posters off his wall... Nirvana, Pearl Jam, Soundgarden... Every last one of them. It was time to grow up.

◊ ◊ ◊

Meanwhile, at Herbert's private training field across town, the kids march along with military precision, bats clenched in their hands. Sergeant Dick heads the line. A PA speaker crackles to life, sending Herbert's voice down over the troops from the comfort of his office. Coach Guy accompanies him, pacing in front of the desk.

"You are the chosen ones," Herbert yells into a microphone device. "You are here because you have what it takes to be a baseball player!"

Coach Guy jumps in. "But in light of your unacceptable loss to the A-Team, we have no choice but to increase the training schedule. All leave is canceled until further notice," he announces.

On the ground below, there are kids running through a marine-inspired obstacle course. Coach Guy watches them from the window.

"A single blow must destroy the opponent, without regard of losses," Herbert shouts, his face reddening as the intensity amps up with each passing second. "A gigantic, earth-shattering blow that will obliterate them!" Herbert is breathless as Coach Guy yanks away the microphone.

"Also, the two soldiers at fault will be dropped from this team," booms Coach Guy. "Strength lies not in defense but in attack! Those soldiers will each have to face their parents and tell them he lacks the strength to fight another day."

On the ground below, the kids stand tall, lined up in military order, silently awaiting their fate. Herbert's voice once again booms through the PA speaker above.

"Become strong in spirit, strong in will, strong in

endurance, strong to bear all sacrifice," screams Herbert, wrapping up his speech.

The kids respond in unison with, "Yes, coach! We are here to serve you!"

Sergeant Dick stands guard over the group. "Back on the field, now! Move it," he growls. "Privates Jefferson and Washington, report to headquarters at seventeen hundred." The two kids exchange a look with one another as they watch the rest of their teammates go off for more drills, catching rampant fly balls while fake explosions assault the field around them.

In her chic apartment, Judy talks with Herbert on the phone. She's dressed in her sexiest nightie — mind you, they weren't video-chatting, so the nightie was a personal choice and allowed her to don the persona of ultimate appeal. The shockingly *hot* date the two had gone on a few nights ago had left Judy feeling absolutely besotted. In all her days, she never would have imagined going for someone overweight and nowhere near drop-dead gorgeous — at least not until her drop-dead dud of a husband ran off with a much younger woman. Now, she was on the path to defaulting her interests toward men who didn't get much attention elsewhere. Those were the ones who would stick around and stay by your side like a loyal puppy-dog. Plus, where Herbert struck out in looks, he made up for with style. His wardrobe clearly presented his expensive taste, each piece of clothing always immaculate. Even the fancy restaurant to which he had taken her out was a place Judy would never be able to afford on her usual salary. She had the looks, the confidence, and the local power — and he matched her on two out of three counts.

She purrs into the phone like a smitten schoolgirl, "I'd love to get together soon."

"That would be great, yes. But first, let's talk business," replies Herbert, his tone very matter-of-fact as he lounges in his office. He barely takes a breath before continuing. "With Gordon out of the way and Charlie busy with the team, that just leaves

Abe's piddly gig as the head groundskeeper."

"Yes, and that'll be handled soon. I'll have my boys step it up. They'll take good care of the fields."

"And with that final move, you'll have control over the board votes, won't you?" Herbert asks, knowing full well that Judy would come through with the goods. The fancy restaurant's exorbitant fees were just a minor expense that was already beginning to pay off — a simple tax deduction for the books. Someone knocks rapidly on Herbert's office door. He says to Judy, "Uh, I gotta go."

"Call me after work," she coos just before Herbert ends the call.

"Come in," he says loudly, quickly tucking away his phone. He straightens up in his office chair. The door swings open and in walk Privates Jefferson and Washington. They each take a seat across from Herbert at his desk, feeling the anxiety sink in.

Twelve-year-old Jefferson found himself wishing for the moral support of a parent — but no such luck. *Was his baseball career over before it had even begun?* The wall behind Herbert was covered in a spread of framed black-and-white photos featuring other baseball all-stars from past Giants seasons. Jefferson imagines the guys in the photographs talking to him. They don't have very nice things to say, though... *You're not good enough, kiddo.* Then another one starts in... *See here, I worked hard to land this gig.* And another... *Yeah, you've got to give 110% to every game — not just 100%.* Jefferson looks away, trying to get the players out of his head. Each photo had been framed and professionally mounted, showcasing only the best of the best. Jefferson knew right then and there; his photo would never have the chance to grace Herbert's walls. He knew what came next, but then again, perhaps it was better to be rid of a team so callous. Sure, his parents would have a fit. They had sacrificed not only time but also money just for him to get on this team in the first place. But he wasn't good enough to cut it, so here he was, sitting across from Herbert, who didn't seem the least bit sympathetic.

"Private Jefferson," Herbert begins, "your insubordination

yesterday was unacceptable. You displayed a complete disregard for orders. As such, I have no choice but to let you go. Both of you." Herbert's eyes sweep over to Private Washington for the first time while Jefferson hangs his head, trying to hold back tears. Was there anything he could say that would convince Coach Herbert otherwise? Baseball was his life, but the grim man behind the desk couldn't care less — that much was obvious. He refuses to let his ex-coach see him cry, and the tears are coming on loud and strong. Jefferson hops to his feet and rushes out before he totally embarrasses himself.

Private Washington stares back at Herbert with a confused look. "Why me? I wasn't even there that day."

Herbert looks the kid square in the eye. "Why?" He shrugs. "Well, kid, you just plain ol' suck. Now, get outta my sight before I have you thrown in the brig." Washington quickly gets to his feet and leaves, an unsettled look on his face. Herbert breaks out into an evil chuckle, without any remorse. His only goal is to win — and to win at *any* cost. Looking around the immaculate office, he brims with satisfaction at everything he's achieved thus far. Yes, he had made the right decision. Next step: find the perfect replacement for his team. A player built with the capability to secure the Giants that spot in the World Series.

◊ ◊ ◊

The next morning, Abe mows one of the fields. As he makes his way around to the infield, he spots Judy hanging around by the home dugout. She waves him over. Abe makes his way to the dugout on the mower, cutting the engine once he approaches. Judy hands him an official-looking envelope with his name printed on it.

"What's this?" Abe asks, taking the envelope with a confused look on his face. He opens it and scans the paper inside — a letter with official league branding and the heading, 'RE: Termination of Employment.' Abe stares up at Judy in disbelief. "You're firing me? Are you kicking me off the board too?" Judy shrugs in response. Abe scoffs, completely appalled by the audacity.

"With the upcoming move to our new fields, we on the board feel it appropriate to engage the services of a bonafide landscaping outfit. We thank you for your service."

Abe shoves an accusatory finger in Judy's face. "I know why you're doing this. You—"

"Good day, Mr. Maddox," Judy says as she spins on her heels and walks off the field, heading to the parking lot where her car awaits her. As she takes her seat behind the wheel, she says, "Well, that's one problem solved." Judy turns to look over at Herbert, who sits in the passenger seat.

CHAPTER FIFTEEN

I t was the A-Team's movie night at Gordon's house, compliments of Charlie. Also there to assist him were Teri, Abe, and Jack. When the kids first arrive, they visit Gordon upstairs, where a nurse gives everyone the rundown on Gordon's health. The old man's well-being would need to continue taking priority over any team bonding rituals if he were to make his way back on the field anytime soon. Once 7 p.m. hits, the kids go downstairs where they were instructed to stay, keeping noise and other 'shenanigans' to a minimum. The coaching team of Charlie, Abe, and Jack offered the kids an atmosphere that was more laid back with a bit more freedom in their playing style and schedule, but regardless, the team was excited for Gordon's return.

Now, with everyone downstairs and the night coming to an end, Teri sits closest to the kitchen, in case any of the kids want anything. Teri had made sausage rolls and pizza for them earlier that night, along with providing junk food for dessert. Not that she had come tonight without her own agenda. It was the night she planned to tell Charlie *everything* — if she could gather up the courage, that is. Telling him about Seth would alleviate so much anxiety, and Teri knew it. She constantly worried that someone else would spill the beans before she had the guts to do so.

Everyone looks to be enjoying the night that was slowly coming to an end. Some of the kids lounge on the floor while others are comfy on the couch. Credits from an animated movie roll across the screen, tying up the night's double feature. Sure, the animated features might have been a bit juvenile, but Charlie wanted to avoid filling the kids' heads with explicit content (at least on his watch). Even though he didn't have kids of his own, he was well aware that the parents would be watching him; they had entrusted him to look after their children. As the credits fade out, Charlie looks around the room. Most of the kids had fallen asleep mid-movie, but a few others, including Seth, managed to stay awake until the end. Though, the rest looked to be on their way to the land of Nod as well. Charlie checks his phone for the time; the parents wouldn't begin arriving for another 20 minutes or so.

His recent coaching experience had given Charlie a little insight into what it was like to be a parent. It was like a whole new dimension. No wonder it had been so hard on his dad back then... *Wow, Gordon as his 'dad' — when was the last time he'd thought of him in that way?* When Charlie's mom passed away, Gordon turned into such a cranky, old bastard. Abe was the only one of the two with the ability to tolerate their father. *Hey, maybe that's why he ended up in ministry.*

Even as a child, Abe was compassionate and understanding of others, never taking another's sour mood personally but instead striving to be the person on which they could offload those feelings. Someone else's crappy day didn't have to be *his* crappy day. Charlie's thought process, on the other hand, was the complete opposite from his brother's. In fact, he would attempt some level of retaliation against anyone who challenged him (especially his arch nemesis Herbert) and became defensive the moment a word was spoken that he perceived as a discredit to his name.

Teri was no stranger to Charlie's ways, and he hadn't changed too much over the years, it seemed. She feared the possibility of an explosion once he learned everything that had been hidden from him for so long. But for now, while she watches him from afar, the Charlie she sees across the room looks content in his childhood home. This was the first time Teri had ever seen him so *at home*. Finally, it seemed like he belonged.

Charlie sits there on the couch, his gaze sweeping over the napping kids. He puts himself in their shoes for a second.

They must be having the time of their lives — the friendships, the games, the group get-togethers. Not one of those kids would believe it right now, but Charlie knew these times were going to be the simplest times... The times that they would look back on and reflect, just like he was doing now. In this moment, Charlie's appreciation grows for the childlike simplicity of the kids in his charge. Maybe that 'parenting' gig isn't as bad as it sounds, he wonders to himself. While building up his reputation and career, the one thing he'd always feared were the school talks. After his own years of what felt like torment, Charlie never forgot how cruel young people could be. But these kids seemed so happy. So, for the first time in many years, Charlie takes a page out of someone else's book — he just has *fun*.

The other day, Abe had given Charlie a wise piece of advice. He'd said something along the lines of, 'Teach others the things that one needs to learn.' Abe was on the subject of his own sermon writing, explaining to Charlie what fueled him to keep going. The most humble person you'd ever meet, Abe set out to teach the kids in his youth group about the human qualities that he felt were missing in his own psyche or spiritual experience. Charlie would think along the lines of what wisdom he could impart in order for each of the kids to reach their full potential, whereas Abe was more reflective, always asking God to show him what he needed to learn that he could then share with the teens. For Charlie, that means learning contentment and sharpening his ability for fun, ridding himself of the sole pressure to perform. He debates how to entertain the kids for the remainder of their movie night, and it's then that he spots a pile of haphazardly labeled VHS tapes of home movies sitting beside the media center. He was ready — ready to share himself and his past with the world, or at least with his inner circle.

Charlie abandons the couch and goes over to the media center, pushing one of the videotapes into the welcoming slot of a vintage home VCR. He stands near the TV, watching with excitement as he hits the play button on a dusty remote. The kids begin to stir from their naps, intrigued by the unusual static that momentarily takes over the screen.

Charlie turns to the kids. "Here's a peek at what victory looks like." He returns to the couch, settling back down next to Abe.

"Charlie, I don't kn—" Abe begins but Charlie ignores him.

"This is actual footage of the first world championship Abe and I won together," Charlie explains to the kids, who watch intently. Everyone has perked up by now, staring at the fuzzy display of a Youth League baseball game from eighteen years ago.

A title card pops up across the aging video: 'Youth Summer League World Series, 1992.' On the TV screen, a twelve-year-old Charlie races for home, where young Abe awaits him with a hug and an onslaught of high-fives the moment he crosses the plate.

Young Charlie jumps up and down in celebration, cheering with glee, "I did it! I hit a home run!"

A middle-aged Gordon stomps out of the dugout, heading straight for Charlie. He slaps the kid's hat right off his head. "I told you to bunt, you idiot! Bunt," Gordon screams in front of everyone.

Charlie immediately stops the video, coming back to reality. There are some things that he should just let be, and that moment was one of them. A moment to forget, never to share, not to be brought to light ever again. He looks around the room, embarrassed, his eyes finally landing on Teri, who smiles weakly at him. Kids will be kids, and so, a few of them snicker; some more loudly than others.

Teri abruptly stands to break the mood. She turns to the kids and says, "Kids, it's getting late. Let's clean up this mess and get moving. Your parents will be here soon."

"Aww," murmur the kids, while a few others pretend to have fallen back to sleep. Thank goodness Teri is here, Charlie realizes, while watching her gently nudge awake some of the 'sleeping' kids. If left to his own devices, Charlie would have resorted to payback, waking up the kids with a glass of cold water to the face like they had done to him on the very first morning of training. Although, the parents wouldn't have been too impressed with that, he imagines. *Heck, Teri wouldn't have been impressed either.* Just then, car headlights reflect through the living room windows. They hear the rumble of multiple car engines as parents begin to pull up to the house, waiting for their kids to come through the front door.

Soon after, Charlie and Teri stand in Gordon's driveway, greeting the parents and waving goodbye to the kids. Michelle is the last of the kids to leave. She waves from the passenger seat of her dad's patrol car. Jack has already ducked out, walking the few blocks home, and Abe carries a half-asleep Nicky to the car, leaving behind only Charlie and Teri.

The two step back inside the house to find Seth fast asleep on the floor in a most uncomfortable-looking position. They exchange a smile with one another. Amid the awkward pause, Teri's the first to break the silence, hesitating to speak.

"I should get him home," she whispers.

Charlie places her hand in his, gently caressing her fingers. "You don't have to do that. There's a spare room — Abe's." Charlie and Teri stare into each other's eyes for a moment. They share a kiss. Charlie nudges Seth and leads him out of the room and up the stairs to Abe's old room, which is now set up as a guest room of sorts.

Meanwhile, Teri stays downstairs, exploring the living room and all of its baseball paraphernalia glory. *Baseball is Charlie's whole life; it always has been. Would he be able to make room for her? For Seth?* Tired herself, she'd like nothing less than to sink into the inviting couch, or better yet, a cozy bed. Old habits are hard to break, though, so Teri stays on her feet, anxiously cleaning up for the night. She stops when she hears Charlie coming down the stairs. Teri gives him a direct look. *Could she be so bold?*

"He's not the only one who wants to stay," she says softly. "If it's not too late?" Upon hearing Teri's words, the wild emotions Charlie once knew come flooding back, invading his thoughts. But instead of the anger he once felt toward her for staying behind all those years ago, for the first time he feels an enormous wave of guilt wash over him — guilt that he chose *not* to stay. That guilt is almost immediately replaced by love. The love he once had is still there, and it's more vast than ever before. *It would never be too late.*

"It's been a long time," he cautions Teri. A moment of silence passes before Teri places her hand on Charlie's arm. They leave the rest unsaid, holding each other's gaze, both frozen in time. He makes the first move, taking her hand in his, and they kiss again — this time with electrifying passion, something they both have been longing for.

◊ ◊ ◊

The next morning, Teri awakes and finds herself alone in Charlie's bed. She looks over at the clock on the night table. It's just after 8 a.m. She wonders where Charlie has disappeared to so early in the morning. The day was theirs. No training, no work... Nothing to do and no one to see except for each other. Being in this room, in this way, after all these years now felt a bit strange. It was as though she'd been transported back to her teen years. Almost like waking up the morning after a one-night stand — but instead, she knows the house layout like the back of her hand. The one difference from back then? The big, tall elephant in the room across the hall named Seth.

She didn't have the chance to tell Charlie the truth like she had planned amid their vigorous activities of the night before. Maybe there would never be a right time to break the news about something like this, and the more intimate they get, the harder it would become. She vows to tell him sooner rather than later. Teri pulls on her clothes from the night before and heads to the bathroom to freshen up before going downstairs. The delicious aroma of breakfast and fresh coffee meets her nostrils before she enters the kitchen.

Teri walks in to find Charlie cleaning up after just having cooked up a storm. Her eyes take in the enticing sight... This morning Charlie's looking sharp, showered, and shaved, no longer sporting his three-day stubble. Dressed in well-fitting jeans and a clean t-shirt, he's managed to create an enormous feast, which sits neatly atop the oversized island: coffee, pancakes, fruit salad, and toast. Charlie breaks out into a smile when he sees Teri, looking beautiful as always, despite wearing her slightly disheveled clothes from the night before.

Teri comes over and reaches up to pat his newly shaven face. "Could you be any more perfect?"

Charlie laughs genuinely. "No, I don't think I could." He takes Teri's hand, pulling her close. They kiss.

Once they break apart, Teri nods toward the food. "Why all the food? Don't tell me the team is coming back for breakfast — I mean, I love them, but it's nice to have you all to myself for a change."

"It's for you and Seth," Charlie answers. "I wasn't sure what your usual breakfast looked like, so I wanted to give you some options."

Teri chuckles, not giving anything away. "Should've stayed to find out." *Ouch.* Charlie felt that. Looking up, Teri sees him staring back with big puppy eyes. He's about to apologize, but she cuts him off before he has a chance. "It's okay... We were just kids. You had to follow your dreams."

"But I *didn't* have to, Teri. I wasn't chasing a dream. My fears were chasing *me*. Fears that I would never be good enough. It was something I had to prove — not to anyone else but to myself."

Teri tightens her embrace around Charlie and asks, "Have you done that?" Just as Charlie's about to respond, Seth walks into the kitchen.

He grins coyly at the two for a moment but quickly notices the display of food. His eyes immediately light up. "I guess all this food is for me since you two are gonna have each other for breakfast," Seth says with a smirk.

Teri switches on the mom lever. "Excuse me, mister!" Charlie laughs as Seth hushes and grabs a plate, ready to dig in. He helps himself to pancakes and maple syrup, pouring on a thick layer. The kid looks right at home. Charlie and Teri each take a seat on one of the barstools and pour their coffee, adding in some milk and sugar before sipping it, thankful that they didn't get the third-degree.

◊ ◊ ◊

On the other side of town, Herbert pulls his truck into the driveway just as his housekeeper gets on her bicycle to ride home. It's raining pretty heavily. Herbert rolls down his window and calls out. "Afternoon, Rosetta."

"Hello, Mr. Herbert," Rosetta answers.

"Can I give you a lift?"

Rosetta looks uncomfortable but cordial. "That would be nice. Thank you."

"Great. Put your bike in the back. I'll drop you at the bus stop."

It's better than nothing, so Rosetta pops her bike into the trunk and climbs into the passenger seat beside Herbert. "Thank you, Mr. Herbert."

"It's the least I could do, considering I'm thinking of turning you into immigration instead of giving you that raise you asked for."

Rosetta gasps, instantly panicking. "Please, Mr. Herbert, I —"

"I'm just kidding," Herbert says with a chuckle. "Say, how are those boys of yours doing? Big fellas, aren't they? Gotta be close to six feet by now."

A look of confusion comes across Rosetta's face, but she answers nonetheless. "Uh, well, yes, they are very big boys. They eat too much, I think. But oh, my, are they strong!"

Herbert's eyebrows raise. "Didn't they just turn twelve?"

"Yes."

"Do you think they'd like to come play baseball for me?" Herbert asks with his smile-smirk.

"Oh, Mr. Herbert, I could never afford that," answers Rosetta. "You know I don't make much money," she adds. Right about now Herbert was feeling a bit more charitable than usual.

Plus, he needed those boys on his team. They had exactly what he was looking for: height and stature. With a team name like 'The Giants,' he'd need at least a few larger kids to encapsulate the message he was spreading far and wide — that his team was head and shoulders above the rest.

"Who said anything about money?" Herbert begins. "Besides, I have a feeling you don't really want that raise…"

"It would be an honor for them to play baseball for you!" Rosetta was so excited that she didn't even mind being dropped off at the bus stop in the rain. She couldn't wait to tell her boys. They had a chance to be stars! All they needed was to work hard, follow instructions, and they would make it. Wasn't that what she was always telling them? 'As long as you work hard, life would turn out okay.'

CHAPTER SIXTEEN

A be met with his youth group on Friday night. Instead of pouring out his heart and soul to them through the gospel readings he usually incorporated into their meetings, he decided to share the news about the fields. Most of the teens had played on the Youth League or some other sport at one time or another, but it had been years since then. Abe wondered if they would even care. He told them about his letter to the council and the school board, explaining that the fields were going to be demolished — kaput — if no one stepped in.

Speaking openly about the fields almost felt like a breach of contract. His job was to encourage them along a path of faith and help them to be victorious against drugs. You know, making sure they stayed on the straight and narrow — that was job number one. But with all this talk about the fields, Abe felt that perhaps this was something that could unite them in a way like never before. These teens knew firsthand what it was like to be out on the field. The angst, the pressure... What Abe wanted to instill were the possibilities he saw for the future — a shift from the controlling dictatorship of sports in today's world, especially in the Youth League, to a more democratic one where all would be free to participate at their own level without being forced to give up a sliver of their soul each day in the process.

Much to Abe's surprise, the teens were onboard all the way. They were shocked to hear the news, and they wanted to help. Despite no longer being active participants in the Youth League, it was nothing short of awful to imagine a neighborhood without their fields — *Mr. G's fields*. The place had been home to this national pastime for generations prior, so the idea of it being wiped out forever by a bunch of dime a dozen shops was despicable. They used this issue as fuel to express their anger about how life had treated them thus far. In this particular forum, it was okay to be angry, or so it seemed.

"I thought it was wrong to be angry," pipes up one of the teens, "I mean, from a Christian point of view?"

Abe smiles. Maybe he *was* getting through to them. For the rest of the night, Abe speaks on something he calls 'righteous anger' and how it wasn't something particularly wrong or evil. Instead, righteous anger was something even Jesus experienced throughout his life on earth. Abe tells them the story about Jesus in Matthew 21:12-13, which reads:

Jesus entered the temple courts and drove out all who were buying and selling there. He overturned the tables of the money changers and the benches of those selling doves. "It is written," he said to them, "'My house will be called a house of prayer,' but you are making it 'a den of robbers.'"

It must have taken guts for Jesus to come barreling in and do what he did back then. Standing up against the shopkeepers in favor of keeping their fields would likely take just as much. After dinner, the teens brainstorm war cries that they can use for protests against the council. Abe's pretty impressed with the war cries and chants they come up with that night. He revels in this unusual case of active participation from the teens — a simple reminder that Abe was not alone and that there is indeed power in words.

Two of the boys, Ethan and Michael, come up with this chant:

Bring back the ball to the base!
Don't mess with our place!
Baseball is our community!
Feed off some other local entity!

Daniel and Chris devise this one:

Go home! Back off!

We want the fields to stay!
Don't take away our place to play!
Go find another space to slay!

The few girls in the group, Abigail and Hannah, create the longest one:

We're speaking our minds!
We're doing it tough!
Buy up concrete, not fields,
You corporate greed machine!
Keep freedom alive,
And let the kids dream.
Let them dream!
Let them dream!

◊ ◊ ◊

The next day, Abe performs his groundskeeper duties for what would be the last time (for now, anyway), using the alone time to think about his youth group. He was astounded by the teens' honesty with what they had discussed last night. Were their parents aware of how articulate these so-called 'rebels' could be? Abe vows right then and there to always be the sort of parent who encourages honesty, allowing Nicky to speak her mind, no matter what. That meant he'd need to be prepared to handle *any* topic. The thought concerns him, but he's grateful for Teri's assistance in helping look after Nicky on occasion, with Abe doing the same for Seth.

Breaking his reverie, he notices a small but ominous figure looming near the snack bar. It's Judy, pacing back and forth. She looks to be waiting for something or someone. For a moment, Abe considers driving the mower down there and pleading for his job back — but then he sees Norm and Patrick approaching Judy, and he realizes the effort would likely be of no use.

Abe packs away the mower in the shed and walks off. Wherever Judy goes, she'd whip up a frenzy of change. No one could escape her wild ideas in favor of progress. Since becoming a single mom, it was as though she felt the need to assert her dominance to anyone she came in contact with. Thankfully not all single moms were like Judy; for instance, Teri — she was utterly different from Judy. Abe mutters aloud to himself, "It's not your job anymore."

Over at the snack bar, Teri crouches behind the counter, restocking the shelves with small chip bags and such. Judy, Norm, and Patrick stand nearby. Judy addresses the two of them. "So, here's the rundown, gentlemen. The two of you will take over Abe's duties as groundskeepers. It's that simple." The men exchange a look of uncertainty. Judy prods further. "Do we have a deal?" Norm and Patrick exchange another look; this time, one of resignation. They both turn back to Judy and nod slowly, giving in.

Suddenly, Teri pops up from behind the snack bar. "Uh, Jud— I mean, Madam President?"

Judy jumps at the unexpected sound of Teri's voice but she collects herself quickly, smoothing her hair and forcing a smile on her face. "Yes?"

"Isn't that something that should be proposed to the board and subjected to an official vote?" Teri asks.

Judy forces another smile before replying. "Given that you are not an elected member of the board, Teri, I fail to see how this is any of your business." Teri scoffs. "But since you asked, I'll let you in on a little secret. Norm here will also be taking over Abe's position on the board. Let him know, won't you?"

Teri ignores Judy's patronizing tone. "May I suggest that the league at least buys Abe a parting gift for his years of service?"

"No," says Judy, "you may *not*." She purposely avoids eye contact with Teri. "Next order of business…" Judy turns back to Norm and Patrick. "Given Norm and Patrick's dedication to this league, putting in countless hours to kill the gophers terrorizing the fields, it's the next logical move. All in favor?" Judy and Norm both raise their hands.

◊ ◊ ◊

Across town, Charlie, Abe, and Jack sneak onto the grounds of Herbert's baseball camp. Spotlights move throughout the complex, shining down from guard towers above. The guys crouch down, burying themselves within the shrubs, and look around.

Charlie has a look of disbelief on his face. "What is this place?"

"This is Herbert's vision," answers Abe. "His vision for the future of youth baseball."

Charlie retorts, "Looks more like a military boot camp."

"I think that's the point," Abe whispers. "Remove the joy of participation, destroy the love of the game, and all you've got left is win or lose."

"And when the result is all that matters…" Jack chimes in.

Meanwhile, Charlie shakes his head, shocked. "Parents will pay top dollar to ensure their kids are winners." Abe nods. One of the spotlight beams suddenly hits the three of them, and a siren sounds throughout the campus. "I think we've outstayed out welcome." The guys turn and hightail it back the way they came.

◊ ◊ ◊

Not too far away, Judy and Herbert occupy a table in a dive bar. Herbert covers her hand with his. "I think it's just about set," Herbert starts. "After we win the championship, teams will jump at the chance to buy one of my training franchises."

Judy pulls away her hand. "Do you think they'll pay?"

"Oh, they'll pay," replies Herbert with his classic smile-smirk plastered on his face. "As soon as they see how my coaching techniques have revolutionized youth baseball, we can name our price."

Judy asks, "Have you thought about how much you'll charge?"

Herbert reaches across the table, once again taking Judy's hand in his. This time she doesn't bother pulling away her hand. "Judy, there are only three things I ever think about."

"Oh? And what might those three things be?"

Herbert looks deep into her eyes, mesmerized for the

moment. "Money... Baseball... And—" Herbert brings Judy's delicate hand to his lips.

Now, Judy yanks away her hand. "And my consultation fees?" She smiles coyly.

CHAPTER SEVENTEEN

Teri loves her career as a kindergarten teacher. She had the luxury of spending spring break with Seth, soon after which the joys and pressures of being involved with the Youth Summer League kicked in. She was able to spend a good amount of time with Seth each season, helping to organize the team mom get-togethers and various support groups. It wasn't until this year, with Charlie back on the scene, that she became inspired to start reconsidering the ideas of love and romance. It had been a long time… A *very* long time. Sure, she had dated a few men here and there since he left, but the prospective relationships never went much further than a date or two before Teri broke off the budding romance. Finding the right person wasn't easy, especially since nothing, and no one, managed to live up to her standards in comparison to Charlie. Now, Teri realized how unfair that consideration process had been to the men in her dating pool. They didn't deserve the cold shoulder she would give them after only a few dates. Comparing other men to Charlie hadn't been very fair to him either. She'd romanticized his mere existence so much that even now there would be moments when the *real* Charlie didn't compare as well to the memory she had instilled within from a time long ago.

The beach had been one of their old stomping grounds where they would escape to each summer, in between games, practice, and Charlie's never-ending search for Gordon's approval. It's an unusually warm spring day when Teri and Charlie manage to sneak away from the kids and steal some time together. Charlie had even given Shoeless Joe the day off, leaving him behind to provide company for Gordon. Meanwhile, Abe agreed to help out with babysitting, looking after both Seth and

Nicky while the reconnecting couple takes a time-out.

Teri had dreamed of a day like this for so long. Spending all day with Charlie was a special treat. He doesn't have anything planned, he says, except for a 'surprise' at sunset. They walk along the beach, holding hands like a pair of new lovers. Teri rambles on and on as if talking to an old friend, and Charlie indeed *is* an old friend. It'd been ages since she was granted the freedom to simply relax, for once not having to rush from one activity to the next.

The two of them stop for lunch at an exciting new spot overlooking the ocean. Lunch was simply divine, and Charlie was such good company. Their day so far had been one of serene relaxation, and any nerves from the start of the day had diminished quite early on.

They stroll through the sand, discussing the years that had separated them, just catching up on each other's lives. Charlie speaks about his passion for the game, leaving out his after-hour exploits, all of which now seemed so insignificant. He can no longer imagine why he'd pursued those women in the first place when he could have been with someone as wonderful as Teri all along. But that's behind him, and now he *is* with someone like Teri — the real deal — and he didn't need anyone else. Not now. Not ever.

"So, Abe tells me you're going to be his next guest speaker at the youth group fellowship," Teri says.

Charlie slowly lets go of her hand, looking away. "Yeah. Don't know how I let him rope me into that one. I'm not sure I'm gonna do it."

Teri stops walking and grabs his arm. "What? Why?"

Charlie shrugs. "I'm no good with kids."

"Are you serious? Kids everywhere adore you. Just look at the A-Team… Seth!" Teri laughs, more to herself than to anyone else. "Since you came back, all he ever talks about is the great Charlie Maddox."

Charlie beams with pride. "He's a great kid, Teri. You're doing an amazing job." Teri smiles briefly and then looks away, distracted.

◊ ◊ ◊

Charlie had arranged a lovely sunset surprise for Teri this evening; a gondola ride along the harbor. Such a romantic gesture, Teri thought. She would often see couples enjoying a cozy ride together and always wished the same for herself. None of the men she dated in the past had even come close to being the partner with whom she wanted to share such an intimate moonlit excursion. Teri was the sort of woman who, when she found the right person, wanted each moment to feel special in some way. She was pleased that Charlie seemed to have the same kind of idea. But she still needed to *tell him*. Would her big news put the finishing touch on their already perfect day, or would it all come crashing down? By now, surely Charlie must have considered the possibility, the timeline... The sunset was, like everything else from their day together, *perfect*. Spatters of orange and purple streak the sky like a painting. Teri had never seen such beauty, such natural artistry. Had it always been available to her? Or did it somehow appear even more mesmerizing with Charlie at her side?

Charlie puts an arm around Teri's shoulders while they float along the water in the gondola. A moment of silence passes between them with Teri lost in her thoughts.

"Peaceful, isn't it?" Charlie says, looking out at the water. Teri remains quiet. Charlie nudges her gently. "You okay? You've hardly said a word since dinner."

Teri shakes herself out of it, just enough to respond. "Oh. Yeah, sorry. I'm fine," she answers before going quiet again.

Charlie chuckles. "Maybe you and the gondolier should trade places. She and I can shoot the breeze, and you can be alone with your thoughts." Teri laughs faintly.

She turns to face Charlie and takes a breath. "I haven't been entirely honest with you, Charlie."

"I'm not going to like where this is going, am I?" Charlie asks, letting out a nervous little laugh.

Removing Charlie's arm from around her shoulders, Teri

takes both of his hands in hers and looks directly at him. "Honestly? I don't know." She takes another deep breath and glances up at the gondolier, making sure she's not paying them any mind. "You know how I told you that Seth was the result of a one-night stand?"

Charlie tries to placate her by setting a hand on her shoulder. "Trust me, Teri. I don't need or want those details."

"But you do." Teri sighs. She's unsure of the right words to say. "Have you done the math?"

"What math?"

"How old is Seth?"

Charlie raises both hands in the air out of frustration. "Uh… I'm not sure. Twelve?"

"And how long ago did you leave?" Teri smiles. All at once, the weight from the burden she's been carrying alone for too long lessens ever so slightly.

He starts casually with, "It'll be—" Little does he realize what's about to hit him. Then he suddenly freezes. His eyes widen. "He's… He's mine?"

"Well, *ours*, yes." Upon hearing Teri's response, Charlie moves his weight to the edge of the gondola and lets himself topple backward into the water as though he were a scuba diver.

Teri springs up in shock and peers over the edge. "Charlie! Are you crazy?! That water must be freezing," she yells, staring down into the water. "Charlie?!" There's no sign of him.

Charlie swims back to shore, fully clothed, his night wrecked. Life had a way of boxing him into a corner, and it needed to stop. He didn't want to talk about it. He didn't want to hear about it. All he wanted was to run away, escape the truth — escape reality, like always. He'd never been given the opportunity to talk about his own child back then, and all he had now was the opportunity to avoid it. Teri didn't need him, just like she hadn't needed him *then*.

Meanwhile, Teri remains in the boat with the silent gondolier. Maybe it was part of the whole Venetian experience, or maybe she could only speak Italian? In any case, Teri popped open the bottle of bubbly that was meant to be a shared experience with Charlie. Parenting was also meant to be a shared experience with him... But here they were, years later, and she had blown it — for everyone; herself, Seth, *and* Charlie. As Teri looks over the harbor, she's glad to not be the one steering the boat, and for the first time in a long time, she makes a conscious decision to stop trying to be the 'gondolier' of other people's lives... To stop controlling everything to the nth degree, even in her own life. She thought it was time to let the tide steer her where she needed to be and just go with the flow.

As she downs that first sip of the good ol' bubbly, she feels refreshed and a bit more at ease almost instantly, and believe it or not, for the first time in twelve years... She gets *drunk*.

CHAPTER EIGHTEEN

T hree long trestle tables stand in the church fellowship room, covered with dinnerware and food. The teens, about twenty of them, sit around the tables. Abe sits at one with a group of five teens, including Jack. These teens were a little rough around the edges, tougher and older than their years. But with a plate of hot food set out in front of them, they looked like a pack of gleeful children, hurriedly eating as though it were a race to the finish. That's what keeps them coming back, though — the food and the friendship. Of course, the teens were mandated to attend each Friday night as a sort of warning from the cops to avoid doing real time in juvie, but the promise of a threat was nothing compared to the powerful draw of food and friendship.

Some weeks it would be pizza or fast food, but tonight's meal consists of slow cooker creamy beef and vegetable curry with the tastiest, most flavorful rice. Two volunteers had come in earlier that day to specially prepare the meal for the night. Most of the teens were unfamiliar with home-cooked meals, growing up in families where parents came home from work only to pop a frozen meal into the microwave or where parents and kids had given up on their relationship, with both parties resorting to eating *whatever* dinner, *whenever*.

"Taking drugs is wrong. Drugs are bad. We have our whole life ahead of us," recite the teens in monotone voices. Charlie enters the room amid the teens' droning, curious as to what he's just walked into. Abe hurriedly stands to greet his brother.

He puts a hand on Charlie's shoulder and introduces him to the group of bored teens, some of whom barely bother to look up. "Kids, our distinguished guest has arrived. For those of you who don't know, this is my brother and Minor League Baseball player Charlie Maddox." A few of the kids perk up to look at Charlie. "Mr. Maddox is here to talk about the positive benefits of organized youth sports."

Charlie awkwardly waves and smiles even though most of the teens are staring down at their now empty plates. They don't look impressed. They've heard enough speeches of positivity by adults who try way too hard. 'Positivity' was akin to a modern disease for these teens, and they didn't want the slightest bit of it.

"Why are your 'distinguished guests' always relatives of yours, preacher?" Jack asks with a coy look. "We get it. The Maddox family is holier than us."

Charlie looks a little worried for a second. "Tough crowd," he murmurs to his brother. Abe claps him on the back and then ushers Charlie back to his table, where they both take a seat. Charlie sits next to Abe.

"Eyes this ways, please, everyone," Abe calls to the teens, who reluctantly turn to give the adults a minimal form of attention. "I'd like to kick things off with a quick Q and A to give Charlie an idea where we're all coming from." A few boos and hisses travel through the group. Has Abe overshot the mark this time? Charlie turns to him, giving a doubtful look.

For a fleeting moment, Abe considers putting the conversation on hold... But despite the teens' poor response, he continues. "Raise your hand if you currently do or have ever played an organized sport."

Everyone in the room raises a hand, except for Charlie. Abe nudges him, and after a moment of hesitation, Charlie also lifts his hand into the air.

"Now," Abe continues, "drop your hand if you *don't* feel like your parents have it in for you." The hands around the room stay up. "And drop your hand if you've *never* been in trouble with the law." Only Abe lowers his hand at first. Charlie starts to lower his until he gets a look from Abe. His hand stays up.

"If you've been pressured to play with an injury," Abe says.

Two hands drop. "If your coach has called you names, yelled at you, or insulted you in some way." Three more hands go down. "If you've been subjected to constant criticism, belittling, insults, rejection… And you don't want to feel that pain anymore." Not a single hand drops. For the first time that night, the teens look attentive — for real.

Jack suddenly shouts out, "What's the point of this, preacher?"

Abe stares Jack right in the eyes with a look of compassion. "The point, Jack, is to show that our parents and coaches are as far from being perfect as we are. And that in the loneliness we feel, and in the pain we are subjected to, there is *unity*. A strong commonality." Abe pauses and turns to look at the rest of the teens around the room. "Sometimes we don't see it because we think we're the only ones. But if we're open with ourselves and open with others, we can find a way through… Together." Silence descends over the room. The teens awkwardly look at one another, most hands still raised.

Charlie clears his throat and stands, pulling a folded slip of paper from his pocket. He looks around the room, slightly nervous. After a moment, he crumples the paper and throws it to the floor. "You can put your hands down now, guys." The hands go down. "You know, when I came back to town, I was greeted like a hero. Me… *I'm* a hero." Charlie shakes his head. "But I ain't no hero. I'm just like all of you. Just a little bit older."

Jack yells out, "A little?" The teens chuckle.

"Jack, next time raise your hand if you want to speak and wait until I call on you," responds Charlie, a bit more hardened than the teens expected. Nobody laughs. In fact, utter silence falls over the room once more. Charlie continues. "I'm not going to lie to you, kids. When I was a teen, I would get drunk. A lot."

This time Jack raises his hand — but doesn't wait to be called on. "What's changed?" A few more laughs from the teens… Charlie lets it slide.

"I was trying to fit in. Trying to be cooler than I felt." Charlie turns directly to Jack. "You know what that's like, don't ya, Jack?" The teens laugh, more heartily this time around.

"But trying to be cool doesn't cut it. It just cuts you *down*." Charlie pauses, letting the revelation sink in for the teens. "You need to meet yourself where you are. If you're feeling like crap, just let yourself feel like crap. Feel it." Another deafening silence shakes the room. He may have actually gotten through to some of these kids.

The speech had gone okay. *Better than the other ones*, some of the teens think. Others feel it had just been more of the same old positivity mumbo jumbo disguised by a mouthful of psychobabble. But overall, to their surprise, most of the teens leave the night's meeting with a sense that maybe there was a way to dump the downhearted feelings other than going back to drugs, delinquency, or other dangers.

After the teens have left, Charlie helps Abe in the church kitchen. Abe washes the dishes while Charlie dries.

"You're sure you weren't drunk back there?"

Charlie chuckles. "No."

"What's gotten into you?"

"Thought you wanted something inspiring."

"Sure," Abe answers with a shrug. He pauses a moment before continuing. "That was meant to be inspiring?" Charlie doesn't answer. *Why was Abe so worried?* Abe takes a hard look at his brother. "That wasn't *you* talking. Who's been in your ear?"

Charlie takes an extended pause before finally answering. "Teri told me." Abe's face flashes with a sign of recognition — *he knows about Seth*. Hurt but curious, Charlie asks, "How long have you known?" This time it's Abe who had betrayed Charlie, and he couldn't find the words to speak. Abe was supposed to be the one setting a good example, and he'd let his brother down. The silence is deafening as they both stop moving, frozen in time. Abe had been dreading this moment for almost as long as he could remember. For once and for all, it was time to come clean.

"Forever," Abe says. It's hard to look Charlie in the eyes but he manages to hold his gaze. "I've known about it since he was born." Charlie's mind races. He can't understand what would compel Abe to keep this vital piece of information a secret. How could a minister who is always talking about truth, honesty, and integrity withhold something like this from his own brother?

"You never told me. You never thought, even for a second, that I should know?" Charlie asks, his throat tight.

Abe's face flushes red with guilt. There was no excuse, but he tries to explain his reasons. "Teri needed to tell you; not me. And would it have changed anything? You left. You broke it off. You wanted to wander the world..." Abe scoffs and shakes his head. "The big world... Seek your fortune... Then you walk back in here like the prodigal son and act surprised when Dad doesn't break out his best robe and sandals, crack open an expensive wine, and celebrate like you're the favored son. He's not going to do that. It was never like that. He never even played favorites, really. You made that up. The whole family dynamic... This big thing, this guilt that kept you going..." Charlie's expression turns more and more enraged with each word Abe spews, but his brother just keeps at it. "Just quit it. Tell him you're sorry you left. Be the big man. Tell him you're sorry. That's all. You don't have to coach a team. You just have to be *part* of one."

Charlie is absolutely fuming. *How dare Abe speak to him like that! How could he keep something like that from his own brother for so long?* He can't help but wonder what else Abe could be hiding. Without saying a word, Charlie leaves in a fury of anger, leaving Abe to clean up the remainder of the mess.

CHAPTER NINETEEN

C harlie's first stop is his childhood home. That time has come. He needs to talk to Gordon. See what the old man knows. He can remember Gordon saying things over the years like, 'I know you better than you know yourself.' Charlie's perception of the sentiment was a sort of veiled warning or threat that meant nothing he ever did, thought, or said would ever impress his dad. Nothing from Charlie would ever be seen as fully authentic, fully innovative. He was no better than a cheap imitation. Now, Charlie found himself growing angrier by the second that his own father had known *more* about his life than he himself. Surely, Gordon must also know that Seth was his grandson?

Ugh. Charlie despised the relationship he and his father had. It was fueled by endless angst and conflict. But worse yet, here was Charlie, having been completely blindsided with the fact that he indeed was also a father to his very own son. With all that had gone on, there was no foreseeable way to begin their *real* relationship without conflict and drama. Everything he had hated about the father-son relationship of his youth — especially the emotional distance — were traits Charlie inherited by default in his new (to him) familial status with Seth. What was he supposed to do? Just hug the kid and tell him how much he loved him? *Did he love him?* He'd only just met the boy!

Charlie has known about his 'father' status for two whole days now, and he was desperate to find out how much Gordon knew and why everyone had chosen to keep him in the dark for so long. Having failed to spend much time with Gordon since he returned home, Charlie knew that broaching a major topic like this one would be difficult since their only recent talk had been that of the 'small' variety.

Now, Charlie sits at Gordon's bedside, silently watching the old man sleep. This time he's without any magazine, old photos, or anything else to distract him from truly being *present*. His eyes take in Gordon's slightly thinner frame, really looking at him as if for the very first time. Charlie waits for his dad to stir, but after what feels like forever, he begins to doze off himself.

The infamous nightmare from when he was twelve-years-old once again taunts him the moment his eyes slip shut. While lost in dreamland, he subconsciously wishes for someone to awaken him. Then comes the annoying answer to his silent prayer. *Was that a knock?* Charlie's eyes snap open. There it is again — a pounding knock on the front door. He checks the clock radio on Gordon's bedside table: 5:53 a.m. Who could it be? Too early for the team, surely. Charlie reluctantly pulls himself up out of the armchair and ties Gordon's old dressing gown around him while trotting down the steps to see who's at the door. He sneaks a peek through the window and looks relieved, opening the door to reveal Teri.

Dressed in activewear, she jogs in place, smiling up at Charlie as if the other night had never happened. "Wanna go for a run? Let off some steam?" Charlie just stares at her. *Was she joking?* All he wanted was to slip back into a deep sleep and dream away his current reality. He pushes past her and leans against the porch railing, staring out at the yard. Teri reaches out for him, but he pulls away. "What's wrong?

Charlie takes a moment to collect his thoughts. After a long pause, he bitterly says, "Guess I passed the test, huh?"

"What test?" Teri asks, genuinely confused.

He avoids her gaze, still staring out at the yard. "What if the As hadn't liked me, Teri? What if Seth hadn't liked me? What would've happened then?"

"Oh— I'm sorry, Charlie. I just—"

Finally turning around to face Teri, Charlie's eyes bore straight into her. "I cannot believe you felt you had the right to keep such a secret." Teri takes a step closer, putting a hand on his shoulder, but Charlie pushes it away and continues. "Does Seth know?"

"No. I haven't…" Teri hangs her head. "I haven't worked out how to tell him yet."

"Can I at least be a part of that?" Charlie avoids her gaze, fearing her next words.

Teri looks slightly caught off guard. She replies, "Uh, sure. When do you—" Teri stops short when Charlie turns to face her, expecting a different answer. One he needed to know… The answer to the unspoken *why*. Resigned, Teri sighs and continues. "*Why* didn't I tell you? Think about it. A young mother, gallivanting around the countryside with her lover and a newborn baby. Are you serious? I was terrified. I needed my mother to be there for me; to show me the ropes of being a new mom myself."

"Okay, okay, I get it," Charlie says, surrendering. But he didn't — he didn't 'get it.' He settles into the couch on the front porch, his head in his hands. He never would've imagined starting a family this way… In the dark… With all these secrets just waiting to be revealed… If he ever did start a family, he would have wanted everything to be transparent. *Clear.* Then again, his main focus has always been on the relationship he had with his own father rather than the idea of potentially becoming a father himself. The task of mending that father-son relationship suddenly became top priority for Charlie. Surely all that familial tension, all those past mistakes, must get pitched down the line from one generation to the next, and he didn't want that kind of relationship for him and Seth.

Teri sits down next to Charlie on the couch, keeping her hands to herself this time. She was nervous to make a false move, potentially ruining their progress all over again. She already feels bad enough. "Look… I'm really sorry. I needed to do what was best for Seth back then. I loved you, Charlie. And I still do."

Charlie's eyes widen as if this is all news to him. He asks,

"You do?"

"Yes," replies Teri. "Think we can try again? Maybe talk to Seth?"

"Let me think about it," Charlie answers. Teri nods but can't help wondering what's left to think about after all they've been through. Too many people left too many things for 'later.' They'd wait for what they thought was the right time. They'd wait for life to settle down. It was as though they'd convinced themselves that they could put life on hold while time just kept marching on, never once having the consideration to wait for anyone to finish 'thinking' about things. Teri stands up. She's about to leave Charlie behind for her morning run when he gently reaches out for her wrist.

"I've thought about it," he says before standing up.

"Yeah?"

"Yeah. How about dinner? Sunday night?"

Teri tries not to look overly pleased, but she's about to burst with relief. She and Charlie are back on track, and Charlie is prepared to talk it through with Seth. She responds with, "Sure. I'll call you tonight to run through the details." Teri warms up with a bit of a jog before running off, waving goodbye to Charlie, a smile planted firmly on her face.

She wasn't too worried about the fact that she'd just confessed her love for Charlie, yet he hadn't returned the gesture. But she did find herself wondering... *If he... Did he... Could he?* Teri knew that he had indeed loved her; he'd told her once before. But now? She continues her lap through the neighborhood, clearing away the 'what-ifs' from her mind and moving on with the joy of a new morning.

◊ ◊ ◊

The next day, Teri and a few other baseball mom volunteers mingle by the snack bar. Little do they know, Judy lies in wait, ready to pounce on her unsuspecting prey at just the right moment.

As the moms talk among themselves, chuckling to one another, Judy comes storming over and with the snidest tone says, "Ladies, the league has contracted out the snack bar duties to a management firm moving forward. They are now responsible for running and staffing the snack bar."

"What?" Teri asks, both inquisitive and shocked.

"The new board voted three to zero on a motion to outsource the snack bar jobs because it could save money," Judy replies sternly.

One of the moms cries out in bewilderment, "But we work for free!"

"I was there — they rigged the votes," another mom chimes in, turning to the others. But Judy isn't listening. The decision has already been made, and that was that. Despite an institution such as 'the board,' not to mention the collective of team moms, their power was essentially null and void when it came to Judy's charismatic machinations.

For a moment, Teri finds herself mourning the sudden end of her responsibilities at the snack bar. But at the same time, she feels as though this could be the universe's way of reinforcing to her that it was time to stop trying to run everyone else's life and perhaps focus on her own for a while. You know, 'when one door closes,' and all that stuff... The shift in routine gives Teri a feeling of empowerment, a whole new level of freedom. Even though she disagreed with Judy on a personal level, she knew that a higher power was looking out for everyone from up above, and in the end, it would all work out just fine. Her natural instinct was to fight, but everything within her was saying to let it go. Looking around, Teri can see that the other moms wouldn't be willing to let Judy off the hook that easily. This team mom stuff had been the center of their lives for years, and she knew they'd expect her to be the one who would fight.

Meanwhile, over on the main field, Charlie, Abe, Jack, and the A-Team kids are busy warming up for a practice game. Abe takes over and has the kids running drills, while Charlie and Jack pause for a quick game of catch.

"Jack, have you ever been to New Mexico?" Charlie tosses the ball.

The teen catches it before responding with, "No, sir." He tosses the ball back to Charlie, who catches it.

"A friend of mine coaches the baseball team over at the university there. Might be able to get you a tryout that could lead to a scholarship. Only if you're interested, of course," Charlie offers. He returns the ball to Jack.

The teen snaps up the ball. "Preacher man put you up to this, huh?"

Charlie looks offended since the idea had been entirely his own. "Abe's looking out for lost souls. *I'm* looking out for star players."

"Well, hey, if you think I'm a star..." Jack says with a smile. "May as well give it a go, then." It had been a minute since Jack felt like anyone had faith in his capabilities to make something of himself.

Back over at the snack bar, Judy has already moved in her new workers. One of the dads attempts to buy a hotdog, but unfortunately the new crew on staff don't exactly specialize in the English language. "Can I get a hotdog?" Behind the counter, the worker gives a bewildered look. The dad tries to explain again. "El hot-dog-o." The worker stares blankly, still bewildered. Shoeless Joe walks by just then, and the dad points wildly. "Hot*dog*!"

"Oh, hotdog, sí! Sí," exclaims the worker.

◊ ◊ ◊

In the home dugout, a new and improved Coach Charlie gives a pep talk to his team. He does his best to ignore the fact that he's the father to one of these kids. The most important thing, he tells himself, is to remain indifferent and treat everyone the same as he always did. He'd confront the rest in due time.

"Alright, everybody, we only need one more win, and then it's off to Williamsport. I want you guys to go out there and play your hardest." Charlie pauses and looks over at Abe, who gives him a prompting look. "If we get way ahead of the other team, we'll throttle it back and give them a fighting chance. But until that happens, I don't want to see any slacking off." They huddle up, and everyone places a hand in the middle. "Go As," shouts the team.

The kids pile out of the dugout and onto the field, each running to their assigned positions. Hank stands by, dressed in his umpire uniform, surveying the field. He looks up toward the scoreboard and freezes for a moment — Nicky's climbing up the ladder to the scoreboard. Immediately, he rips off his umpire mask and sprints toward the little girl.

"Nicky," Hank's voice booms, "get down from there!" Nicky looks down at the ground beneath her, giggling. "Get down, Nicky, please!" She climbs up the next rung and suddenly loses her balance. One hand slips off the metal rung, and before realization sets in, she's dangling. "Hold on! Just hold on," shouts Hank.

By now, Charlie and the other adults run over, along with the kids, all of whom watch, terrified. Nicky loses her grip entirely and falls. Her head thuds hard into the ground. She lies there, motionless, while Abe rushes to her side, immediately calling for an ambulance.

◊ ◊ ◊

Nicky lies in a hospital bed, connected to all sorts of machines. She looks so innocent, so vulnerable, so weak — the complete opposite from how she usually looked while on the field. Charlie, Abe, and Teri are scattered around the room. Charlie sits with his head in his hands.

Teri sets a hand on his knee. "It's not your fault, Charlie," she whispers.

"I was supposed to be watching her. That makes her my responsibility," Charlie answers in a hushed tone. He turns to face Teri. "Still think I have paternal potential?"

An exhausted Hank suddenly rushes into the room, panting. "No, no… It's my fault… It's my fault she fell."

"Blue—" Abe says, using Hank's old nickname, creating an immediate connection that hadn't been dusted off in ages. "It's okay — come on, let me buy you a cup of coffee." Abe puts an arm around Hank's shoulder, offering some gentle comfort as they make the short walk to the vending machines down the hall.

"Oh, yeah? It's my job to stand at the edge of the rye field and keep them from falling." Hank sighs, shaking his head in shame.

Abe tries another tactic to comfort the older man. "Kids are going to get hurt. It's part of growing up. We can't protect them forever."

"But when they fall, they change, and nothing is ever the same." Hank stares off into the distance, perhaps remembering an unfortunate event from long ago.

They reach the vending machines. As they come to a stop, Abe steps in front of his uncle and faces him with a serious look. "Uncle. She will be fine. Saving everyone? It's not your job. We do the best we can."

"I could have been there for you, at least," Hank replies. Now, Abe isn't the kind of guy who needs anyone to 'be there' for him. Instead, he depends upon his faith rather than the failure of men.

Abe inserts his bank card into the vending machine, and before long, two steaming cappuccinos warm his hands. He passes one of them to Hank, who immediately sips the scalding beverage without so much as a wince. A bit of color quickly returns to the older man's face. The soothing touch of a warm drink had been a great suggestion on Abe's part for a time such as this.

The two of them walk back into the hospital room, reconvening with Charlie and Teri. Not a moment later, the doctor enters the room. Charlie's eyes widen as he stares nervously at the man in white. Abe steps forward, suddenly anxious but keeping his cool.

The doctor tells them, "She has a concussion, but she's going to be fine." Everyone breathes an audible sigh of relief; most of all Hank. Teri comforts a relieved Charlie.

"How long is she going to be in for?" Abe asks.

The doctor looks down at Nicky's chart for a moment

before returning his gaze to meet Abe's. "We need to keep her overnight for some routine tests and observation."

Abe nods. "Thanks, doctor." The doctor gives a curt nod before exiting the room.

Spending the night in Nicky's hospital room, Abe sprawls out across multiple uncomfortable waiting room chairs and remains patient for all the tests to come back. Thankfully, she was stable and would be released later that day. She was one of the lucky ones, the doctor had told him.

That morning, Abe holds Nicky's hand, praying at her bedside, when Charlie walks into the room. The last few weeks have really been a whirlwind for Charlie. He'd gotten to know his brother pretty well in a short span of time, and surprisingly, he was coming to like him quite a bit too. Charlie reaches out and sets a hand on Abe's shoulder, giving a reassuring squeeze. They were family, and Charlie would be there, no matter what happened.

Charlie breaks the silence. "How is she?"

Abe looks up at him. "She woke up briefly before. Mumbled something about popcorn, and then drifted off again." He suddenly glances down at his watch, brows furrowed. "Aren't you supposed to be on the field right about now?"

"We forfeited. Want coffee or something? You should get up, walk around." Abe shakes his head. "I'll stay with her for a bit," offers Charlie.

"Thanks, but I'm fine," Abe replies. A long moment of silence passes before he continues. "She reminds me so much of her mother. We'd gotten married right before she died... I said I'd look after her like she was my own. I promised." Abe looks down into his lap while Charlie silently acknowledges his brother's tragedy. "Did I hear you right... You forfeited a game?"

"We took a vote. I couldn't get them to play. What a lousy coach I am, huh?" This time, it's Charlie who's shaking his head — but in regret. Abe looks taken aback. Maybe even a bit choked up. The kids had decided on their own... *Wow.*

Abe nods and says, "Sometimes there are more important

things than the game." Charlie looks pissed as if Abe had just said something truly sacrilegious. Despite the speech he'd given to those teens about keeping it real, despite not having the heart to become the dictator that Herb professed to be, and despite his rejection of the military-like precision, the hierarchies, the nonsense of Herb's regime, the game was still *everything* to Charlie.

But to keep the peace between he and Abe, Charlie manages to bite his tongue. "I'll get you a coffee," he says, extending an olive branch. As he exits the room, the A-Team kids come streaming into the room, surrounding Nicky's hospital bed. After all, Nicky is far more important than baseball.

CHAPTER TWENTY

S unday night couldn't come fast enough. Before Charlie returned to his hometown after a decade of leaving it all behind, he could only ever dream that Teri would still be around, unmarried, and open to the idea of getting back with him. Yes, *him* — an unreliable bloke who followed the scent of the game and the competition rather than the solidity of commitment and family. Never once would he have imagined this kind of life for himself; the life that he was suddenly considering. It was a whole new world for Charlie, one that was slowly revealing itself to be a real possibility.

In preparation for Teri and Seth to arrive, Charlie whips up a simple Waldorf salad, with an array of varied toppings including walnuts, apple, celery, and a bit of onion with a homemade mayonnaise dressing. All the time spent mindlessly watching cooking shows in between games and training had finally paid off. He rarely was given the opportunity to cook for others, so on the occasion that he did, he gave it his all, creating a delicious yet simple meal with fresh ingredients.

Charlie wanted everything to be perfect for Teri and Seth. In the backyard, he fires up the barbecue and prepares to cook up some fish or steak... Or both. It was like their first breakfast together all over again. He couldn't recall if Teri had a preference for fish or steak. What did she used to eat back then? Who knew if she still liked the same things all these years later, but either way, he couldn't recall because he hadn't cared enough at the time. And when he finally got her to accept a dinner invitation after his homecoming, he'd been over the moon just to be spending time with *her* rather than the plastic-filled Barbie doll princesses he usually dated back in New Mexico. Cooking for kids and their finicky palates intimidated him a bit, since he had no experience with that, so he decided to err on the side of caution and keep things simple.

Setting foot in his childhood backyard immediately transports Charlie back to happier days. Although his relationship with Gordon was strained from back then, the relationship he'd built with this magical place brought only solace. The backyard was where he would run to as a child, seeking comfort when life was being unfair. How fitting that his old safe place was about to serve as the meeting spot for such an uncomfortable topic as this. It was here that a young Charlie had practiced his pitching by aiming at the big red 'X' he once carved into his favorite tree. The yard itself was so vast that it was like escaping into another world. Now, here he stands as an adult. This whole process — coming back home, coaching Gordon's team, discovering he was a father himself — has been an introduction to an unfamiliar world he could never have chartered himself.

As Charlie stands lost in thought, Gordon creeps up behind him in his wheelchair. The old man gives his son a long look but doesn't say a word. Sensing his disapproving presence, Charlie turns to Gordon. "We didn't lose. We forfeited. There's a difference."

"You walked away from the game. That's a loss in my book," snaps Gordon.

"Oh, yeah? Your book's old and musty and half the pages have fallen out. We've got a new book these days. One that says a little girl's well-being is far more important than a win."

Gorton snorts. "I've been on my deathbed, and still, you've kept on playing. Why's she so much more important than me?" Before Charlie can answer, the sound of two car doors closing steals away his attention. Then comes a knock. Teri and Seth have arrived.

Charlie calls out, "Back here!" The gate leading into the backyard swings open... Charlie notices that Teri seems a bit nervous — quite the opposite from her usual cool and confident self. He understands, though; he's nervous too. Hoping to diffuse the tension, Charlie asks Teri to pick out some music to play on the outdoor speakers. Before long, the three of them (including Seth) enjoy the soothing sounds of Canadian jazz singer Ann Vriend's 'The Knot Song.' This particular song was especially appropriate for this moment in time between Charlie and Teri. Their own vulnerabilities paired with the upbeat song's lyrics blended perfectly. As the song goes, 'There's so much left still to untangle...'

◊ ◊ ◊

After dinner, sitting side by side on the outdoor lounge, Charlie and Teri unwind with a glass of chilled white wine. Gordon sits there in his wheelchair, still somewhat alert, with a blanket draped over his legs. Charlie was surprised to see Gordon join the group tonight but felt it was a good sign. The added presence also helps take some of the focus off the elephant in the room... Gordon mumbles something about it being his nap time, but Charlie ignores him. The old man senses something brewing in the air and thinks it best to make himself scarce.

Meanwhile, Seth practices his pitching in a pop-up pitching and batting cage, complete with its own lighting. The sun has just about disappeared over the horizon. By the end of the night, the secret would be out for good. The remaining adults watch Seth, and Charlie reflects on the privileges he and his brother had during their childhood. So many of these kids dealt with the pressure to perform without the means to practice in their very own backyard. Sure, they could *practice* — but unless their parents had the unique ability to equip their backyard with the tools needed for their kid to practice and practice until they reached the point where some elusive talent agent lurking in the back of the bleachers would pick them out of the hundreds, thousands even, and make them a star? It was an unrealistic goal, and only a rare few would be the ones to make it. Charlie had been one of them. He still has yet to hit the *big*, big time with the big bucks to show for it — but that pressure...

There was no way Charlie would be responsible for

putting that kind of pressure on his own son. Seth could be a surfer… A doctor, lawyer, retail sales assistant, car washer… He could become anything he wanted. The way Charlie feels, it's not the parents' decision to select their child's life path, and he was glad that Seth had been blessed with Teri as his mother. She's passionate about the game, loves cheering on their son, and has a good head on her shoulders. Of course, they hadn't planned on Seth's arrival, but it couldn't have worked out more perfectly. *Did the game really matter? Did any of it matter? Was Abe right?* There shouldn't be any hierarchies in a child's game, but yet, all Charlie can think about is getting his team to Williamsport — and to hell with Herbert and the rest of them. In fact, even the LA Dodgers hadn't crossed his mind in over a week. He considers giving Earl a call tomorrow for an update, or should he just leave it?

Charlie gets out of his head and refocuses on Teri, who sits beside him in silence. He asks her, "So, how are we gonna do this?"

She turns to face him. "Honestly, I have no idea."

"I could put my Darth Vader costume on, and—" Charlie smirks.

"What? Cut off his hand?" Teri laughs. "I don't think he'd get the reference, anyway."

Charlie's face distorts into a look of shock. "You mean he hasn't seen *Star Wars*?!"

"Afraid not," replies Teri.

Charlie shrieks, "None of them?!" Teri answers with a firm shake of her head. Charlie lets out a deep sigh. "In that case, I take it back. You haven't done an amazing job at all. It's been mediocre at best."

Teri playfully jabs him in the ribs. "I guess we just… Tell him."

"I guess." Charlie looks across the yard at Seth and then back at Teri. "You nervous?"

"Yeah. You?"

Charlie comes up with a clever baseball metaphor to lighten the situation. "Like we're on deck with bases loaded in the bottom of the ninth."

"Well, then, let's smack it out of the park." She gives Charlie a nervous smile, and he returns a weak one of his own. Teri calls out to her son — *their* son. "Seth?" The boy looks over at his mom. "Can you come here for a minute?" Seth hurries over to Teri and jumps into her lap. Before she has the chance to chicken out… "We've got something we need to tell you."

Seth blurts out, "Are you getting married?" Anyone with eyes can see the sparks flying in the air every time the two were together.

Charlie clears his throat, suddenly flustered. "Seth—"

"Am I in trouble?" The boy looks nervous.

Teri steps in. "Not at all." She pauses before finally spitting it out. "You know how I told you your father passed away?"

"Uh-huh."

"Well, that wasn't true. I'm sorry I lied to you, but it's what I thought was best at the time…" A tear wells in her eye. "Your— Your father…" Teri trails off, quickly losing the nerve.

Luckily, Charlie takes over. He looks at Seth and takes a deep breath. "It's me, Seth. I'm your dad."

Seth's eyes immediately light up with glee. His eyes dart from Charlie to Teri and back to Charlie again. "You mean it? Really?" Teri, now lightly sobbing, can only nod. Charlie pulls Seth into a hug, holding his son for the first time after all these years. The kid is over the moon to find out that his hero is actually his own father. Countless questions flash through Seth's mind, but unable to speak, he can only return his dad's embrace instead. Teri watches Charlie and Seth, her heart nearly overflowing with love. Charlie returns her gaze and sniffles, giving Seth's back a pat as they pull away from one another. "Anyone feel like dessert?"

Seth shouts with delight, "Best day ever!" And that was that — the cat was out of the bag, and everyone could now get on with the rest of their night, stress-free. It all felt a bit surreal to Charlie. An instant happy family… *Could it be true?* The three of them eat their dessert in comfortable silence with the soothing music filling in the gaps.

Before the family get-together comes to an end, Teri and Charlie talk with Seth about keeping their situation under wraps until the end of the season. Keep it a secret that Charlie was his dad? Sure, he could do that. After all, he'd lived his entire life until now thinking that his father was dead. Seth thinks back on a conversation he'd once had with Casey. Had *he* known? He must have, imagines Seth — but if so, how? Had the other kids suspected the same, or were the rest of them as clueless as he had been? Seth couldn't be more thrilled by the sudden reveal. He'd always felt like he missed out, not having a dad. But now that Charlie indeed was in his life, the boy ponders what this means for the future. Would Charlie leave them behind again? Was he really going back to New Mexico? Would their father-son relationship be limited to holiday visits and video calls from miles away? Seth decides to wait until he and Teri return home to confront the multitude of questions swimming around in his head. But for right now, he was glad to know it wasn't just him and his mom fighting the world alone. Finally, there was someone else he could turn to when his mom just didn't understand. He feels complete for the first time.

Teri thanks Charlie for the wonderful meal before they leave for the night. They exchange words of relief that, all things considered, the reveal of the secret they both had so violently feared in fact turned out to be a most positive experience — for everyone. Teri had indeed been the most fearful of the two, internally freaking out every time she thought about having to confront something she had withheld for so long. But here it was, finally out in the open, and it had been much less awkward than she could have ever imagined. She was relieved that Seth was pleased rather than angry about the truth, despite understanding that he had been lied to all this time. They would discuss that later, though; just the two of them... That she'd never wanted to lie to him, and that she'd never do it again. How endlessly regretful she was for not being strong enough to tell him the truth sooner.

Lying in bed later that night, Charlie finds it difficult to sleep. He wishes for Teri to be cozied up in bed beside him. In his mind, living together would be the next step — but to make such a huge transition so flippantly wasn't realistic, and it wouldn't be fair to anyone. Charlie's mind races with countless thoughts, no end in sight. He thinks about what it means to be a father. The consequences it would have on his life. Until the wee hours of the night, he can't help but wonder... Would he wake up one day and realize he'd transformed into some critical, intolerable old man too? Or would he escape the curse of his own father? Charlie hates the way Gordon had criticized the team's decision to forfeit in lieu of supporting Nicky, who they considered one of their own. But then it dawns on him... Gordon's never truly gotten to know his own team. Their reaction to a crisis such as this might have been a bit extreme but nevertheless appropriate. *Had* Charlie been too soft on them? Would he need to amp it up and relinquish the little bit of freedom and comfort he'd increasingly allowed the kids over the past few weeks? Now not only was he plagued by insomnia but also indecision. Such a time like this called for only one thing. Nothing calmed his soul more than hitting the ball out of the park. He would imagine every uncertainty, every terrifying thought, every indecision flying up and away with the ball, following the trajectory of the wind until they had flown so far that they'd never be able to find their way back.

◊ ◊ ◊

Charlie grabs his bat and ball before ushering Shoeless Joe into the car. An impromptu late-night training session would set him at ease — not that he needed the practice now. With the team's forfeit, Charlie now had little faith that Brian Ragsdale was going to come through and fulfill his end of the bargain, securing that meeting with the Dodgers. What a name, anyway. The *Dodgers*... Did he really want to join a team that represented everything he disliked about himself and his past? Constantly dodging it all — commitment, responsibility, family, and even love.

When they reach the field, it's completely empty as expected, lit only by a few street lamps. Peaceful silence engulfs them. There was no game, no reason for any light to shine, and the ones that did provided just enough for Charlie to hit that ball — *that stupid ball* — the one with Charlie's initials that Hank had saved for him through all those years. He steps up to the plate, tosses the ball into the air, and slams it. Each time Shoeless Joe fetches the ball, the same as usual, and Charlie keeps hitting it, crushing it further and further afield each time. He begins to sweat after a while despite the coolness in the air, but still, he continues on. Charlie needed to let off all that steam, and hitting something so hard was the kind of release he had grown to need. Well, it was that or a drink, and he was well aware which was the least destructive of the two. Whenever the bat meets the ball, it's like a unique melody, each more beautiful than the last, and with each hit, Charlie finds himself hoping for the wind to swallow that godforsaken ball — for good.

It's been just over an hour when Charlie manages to achieve his mission. He smashes that ball right out of the park, and he hopes, out of existence. When Shoeless Joe comes running back without the ball in his mouth, Charlie can't be happier. He rolls around on the ground with Joe, rewarding him for doing the opposite of what he had been trained to do. Of course, the dog hasn't the slightest clue as to what the big deal is. Why the celebration? When he settles down, Charlie is both laughing and crying at the same time.

"Problem solved. Let's go home, old mate," he tells Joe, who follows him back to the car like the loyal friend he is. Charlie drives home, and for the first time in a long time, he feels nothing but joy; pure *joy*.

CHAPTER TWENTY-ONE

C harlie and Abe sit on the hood of the Mustang, each with a beer in their hand. It had been another tough day for the two, starting bright and early with the A-Team's training and ending with a viewing of Herbert's team as they played an unscheduled game against one of the top teams in another district. Arranging these supplementary games is just another step in Herbert's latest strategy. Connecting with the all-star teams work, to his satisfaction, to both strengthen his players and frighten the living daylights out of them.

The brothers had stayed behind to watch the game plan, hoping to come up with an angle to use on their own team. As he sits there, Charlie finds himself wondering whether the kids' sheer love for the game would have a chance to win over fear. He hopes so... Forcing them to operate with fear could easily destroy their love of the game.

The A-Team doesn't have nearly half the regimental discipline of Herbert's team, who just happened to be running cross-country across the field after their game today. It takes real stamina to consistently train every few days, especially at that level, maintaining focus on the possible prize waiting for them at the end — a spot at the World Series. Only once before had it happened, and that was when Gordon was in his prime as a coach. Now, Charlie has some big shoes to fill. He felt reassured with having Abe onboard, knowing that they were in this together. But ever since Nicky's accident, Abe's been less focused on the team, often needed elsewhere.

As the brothers sit there, Charlie breaks the silence and asks, "How's Nicky doing?"

Abe swallows his sip of beer before answering. "She's okay.

We'll need to follow-up with the doctor in a few months, but other than that, she's back to being the happy, carefree child I know and love. Colleen's looking after her. That's Samantha's mom, so Nicky's grandma. We've been spending a lot of time over there lately. Between work, coaching, and the youth group, I've been needing a bit of support."

Charlie nods his head slowly. A few long moments of silence pass. "That must've been so scary for you, man," says Charlie. "I'd have freaked out in a major way if that had been my son."

"Listen to you," Abe says with a laugh, "'My son.' Never thought I'd hear those words coming from you."

"Well, Abe, life is full of unexpected turns."

Abe holds out his beer toward Charlie. "To unexpected turns." The brothers knock their drinks together. Then Abe turns back his attention to the field up ahead where Herbert's team continues their drill. "You reckon we can beat them again?"

"Not a doubt in my mind. Herbert knows we can too."

"What makes you say that?"

"We've got the As tied with the Giants for first place, and *Judy* decides, all on her own, to move for a best of three to determine the champions? And don't forget replacing Hank with one of those robot umpires." Charlie scoffs.

"You don't think it was Judy's decision?"

Charlie laughs before he continues. "Judy doesn't make decisions. She's just Herb's puppet. He's got his hand so far up her—" He shakes his head and stares straight ahead. "Look, I understand why you didn't tell me about Seth." Abe makes eye contact with Charlie. "Who knows whether I would have come back even if I had known."

Abe smiles. "You would've."

"You think?" Charlie asks.

"Sure," replies Abe. But still, Charlie remains doubtful.

Over on the field, Herbert's wrapping up his team's training after yet another successful win against a higher-ranking team. *Impossible*, Charlie thinks. Fear and love, that's what it was. But right about now, it seems like fear's the one gaining ground.

Herbert walks up to Charlie and Abe with two beers in his hand. He hands one of them to Charlie. "Truce?"

Charlie looks at Abe and rolls his eyes. "Sure, Herb," he answers, taking the beer.

"May the best team win," says Herbert. The two of them toast. Charlie takes a sip of the beer and immediately spits it out. *Nothing worse than a warm, flat beer.* Herbert smiles and pets Shoeless Joe, knowing full well that Charlie had fallen for the ol' warm beer trick.

◊ ◊ ◊

Later that afternoon, Charlie replays the tape of Gordon hitting the twelve-year-old version of himself after making the winning run for the Youth Summer League World Series. He relives the moment, over and over, like it was yesterday — and for a moment, he's back there.

A younger Gordon's in the middle of instructing Charlie when the kid blurts out, "I want to hit a home run for you, Dad." Gordon backhands Charlie across the mouth as soon as the words escape him.

"Home runs don't win ball games. Base hits do," snarls Gordon. "Now, get out there before I beat the crap out of you. *Again.*" He looks away, avoiding Charlie's hurt gaze. "And watch for my signals."

Charlie stands at the plate, where the pitcher delivers a wild one. When the catcher misses the ball, Abe and Luke scramble to make a double steal, with Abe ending on third base.

Gordon signals Charlie, mouthing the words, 'Bunt, you stupid idiot.'

Next, the pitcher releases a fastball. As it speeds across the plate, Charlie swings hard and misses the pitch.

Gordon signals at Charlie again, more urgently this time: 'B, stop, U, stop, N, stop, T, stop. You idiot.' The pitcher's next throw comes low and outside. This time, when Charlie swings, he crushes the ball out of the park.

Charlie comes back to his present reality, suddenly turning off the TV. He gets up from the couch, grabbing his keys, and walks out the front door. Shoeless Joe follows closely behind him and leaps right into the Mustang.

A few minutes afterward, Charlie pulls into the parking lot of the high school where he used to play ball. He makes his way over to the baseball field and stands on home plate, staring out into the greenery, dreaming of a life where what he had just watched on screen didn't happen. Herbert walks up, stopping a few feet behind Charlie. He clears his throat for attention.

Charlie turns to look, his eyebrows bunched together in anger. "To what do I owe the displeasure?"

"Are you following me? You watched my team all day long."

Charlie shrugs casually. "No crime for being in the bleachers or the parking lot."

Herbert hesitates momentarily. "Look, I'm here to visit Judy. She's working late tonight." Charlie gives a look like he hasn't the slightest clue as to what Herb's talking about. "We're an item, if you must know." Then Herbert reveals an open hand, and inside lies something Charlie would rather not see — it's the ball with Charlie's initials on it. "This belong to you?" When Charlie moves to take the ball, Herbert holds it just out of reach, tossing it up and down in his meaty hand. "You know, Charlie, sometimes I wonder which of us is *really* the 'bad guy.'"

Charlie gives his arch nemesis a look as if he's off his rocker. "Really? You have to ponder that?"

Herbert shrugs. "I got my flaws too, Charlie. I'm not denying that. Hell, it's no secret I'd rather have a million dollars in my own pocket than give a buck to the poor. But you, my friend... You're not half the saint you think you are."

"Oh, is that right? And what have I done, Herb? What am *I* guilty of?"

Again, Herbert messes with the ball, tossing it up and down before answering Charlie's question. "Back in senior year... Know how I'd start my day?"

"With a glass of freshly squeezed puppy-dog blood?"

Herbert chuckles, unfazed. "I'd start each and every day thinking about you, Charlie."

"I'm flattered," Charlie snidely remarks.

"Every day, I'd go to school and think, 'What's he going to do to me today?' Stuff me in a trash can? Shake me down for money? Smash my paintings? Set off firecrackers in my locker?" He pauses and tosses the ball up and down once more, focusing on it steadily. Then he looks Charlie in the eye. "I never even had the courage to hate you. All I could feel was jealousy. You had it all — the popularity, the car, the girls. And that stupid Letterman jacket you wore? Hell, it might as well have been a crown. You were the king, Charlie, and the rest of us were merely your loyal subjects. Or worse."

That strikes a nerve. Charlie turns to stare Herbert down, closing in on him ever so slightly. "Look, *Snot Nose* — I mean, Herbert. I was just a kid. I didn't—"

"Do you know how long it took me to stop hating myself? To realize it was you — not me — who had it worst of all? You were simply treating everyone else the way your old man treated you."

Charlie's expression softens. "I'm sorry, Herbert. Okay?" Herbert scoffs in response. "Look, come on, how about we leave it all in the past and just let our teams play ball?"

Now, Herbert laughs. He shakes his head solemnly and looks out across the field. "Play ball? This has nothing to do with baseball. It's not even about money. This is about my team crushing your team. The same way you crushed me." Herbert rips the bat from Charlie's hand and tosses the ball into the air. He smashes it deep into the outfield. Shoeless Joe takes off after the ball.

Charlie begins to walk away. "I'm out of here."

"Darn shame what happened to your brother back in high school," Herbert begins, causing Charlie to slow down. "The accident and all." Charlie freezes on the spot. Now Herbert's the one to walk away, free and easy.

Meanwhile, Joe turns back around and barks at Charlie to keep going but he doesn't, stuck in a sort of trance. His mind flashes back to that moment — the 'accident,' as Herbert had called it. Being on the field of his youth, it didn't take much for his brain to wind its way back down the familiar path.

Many moons ago, right here on this field, it had been a warm spring day. The brothers warm up for the impending game. Charlie's on the pitcher's mound, and Abe is at home plate, standing at the ready with his bat up in the air. Over by the bleachers, Gordon talks to a scout from UCLA. From the mound, Charlie notices Gordon pointing to Abe. Charlie shakes his head in anger, and with a fitful scowl on his face, he winds up and puts every muscle into his next pitch to Abe. Suddenly, the baseball connects with Abe's collarbone. Before Charlie realizes what's happened, Abe screams in pain and drops to the ground, the ball landing right beside the plate. Gordon runs over to the boys with shouts of concern.

They call an ambulance and rush Abe to the hospital, where he lies in a bed. Abe doesn't look too bad at the moment except for the unshakable wince of pain on his face. The doctor addresses Gordon but Charlie listens in, terrified. "His left collarbone is shattered in two places." Gordon grumbles with an exclamation of disdain. The doctor continues. "Now, I have to warn you. If it doesn't heal right, he may never play baseball again."

"Thanks, doc," says Gordon before the doctor leaves the room. He turns to Charlie and instantly strikes him down with one powerful swat. He spews, "You did this on purpose!" Charlie runs off.

"Charlie, wait," shouts Abe with as much volume as he can muster — but it's too late.

Meanwhile, back over at the fields all those years ago, Hank picks up a baseball that sits casually beside the plate. He pulls a pen from his pocket and writes the infamous initials: 'CM.'

From the hospital, Charlie jumps into his Mustang and

drives over to Teri's house. He throws pebbles at her second-story bedroom window until she opens it and waves him up. Charlie hurriedly climbs the tree nearest the window and slips inside the teen girl's room. He sits on Teri's bed and takes a breath. Teri joins him on the bed, and Charlie clasps both of her hands in his. He can barely contain himself.

"I'm leaving tomorrow to go play pro-ball," Charlie tells her. "Come with me."

Teri's eyes widen in shock. "What? And give up my scholarship?"

Charlie stares down at his lap. Tears begin to form in his eyes. "Please. Come with me," he says, his eyes slowly finding Teri's.

"You know I can't. I'm going to UCLA this fall."

"Please. Come with me," he repeats desperately.

"Why don't we sleep on it and talk in the morning?" Teri looks confident with her suggestion, but then Charlie begins, ever so softly, to kiss Teri. The kisses progress, becoming more and more passionate by the second as though there were no tomorrow. They both knew there would be no chance of sleeping tonight...

Luckily, Charlie hears Shoeless Joe's repetitive barking, and it brings him back to the present. Joe drops the initialed ball in front of Charlie, and Charlie picks it up. He just stares at the ball... Then he stares at the field — the silent field that gives him no grief. *It's just a field*, he tries to convince himself. But nevertheless, all it reminds him of is the vengeful crime of jealousy he'd committed against his own brother. There was no escaping this; not ever. He winds up and throws the ball into the outfield as hard as possible. With a whistle, Charlie turns on his feet and heads back toward the Mustang. Joe takes the signal and comes bounding after him. Charlie hopes another beer or some sleep would at least help tone down the memories. Otherwise, he didn't know how much more he could take.

◊ ◊ ◊

Finally Abe receives the news he'd been waiting on, but

unfortunately, it's nothing like the welcome response for which he had hoped. He reads it in silence.

Dear Mr. Abe Maddox,

I am writing to inform you that we received your letter to protest against the demolishing of Mr. G's Fields. However, the fields have been earmarked for development for many years now, and the council believes that the community has many such recreational spaces to indulge your passions and proposals.

The longevity of American baseball is not dependent on whether these fields in question remain standing. Please refer to the attached map of the local area where I have taken liberty to sticky note the available fields to be used as possible spaces.

Please consider these spaces, and you are welcome to inquire further about using these fields to expand the potential of an already thriving institution. We at council appreciate your dedication and understand the legacy your family name has been in the community. We recommend contacting the Randwick Group at your earliest convenience. As the developers of this site, they can tell you if it would be amenable to maintaining this legacy by possibly naming a section of the shopping center after your father.

Sincerely,
Leonie Clarke
Planning Commissioner

Abe sets down the letter onto the table and lets out a deep sigh. He feels betrayed... Downhearted... He didn't want his family name to appear in a stupid shop window like some abandoned, lonely, orphaned pet. He didn't want to consider other 'recreational spaces.' What he wanted was for the fields named in his father's honor to *remain* in his name. It wasn't about the game per se.

Sure, Abe believes kids of all abilities should be given the chance to play the game, but regardless, his dad's name should be retained as something special. Mr. G deserves that much, doesn't he? It was about everything Mr. G had done for the town throughout the years, helping to maintain the community spirit in that place. Abe imagines young people hanging outside the future shopping mall, keeping themselves entertained by smoking and drinking; maybe dealing drugs. Everything that was the total opposite of what he now so strongly believed in. Who needs retail therapy when a good run around the bases can perk up any foul mood just as effectively?

Abe squishes the letter into a crumpled ball and throws it into a nearby bin. *Ask and ye shall receive.* Obviously, it hadn't been part of *His* plan. What was Abe not wanting to accept about this whole scenario? He prays vigorously that night, begging for a revelation about the whole thing.

CHAPTER TWENTY-TWO

O ver at the snack bar, Judy, Abe, and Charlie discuss more impending changes to the fields' management. The original replacements Judy hired didn't work out so well, and additional resources had needed to be called in. Abe, with the voice of a preacher on a hot Sunday morning, shouts, "Can I get an 'amen' for us being under new management here at the snack bar? The Lord Jesus truly does work in mysterious ways."

"Preacher, we are here to discuss the organization of the teams," Judy says.

"I thought we were here to discuss the management."

"Well, seems we all have our own little agendas, don't we?" Judy's response is both firm but patronizing.

Charlie chimes in with, "Abe, I thought you wanted to speak about the possible transformation of the fields?"

"No, Charlie, we need to first *find* another field to transform," replies Abe. "Don't you recall? I received a letter from the city council, stating that my campaign was unsuccessful."

"There must be something else we can do—"

Judy acts as a mediator. "Charlie, we're not here to talk about doing something else."

Charlie opens his mouth to speak but Abe shushes him, and Charlie shushes him right back. They both start fake slapping each other.

"Boys—" Judy holds up two fingers to silence the brothers who appear to have lost a little of their solidarity amid the conversation. Abe and Charlie remain silent under Judy's hardened gaze. "At his father's request, Casey will be traded to the Giants for Emily Jones," she says. Neither Abe nor Charlie have the courage to buck against Judy for fear that her icy glare would turn them into stone. Finally, Charlie can't stand it any longer. He bursts out, "Emily Jones?! She's a six-year-old in T-ball!" Judy shrugs like she couldn't care less. "Isn't the coach supposed to pick their own replacement players?"

"No, I'm afraid it's the league president now who has the obligation to determine who the replacement player will be in order to fairly balance out the teams." Judy smirks. Charlie's lip nearly forms into a snarl.

Abe pipes up. "Charlie, it's not that bad. She's a little weak at batting, but she's great at catching fly balls."

Charlie ignores Abe's comment and takes a step toward Judy. "The head office will hear about this," he challenges.

Judy's tone warps into one that's much softer, much more delicate. She reaches out and strokes Charlie's hair. "Charlie-boy, go right ahead. By the time they decide that you're right, it'll be too late." She pauses and leans in as if going to kiss him. "Why don't you come over to my basement, and I'll make it up to you." Then she turns her head away, just short of kissing him, and walks off. "Like it or leave it," she says without looking back.

Abe continues on as if nothing has happened. "Look, Charlie, I was joking. This kid isn't some pawn in a game; she's a kid. We'll cope no matter who's on the team. Remember Gideon?"

"Who?"

"He fought against the Midianites. God asked him to reduce his men to three hundred. They were fighting over one hundred thousand men."

"What was the point in that?" Charlie asks in complete frustration.

"God wanted to show Gideon that it wasn't about fighting in his own strength. It was about God's strength."

Soon after, the brothers go their separate ways. Abe goes to lead that night's youth group while Charlie drives over to Teri's place. He racks his mind during the drive, plotting out the next move in regard to Judy's recent shift in league orders.

Minutes later, in Teri's living room, Charlie sits on the

couch with a beer in his hand. Shoeless Joe has a splash or two of the beer in his to-go water bowl, and the dog happily slurps it up. Teri accompanies Charlie on the couch.

"It gets better," Charlie tells her excitedly. "Herbert wants to begin selling his baseball franchise to other leagues."

"Why would any other league want to buy into his master plan for world domination? It's like *Moneyball* for kids." Teri chuckles to herself.

Charlie shrugs and takes a long swig of his beer. His eyebrows raise as though he's just remembered something. "Oh, here's a donation for Nicky." He pulls a money clip from his pocket and tosses it onto the coffee table. "It would've been more, but the pizza party went over budget."

Teri stares down at the money, giving it a thoughtful look. "Is that your pocket change?"

"Very funny," Charlie quips.

"What? I thought all baseball players made millions."

Charlie shakes his head. "Only the lucky few. The rest of us make eight hundred bucks a week, plus a six-dollar per diem when on the road."

"Guess I was right to go into teaching instead of sports... It pays better," she says with a coy smile.

"Well, I went into it for love, love," he teases back. Teri smiles. Looking at Charlie, she realizes just now how much she had missed him and his funny banter. In fact, she can't remember the last time she smiled this much; it had been so long.

◊ ◊ ◊

Abe had only recently been notified that his campaigning failed, and the sadness and frustration weighs heavy on his mind. The pastor confronts the familiar group of teens later that night, spreading the news that their request had been denied. They'd certainly done all they could think to do — various online petitions, fundraisers, street campaigns — but the big bucks always beat out the little guys at the end of the day. Capitalism and retail therapy would win out anytime.

One of the teen girls pipes up. "I thought you said we can ask anything in God's name, and He will make it happen?"

Abe hesitates before responding. "Yeah, I said that," he reluctantly admits. "I mislead you, and I was wrong." The teens look shocked, exchanging looks with one another, eyes wide. For most, this was the first time they'd heard an adult admit fault. Abe continues. "You see, the Bible says, 'You may ask Me for anything in My name, and I will do it.' John chapter fourteen, verse fourteen. But we weren't asking for this to happen in *His* name… To glorify *His* name… No." Abe sighs deeply and looks around at the attentive teens, who for once stare straight back at him. "We were asking for this to happen in *my* name and in *my* biological father's name — not in my heavenly Father's name. You see, what *we* want and what God wants are sometimes two different things." Then he shrugs as an afterthought. "*He knows* what's best for us. *He knows* what we need to hold onto and what we need to release. Maybe something has taken hold of your life in the form of an idol or an obsession. You've probably seen it happen with your friends, family members… But I guess that's why you've really got to form your own relationship with the Man upstairs. Don't just take my word for it," he says in closing.

Abe hopes his words are enough to inspire some follow-up questions from the teens. He couldn't be the only one they relied on to bring the truth of Christ to them; otherwise, they'd have nothing more than a distant 'secondhand' version of faith. The only way anyone can start to comprehend God's love is to know Him for themselves, Abe ponders. That night the group says grace and eats dinner in relative silence. This week's volunteers had prepared a homemade roast chicken and salad dish — simple yet delicious.

The news of the campaigning ending so quickly had been a bit of a blow to the teens' already downhearted spirits. Once again they had fought hard with nothing to show. Just another failure in their lives, it takes them right back to those wasted years where they had played hard on the field. Blood, sweat, and tears pouring out, and still, nothing they did could impress or even satisfy their folks. Nothing would ever make them 'good enough' in their parents' eyes. The only shift to the parent-child relationship wouldn't come until the teens spiraled out of control, whether with drinking, drugs, or some other escape. It wasn't until the teens were caught on the wrong side of the tracks, usually in a damaging situation, that their parents stood up and took notice. Only then would the relationship change — and it was hardly ever a change for the better.

More often, the parents withdrew, giving up on their own children, and some even disowning them completely. And from what Abe had told them, the teens knew that trying to impress God wouldn't work either. Luckily, though, their Creator was already impressed with who they were, and no matter what they did, nothing would change that — according to Abe, anyway. With this new mindset, still they wanted to fight. They felt a driving need to *show* how much they supported Abe... To give back to him and the Man upstairs for caring... For *loving* them. But as they sat there that night in the relative silence, they realized something. They didn't have to *do* anything in order to receive more love. Instead, they already were loved, and the only thing they had to do was let the true Author of love *love* them.

◊ ◊ ◊

The next day, the league holds a fundraiser in honor of Nicky, helping to raise money for the hospital bills she's incurred. A large banner strung across the batting cage reads: 'Silent Auction — Nicky Maddox Fundraiser.' Just below the banner sits a long table filled with gift baskets from each team.

Charlie, Teri, and Shoeless Joe wander around the field. Seeing how many people know and love Abe and the family he'd made for himself left Charlie a bit awestruck. If it had been *his* kid who fell, would there be this much support? *There it was again...* That green monster attempting to rear its ugly head once again, trying its hardest to destroy the solid relationship Charlie was forging with his brother. Nicky deserves to reap all the benefits from this fundraiser as should any other neighborhood child. They peruse the table piled high with gift baskets.

"See anything you like?" Charlie asks Teri.

"Hmmm," Teri says as her eyes glaze over the items on the table. "Anything with perfume, skincare, makeup, linen — oh, or chocolate — that's for me."

"Makeup? No need; you're already perfect just as you are," Charlie coos flirtatiously. Teri rolls her eyes in response but a genuine smile plays upon her lips. It was nice to hear such romantic words for a change. Charlie spies a dog-themed gift basket that's been donated from his and Joe's favorite coffee shop, The Park Bench Café. Shoeless Joe comes over and sets a paw onto the gift basket, barking at Charlie for attention. Charlie smiles and gives Joe's head a pat. After all, he's spot on with his choice — an outdoor cafe that serves dogs as well as their owners.

Meanwhile, Judy stands on stage and speaks into a microphone. Her voice booms out over the sound system. "It's such a tragedy, what happened to poor, sweet, little Nicky and this league. Pastor Abe has asked that everybody stop by his church to say a prayer for her. It's the least we can do, anyway." Judy dramatically sniffles away invisible tears before continuing. "Let's have a moment of silence for little Nicky." Judy and those in the crowd, scattered around the field, bow their heads simultaneously. After a brief pause, Brian Ragsdale suddenly runs onto the stage and hands a note to Judy. Her eyes widen as she reads the note. "I've just received notice that Charlie Maddox has bid four thousand dollars on the romantic weekend getaway basket."

Charlie looks up at Teri, confused. "I did?" Everyone applauds. Teri nods her head, urging him to take the cue. Charlie walks to the stage to accept the basket. Once on stage, Judy gives him a hug and looks out over the crowd. "I'm sure I speak for all the ladies here when I say I'd *love* to be the one joining you, Charlie." She winks and then tries to give him a kiss but he quickly turns away.

As the fundraiser comes to a close and everyone's nearly

cleared out, Charlie loads his gift basket into the Mustang. Teri follows closely behind with a basket of her own, brimming with all kinds of girly things. Charlie turns to her and asks, "So, when are we going on our romantic getaway?"

Teri just smiles at first. "Who says I'd go with you? Maybe I've got my eye on ol' Herbie. He's kind of cute, you know, and he's a politician to boot." She and Charlie soon burst out laughing before getting into the car and driving off.

The Mustang pulls into a church parking lot. "Hope you don't mind, but I gotta go pay my respects." Charlie gets out of the car and peers down at Teri. "You coming in?"

"No," she says, shaking her head, "you're on your own for this one."

Charlie watches Teri for a moment with a puzzled look on his face. Doesn't she care about Nicky? Or maybe it's the whole idea of church she has issues with. Either way, he'd need to put that conversation on hold for another time.

Teri gets out of the car. "You know what? I'll walk back. The house isn't far, and you can bring me my gift basket when you pick me up tomorrow. We can discuss plans for our special getaway then." The two kiss before parting ways until the next day.

Charlie walks into the church and down the aisle to the front, where he kneels before a gigantic photo of Nicky. Moments later, Abe enters the room, dressed in his church robe. Charlie's just about to take a seat in one of the pews.

"Got a minute?" Abe asks. Charlie turns around as his brother strides past, heading up to the pulpit. "I want to take this week's sermon for a test drive."

Charlie hesitates. "I gotta get back to the field. Just stopped by for Nicky..."

From the pulpit, Abe stares him down. "Don't worry, you won't be struck by lightning. Plus, I'll skip the boring parts." Charlie rolls his eyes but stays put in his seat. Abe takes a moment to review his notes before beginning. "Cain is doomed to wander the earth in the land of Nod, somewhere east of Eden, protected by the mark of Cain, which is thought to be a canine." He steps down from the pulpit and approaches Charlie. "The word 'Nod' actually means 'wandering' in Hebrew. So, it's a term more descriptive of Cain's life than his actual wandering."

"Your veil's a bit thin here, Abe. I came home."

Abe stares into his brother's eyes. "Cain still lives in an internal 'East of Eden.' If we think of Eden as a place in the human heart, Cain exiled himself from life and love."

Charlie lifts his arms to the heavens and dramatically proclaims, "Gordon favored Abe."

"At no point did *Cain* seek to make amends for his irresponsible actions," Abe replies. Just then, the church choir enters for their weekly practice and breaks out into 'Amazing Grace.'

"I reacted! I was jealous! Okay?" Charlie says, cracking under the pressure. Abe gives a knowing smile and a slight shrug. A serious look comes over Charlie's face. He stares straight ahead at Abe. "I'm sorry. Forgive me, brother."

The two men freeze, staring at each other. Suddenly Abe grabs Charlie around the neck and gives him a noogie. The brothers playfully struggle. Charlie hops to his feet and quickly dominates, giving Abe a mean wedgie in return.

◊ ◊ ◊

Charlie and Abe pay a visit to Jack, where they bid him farewell on his new scholarship. Jack's currently living at his dad's house, but according to him, the older man doesn't seem to care or even acknowledge the fact that his son has landed such a great opportunity. On the teen's bedroom wall, there's a handmade poster of Charlie and Abe. The brothers watch as Jack packs his suitcase.

"Thanks for the scholarship, even if it is way out in New Mexico," Jack says to the brothers. His excitement is palpable, with a happiness he hadn't felt in years. "I'll miss you guys, but I imagine it'll be nice to have a change of scenery."

"Glad to help. Besides, my friend jumped at the chance to get you with your virgin pitching arm."

"Oh, yeah?" Jacks asks with a smirk.

"Sure. He's seen way too many kids who've blown out their arms by pitching too many curve balls before they even get into high school. You're a rare find," Charlie says, with a genuine smile on his face.

Abe pipes up, smirking. "Remember to bring your Bible. It might come in handy when you can't find a hammer."

Jack guffaws before handing Abe a key. "It's for my private locker at the fields. Now you guys'll be able to go out with a bang," says the teen, with a sly grin.

CHAPTER TWENTY-THREE

Teri and Charlie sit on Teri's living room couch, discussing plans for what to do about their most recent predicament. The other team moms were putting the heat on Teri, expecting her to lead them in the charge of turning this thing around. Charlie worries that if they allow Judy and the board to continue making changes without proper consultation, who knows what would become of the league. He suspects that Herbert is the one pulling strings behind the scenes, and that's another problem in itself.

"What if we stage a rebellion? Oust Judy from the presidency and take over ourselves?" Charlie suggests.

Teri slowly turns to look at Charlie with a doubtful look. "A rebellion? Always trying to find an excuse to wear that Darth Vader costume, aren't you?"

"Well, technically Judy would be Vader. I'd be more of a Luke."

Teri laughs. Then she sits up, struck by inspiration. "I got it. We call an emergency meeting with the other parents and tell them exactly what Judy and Herbert have been up to."

Charlie's face suddenly lights up. "Then we have them vote me in as league president, and I kick Judy out the first chance I get."

Teri snaps up her phone and immediately gets to work. "I'll post an update to the league's private community page, along with an invite for an emergency meeting, calling all team parents."

"The community page?" Charlie asks.

"Sure." Teri sends off her invite with a final tap to her phone. "And off it goes to eighty-five parents."

Again, Charlie's face lights up with an idea. "Let them know there's a romantic getaway up for grabs for one lucky couple who attends the meeting — free babysitting included. That'll get 'em to come out on such short notice."

Teri shakes her head, disagreeing with Charlie's hopeful initiative. "It should be a mom's getaway from the family, with dad staying behind to watch the kids. Lord knows we deserve it."

"You got a point," Charlie replies.

Before speaking, Teri gives him a long, hard look as though trying to read him like a book. "Do you really think you're up to the challenge of possibly sticking around long enough to run for the presidency? Isn't that a little below your professional league status?" She smiles, warming his heart.

"How long of a process are we talking?" Charlie asks with uncertainty in his voice. When Teri's smile wavers ever so slightly, he carefully rethinks the next words coming out of his mouth. "Never mind that. Count me in. Can't let those kids down, huh?" *Can't let Teri down again is more like it.* Charlie smiles wide, and Teri matches his expression.

◊ ◊ ◊

On the other side of town, Judy sits opposite Herbert in his lavish office space that ironically overlooks his baseball bootcamp. Her phone dings, signaling a new app notification. She's quiet for the moment, intently focusing on her phone screen. An evil grin crosses her face. "Those idiots," she murmurs aloud. Herbert's too distracted with himself to hear her.

He leans forward with both arms on his desk. "I was thinking, Judy... Since I got outbid by that bumbling lummox for the romantic getaway at the fundraiser the other day, how about we go on a little getaway to your secluded basement instead?"

"We'll see," Judy responds dismissively. "But tell me, Herbie. What shade of green are you going to be when I'm the one to win that romantic getaway with Charlie?"

"Sounds more like an insurance policy." Herbert goes to kiss her but she turns to avoid it.

"A girl's gotta protect herself."

Intrigued, Herb asks, "Oh, really?"

"We'll talk about this later. Right now I have somewhere to be." Judy abruptly stands up, collects her things, and leaves the office.

◊ ◊ ◊

Teri, Abe, and Charlie, along with a group of forty or so team moms and a few team dads, stand just outside the snack bar. Teri leads the charge, addressing the parents. "So, that's it, everyone. Our esteemed 'Madam President' has been plotting against us this entire time. But now, with Charlie here, it's about to bite her in the a—"

Suddenly, Judy steps out from hiding. She holds a small barrel in her hands. "Unfortunately, though, there's one itty-bitty clincher," she begins. A few of the parents gasp while others cower. Judy continues with, "The president-elect must have served as an elected officer on the board, in good standing, before taking office as president. Charlie Maddox, therefore, is ineligible for the position." She turns and looks straight at Abe. "If only Abe still had his position on the board," she says, a patronizing tone in her voice.

Abe's eyes widen in complete disbelief. "Wait, what?" He casts a sidelong glance at Teri, confused.

Judy smiles happily at the scornful faces around her. "Gee, Teri must have forgotten to mention— Oh, well. Sorry to rain on your parade, folks." Teri puts a hand to her forehead and mouths 'sorry' to Abe. Then Judy saunters up to Charlie and coyly wraps an arm around his shoulder. "Perhaps I could lighten the mood by taking this opportunity to announce who will be joining Charlie on his romantic weekend getaway." She pulls a scrap of paper out of the otherwise empty barrel. Not even bothering to look at the paper once, she tosses it to the ground. "Oh, fancy that. The winner is *me*." Judy smiles smugly at Charlie and then throws the barrel aside. She shoots one last venomous look at the team parents and walks away.

"Well, *that* really stunk up the place," Teri says loud

enough for Judy to hear. The vindictive woman stops in her tracks and then turns back. "Charlie, do you want to take me for a ride in your Mustang? I'd love to wear your Letterman jacket." Judy's eyes lock onto Teri. "Oh, I'm sorry, Teri. Do you mind if I flirt with your boy?" Teri gives Judy 'the look,' and Judy makes a cat clawing motion in response.

◊ ◊ ◊

Teri, Charlie, and Abe decide to go back to Teri's house to wind down and take stock of their emergency meeting with the team parents. "I'm such an idiot," Teri says on her way in from the kitchen. She hands the guys each a cold beer and paces around. "I never would've thought she'd still be in the group. She never shows up for the meetings, never participates…"

Charlie scoops up Teri into a hug. "This is not your fault, Teri. Besides, that plan might not have worked, anyway. We'll come up with something else."

"Why bother? We can't possibly win, Charlie. The game against the Giants is just a battle. Herbert and Judy — they'll win the war." Teri almost instantly regrets the words as they tumble out of her mouth. As head team mom, she'd always been the A-Team's biggest fan and would continue to support them (and Charlie) no matter what — but there was a part of her that felt it could be time to embark on life's next chapter. Maybe such a resolution like this had come about for a reason. Teri's mind races… Should she try convincing Charlie to just let it be — to let it go? Then again, she'd never seen him so truly passionate about anything before, and it had in fact taken this 'problem' to unite the brothers. The problem had become an unexpected solution and ultimately the key to forging their relationship. Everyone needs something to unite against, something to fight for, and Youth Summer League was in their blood. They had been born into something so strong that spanned decades, and it wasn't something that could be abandoned overnight.

"Hey, Abe, wanna turn that off and join us?" Charlie calls out over the blaring TV Abe's eyes are fixed on. Abe doesn't respond, so Charlie goes over. On the screen, a news reporter talks about civil unrest and the protests going on in Europe. The next moment, they cut to a break with a cheesy used car dealership commercial — one that really works to bring in the crowds on a consistent basis:

> *"Hey, people, I'm Cal Worthington, Jr. We have so many cars on the lot that we're having our biggest sale ever under the big top. There will be elephant rides, clowns making balloons, and popcorn. If I can't finance you, I'll put my head in a tiger's mouth. That's right, people, you heard me. I carry all my own paper, so I can finance any deal in town. Bring down the whole family, and I'll see you there."*

Charlie stares at the TV, mesmerized. As the commercial ends, he slowly turns to look at Teri, a huge grin spread across his face. "You may be right, Teri. Maybe we can't win this. But we can teach ol' Herbert and his boys a lesson they'll never forget."

CHAPTER TWENTY-FOUR

I t's time for the big game. Families, small and large, already fill the stands. Even some unlikely spectators like grandparents and older siblings have come out for the day. Many of them had never been to a kids' baseball game until now.

Several parents wait in line to buy their tickets. One grumpy father turns to another and comments, "You believe this? Charging us to watch our own kids play... They'd better win." At the front of the line, another parent has difficulty communicating with the cashier who apparently doesn't understand English.

The A-Team kids warm up on one side of the field while the Giants warm up on the other side. Off in the distance, a few construction workers tear down the iconic sign that reads, 'Welcome to Mr. G's Fields.' Abe watches the workers, taking his own personal moment of silence to commemorate what he considers to be the official ending of an era.

Fighting against special treatment for 'team favorites' was something Abe had done for so long. The irony, however, was that he had also fought for the fields to remain in the name of the one and only Mr. G — or for the fields to remain as *fields*, at the least. Regardless of Abe's good-naturedness, there was a tiny sliver of him that lacked integrity. He'd wanted his old man to still be singled out among the crowd. For his own family name to be honored. Abe comforts himself with the thought that no matter *where* they play, the game would still go on.

In the A-Team's dugout, Charlie gives the kids his pre-game pep talk. "We've got a doubleheader today and another game tomorrow, so don't overexert yourselves." He looks around at the anxious faces staring back at him. "You can do this, team.

I know you can."

Across the way, in the Giants' dugout, Herbert does his own little pep talk; one filled with fear, fire, and brimstone. "You still have a chance to redeem yourselves, boys, to me, to your parents, and to God. But you'll need to work hard — over and above everything you have ever known. Can you do it?" A few of the players gulp and exchange looks with those around them amid the silence before Herbert continues. "Who knows. I hope you can, for your own good. What about those who don't step up to the plate? Your contract with this team can end at any time; you mark my words. Today we show no mercy."

Charlie builds up his team as a good coach should. "You have the energy, the enthusiasm, and most of all, the love of the game."

Herbert barks at his players like nothing they do could warrant even a simple high-five as far as he's concerned. The best the kids can hope for is to perform well enough to remain in the game (*and* on the team). "It's not good enough just to 'do your best.' You need to be perfect, and with the enemy on retreat."

Charlie talks strategy with the A-Team. "Seth will be pitching in the second game only. A couple of you guys will step up to pitch during the first. I have faith in every single one of you, and I know you'll come through, even outside of your regular positions on the field. You can do it. Step outside your comfort zone, trust me, trust your team, and we'll come through today just fine."

"We must show them no mercy," Herbert continues over in the Giants' dugout. "Cut them down, or you will see me at the end of this game cutting *you* down, my friends." He uses the term 'friends' lightly — patronizingly, even — as though this *friendly* word can help soften the blow of his verbal assaults.

"Win or lose, we all still have to get up the next morning. You have family and friends. You still have to go to school. It won't be the end or the beginning of the world, no matter the outcome," Charlie says with confidence, completely on a roll, doing his best to reassure the kids that whatever happens *on* the field shouldn't affect their self-esteem *off* the field. "You're all incredible human beings who are here to have fun. Be the best you can be, and always know you're not alone; we're in this together."

Herbert barks again at the Giants. "We will attack with everything we have and not stop until total and complete victory is ours."

"And finally," says Charlie, "we must all respect Casey's decision to leave us and play for the opposing team. Despite that, we continue to support him because he is one of us. Now, I'd be devastated if anyone else chose to leave our team but it's ultimately your choice. I hope I'm providing the leadership you need to see lifelong success, and I am confident you have what it takes. So, let's express the freedom to be here on the field today and play like it's truly a privilege to be here. For me, it's a privilege to be coaching you. I've had the time of my life over the course of this season, so let's get out there on that field and have the time of our lives."

The kids all stand up and crowd around in a huddle with Charlie. "Let's go, A-Team," everyone shouts. As the huddle breaks apart and Charlie and the other players head out onto the field, Casey walks into the dugout. Seth stays behind and watches him pack away some of his gear into a ball bag.

Casey looks up, only to lock eyes with his friend for a split second. "My dad got me traded to the Giants."

"But *we're* your team, Case. You're an A."

Casey shoves his cup into the ball bag. "Not while you're here. The best I can do is a 'B.'" He zips up the bag. "Besides, he's only coaching because my dad's paying him." Casey storms out, leaving Seth standing there in shock.

◊ ◊ ◊

It's almost time... In the Giants' dugout, Coach Guy frantically works to book up a robotic umpire. Despite pressing all the buttons, the robot doesn't start up nor respond at all.

Over the loudspeaker booms the announcer's voice. "I was just handed this note. Today's game was supposed to feature the debut of Robbie the Robotic Umpire. But unfortunately, due to technical issues, our head umpire Hank will be stepping in."

Next to the bleachers, a content Gordon sits unsuspectingly in his wheelchair with a blanket draped over his knees. Next to him sit Teri and Nicky. The day is warming up to be a good one, he thinks. Teri's voice suddenly interrupts his thoughts.

"If your doctors knew the two of you weren't home in bed —"

Nicky pipes up. "It's okay, I won't say anything." She turns to Gordon. "How about you, Grandpa?"

The old man turns to Nicky with a hint of a smile. "Your secret's safe with me, kid."

Meanwhile, the two teams, along with their coaches, stand at attention on the field. Abe whispers to Charlie, "Watch this," before sending a hand signal across the way to Herbert.

Herbert translates Abe's signal aloud. "It was me who outbid you on eBay for the signed Mickey Mantle photo." Herbert lunges at Abe, and a full-blown fight nearly breaks out, but luckily Charlie and Coach Guy manage to keep the two men at arm's length. Everyone else just watches — some with concern, others with confusion, and others still with amusement.

Nicky scrambles her way toward the announcer's booth. A few moments later, her voice screeches over the loudspeaker. "Can't we all just get along?" Abe and Herbert start to go at it again, but then Nicky, attempting to be the peacekeeper though totally ill-equipped for such a role, recites the Pledge of Allegiance.

Everyone below on the field freezes and covers their heart with their right hand, joining Nicky in reciting from right where they stand. "I pledge allegiance to the flag of the United States of America, and to the Republic for which it stands, one nation, under God, indivisible, with liberty and justice for all."

Afterward, there is peace for but a moment — until Herbert breaks away from his team. This time he approaches Hank and points at Michelle. With a smug look on his face, he spews to the old umpire, "Per rule seventeen, section forty-two, I demand a cup check on all players — especially the girl."

Teri stands up in the bleachers and shouts, "You trying to get a girl thrown out of the game because she beat your team?" The crowd of parents boos loudly, led by Teri.

Back on the field, Michelle steps forward, seemingly unbothered by Herbert's ploy. Instead, she outsmarts him. "I got one. You want me to do a drum solo to prove it?"

Hank ignores the nonsense, lowers his mask, and takes his place behind home plate. "Play ball!"

A few minutes later from the A-Team's dugout, Charlie and Abe watch as new players Frankie and Benji, both over six feet tall, with uniforms that are comically too small for their hulk-like bodies, enter the Giants dugout across the way.

Abe and Charlie exchange a look before Abe asks, "What's with the giant twins?"

Charlie nods. "Herbert's replacement players. A couple of his regulars suddenly got *ill*.'"

"Oh?" Abe asks with a look of concern.

"Yeah, something called the 'short on money syndrome.'" Abe rolls his eyes at Charlie. "Having to fork out the big bucks to line Herb's pockets... Some of the families can't afford that forever, and their kids have to drop out."

"Well, bro, in that case we're in trouble."

"Doesn't matter. We're going out there to play the game — and that's what we'll do."

Over at the announcer's booth, the announcer sits alongside a mystery guest, who wears a paper bag over their head, with holes cut out for the eyes and mouth. The announcer begins,

"We have an exciting doubleheader coming up today. And even more exciting is our lineup of mystery guests on deck. Our first guest is the 'Unknown Announcer,' Murray Langston."

"Thanks. I'd like to say—"

The announcer cuts him off. "I'll do the talking. Thanks, pal."

With the Giants being the visitors to the field, they would bat first. These fields — Mr. G's Fields — were home to the A-Team, and they were proud of this land. Well, at least, it *had* been their home. Tomorrow these very fields would be taken over by the new management, and they were keen to get started on making their new home for retail therapy.

The top of the first inning is all about showmanship — psychological strategies, to be exact — but the Giants don't waver. They are cool, calm, and collected, having been trained well to hide any emotional urges, no matter how slight. The A-Team manages to strike out the first two batters but the team still goes on to score three runs right out the gate.

Now, the Giants are not ones to hold back when it comes to playing the field. Their best pitcher comes out first — a strategy completely opposite from the one adopted by Charlie, who chose to wait a while before moving Seth, the A's best pitcher, into this pivotal role. Instead, Michelle pitches at the top of the game, keeping Seth waiting in the wings until they really need to come down on the opposing.

In the A-Team's dugout, Charlie turns to the kids. "Seth, you're up first. Michelle, you're on deck." Seth and Michelle get up from the bench to prepare.

The bottom of the inning starts off with an ironic pairing — Casey pitches to Seth, who strikes out at the plate. The next two batters following Seth strike out just as quickly. This inning's resulting score was disappointing, but it was just the beginning, after all.

The announcer calls out the current scores for each team, encouraging the As to give the visiting team a run for their money. The scoreboard reads:

INNING #1

A-TEAM — 0

GIANTS — 3

The A-Team takes to the field at the top of the second

inning. Again, Michelle is on the mound. Teri watches from the bleachers, biting her nails, wondering when her boy will take over. They needed to do something before it was too late, and with two players already on base, Frankie slams one deep into the left-center field. The two on base make a run for home, scoring two more for the Giants.

Over in the A-Team's dugout, Abe mutters to Charlie, "You ready to put in Seth yet?"

"I need him for the second game."

"Doesn't matter now. All they can get is seven more runs, and the game is over," Abe reminds his brother.

Charlie turns to look at Abe, his brows furrowed in confusion. After a moment, a look of realization crosses his face. "Ohh, you weren't— the board did away with the mercy rule this past meeting. We now *have* to play six innings per game, regardless of the score."

"Sounds like it'll be an exceedingly long day."

"Right, and I can't have Seth pitch twelve innings. It'd destroy his arm."

Back over in the announcer's booth, the Unknown Announcer has been replaced by a mime in whiteface and a black and white costume. His mouth and eyes are dramatically outlined in black. The announcer asks the mime, "Your thoughts on the game so far?" The mime pinches his nose.

On the field, Benji effortlessly hits one that nearly sails right out of the park. The left fielder leaps into the air and snags the ball. The runners on the second and third base tag up, but the left fielder rifles the ball to the third baseman, who tags the runner out and then rockets the ball home to the catcher.

"Out," shouts Hank.

From the Giants' dugout, Coach Guy screams back, "He was safe!"

"Let it go," Herbert says, patting Guy on the shoulder. "We need them to get *some* outs. I don't want the game to end on technicalities."

Mention of the rules makes Guy even more ferocious. He

snarls at Herbert. "Like it's dark, and we're still in the second inning?"

"No, I want them to have hope. Without it, they won't play." Herbert smiles, satisfied. On the scoreboard:

INNING #2
A-TEAM — 0
GIANTS — 5

The crowd, mostly on the side of the A-Team, yells out words of encouragement. Someone shouts, "Hit the ball out of the park!"

"Go, Michelle! Focus," calls out another spectator.

"Just hit the damn ball," booms another. Those in the stands crave even the slightest taste of victory — today more than ever, this being the last time the A-Team would play on their home turf. They want to see *something*. There had been rumors circulating around town that this day would be one to remember. Even a few news vans were in the area on standby. It wasn't every day that the field where a national sport was played got usurped by something as dull as retail. The game was intense but slow.

Some of the younger kids who had come to watch their siblings play were getting bored. The game had reached a standstill, and so, the kids decide to begin their own game on the adjacent T-ball field. Several parents come over to supervise, giving them respite from the screams and frustrations on the main field. Even Gordon wheels himself over to watch the younger players — mostly out of curiosity. Besides, as much as he'd rather not admit it, he knows the A-Team is safe in the caring hands of his two sons.

On the smaller field, Nicky hits the ball into the outfield. Three kids simultaneously dive to the ground. Whoever scoops up the ball first throws it to the first baseman as Nicky makes a break for second base, not even bothering to look back. The first baseman misses the toss from the outfielder.

Now the pitcher chases after the ball, quickly scooping it up, and throws it to second just as Nicky slides. Her determination to reach the base safely was so evident that when the dust clears, revealing Nicky's position as two feet shy, the second baseman drops the ball and beckons for her to stand up. The two lock arms, running to second base together — and Nicky is *safe*.

From the sidelines, the parents cheer on this friendly turn of events. The second baseman then picks up the ball and throws it back to the pitcher. Still, the bystanders clap and cheer wildly because they have witnessed something very unusual — a friendly game where the word 'competition' doesn't seem to exist between the children.

Gordon at first looks irked by what he sees playing out on the field. Ordinarily he'd yell and scream at anyone who dared to defy the game's competitive edge. But this time, the old man experiences the sheer joy of watching a game where the players have no desire to seek the blood, sweat, and tears of their opponents. Embracing this alternative way of playing the game for the first time in his life, he whispers to himself, "Good job, Nicky. You made Grandpa proud — again."

The T-ball game carries on. Several five-year-olds try their best to hit the ball off an air-powered tee. By now, even more of the crowd has migrated to watch the kids play, seeking solace from the disappointment of the main game's underwhelming action.

Nicky races off the field after getting tagged out on base (everyone's got to get out some time) and runs over to Gordon, who welcomes her with a high-five. The next kid at-bat hits the ball but runs in the direction of the bathroom instead of first base.

Soon, the crowd is larger than ever. One of the kids in the outfield stands there with a glove on his head while another is getting chased around the field by a kid holding the ball. Shoeless Joe joins in on the fun and gets tagged out at first base. The playful dog absolutely loves being out on the field with so many adoring young fans, and it shows.

While the self-organized T-ball game provided a welcome change from the intensity of the main event, after a while it was time to head back. Gordon hugs Nicky, who walks by his side, and the two of them return to watch the A-Team strut their stuff.

In the announcer's booth sits a homeless man who appears not to have taken a shower since the state announced drought warnings in an attempt to cut down on water waste. The only problem here was that nobody had told this guy it was still okay to shower — encouraged, in fact. The announcer asks the homeless man, "What do you think of the young and mighty Casey Ragsdale?"

The announcer holds up his phone to the homeless man's mouth as he mumbles into it. Setting the phone beside the microphone, he taps a button and the phone spews out words: "Casey Ragsdale does so many other things so well. It's hard to jump on him when he's hitting below .730 — but if he keeps hitting .690, he'll do well."

Now, it's the bottom of the third inning. The Giants play the field, and it looks like the relentless hold they have on the A-Team isn't about to break or bend even in the slightest.

Back at the A-Team's dugout, Charlie watches Casey prepare for his at-bat. The frustration builds as he realizes that Casey has become the Giant's star player, and it was likely all Herbert's doing. Just another manipulation tactic. Charlie does a hand signal and then pantomimes picking his nose.

From across the way, Herbert interprets Charlie's signal, reciting, "I'm so talented that I can pick my nose and coach at the same time." Herbert makes a move toward Charlie, but Guy puts an arm out to stop him.

The game progresses onward. Finally, the A-Team has scored their first run! Michelle reaches home plate, officially breaking the spell the Giants had over them all day. Maybe Charlie should joke around more often... The dugout's atmosphere could certainly benefit from a bit of light entertainment. On the scoreboard:

INNING #3
A-TEAM — 1
GIANTS — 8

At the top of the fourth inning, three Giants batters strike out — but not before three of them cross the plate safely. By the bottom of the fourth, with the A-Team at-bat, Casey is really feeling the pressure on the mound. The scoreboard reads:

INNING #4
A-TEAM — 3
GIANTS — 11

Top of the fifth inning, and it's time for the Giants to return to the plate. As usual, the players are cocky, proud, and flaunting their success. Starting off, Frankie crushes the ball, sending it out of the park for another home run. Two strikeouts follow for the Giants, but they still manage to score with the next three crossing the plate.

Michelle, exhausted but yet fighting to stay poised and focused, pitches with everything she's got, sweat dripping down her face. She's not giving up without a true fight, and she knows her teammates will back her up, all in position to catch any ball that comes their way.

The seventh Giants batter steps up to the plate next, with two out and four home so far. He gets a piece of the ball for a pop fly, but Sarah makes an incredible play, catching the ball way out in left field.

Next, the A-Team takes their turn at bat, with Casey still on the mound. Slowly improving, they manage to get four home runs — but is it too late? On the scoreboard now:

INNING #5
A-TEAM — 7
GIANTS — 12

From the A-Team's dugout, Charlie peers up at the

scoreboard, clearly frustrated. He can see that Michelle's energy is waning. With only one more inning left to this game, he considers swapping her out for Seth. He's conscious of the fact that they still have another game to play today, but at this point there are no other options.

"I've got to end this," Charlie says under his breath. He brings in Seth to pitch for the sixth and final inning of the doubleheader's first leg. Before Seth goes out to the mound, Charlie tells him, "On the third pitch, I want you to look for my signal."

Once on the field, Seth pitches two fastballs to the Giants batter — both are strikes. Seth puts his glove to his mouth and looks over at Charlie for the next signal. *Another fastball?* But Seth nods at Charlie and begins his windup. He releases the pitch. Sure enough, the batter swings late, not expecting another fastball, and misses it by a mile. That's strike three. Next batter up...

Seth's pitching talent is sharp. He's got a strong arm and great aim. It's a dream of his to one day become the sort of pitcher who's known for achieving an 'immaculate inning' like his other baseball hero, Garrett Richards. An immaculate inning is a total of nine pitches (nine strikes) and three outs. Despite the strong beginning, Seth has a long way to go.

The next Giants batter gets a piece of the ball on the second pitch and makes it to second base. Seth's concentration begins to slip, letting the third batter walk. The fourth batter to step up to the plate gets the player on second all the way home, but in a surprising turn of events, one of the As snags the ball on the third base line, putting an end to their opponents' momentum. The fifth batter makes a hit, but it's an easy out when one of the As, Glen, catches the ball. Seth's confidence returns and his form improves, inspired by his team's performance, and he winds up pitching three strikes in a row to the sixth batter.

The announcer's booth is fired up as everyone witnesses the tension on the field. Back in the guest seat is the Unknown

Announcer (Murray), who still tries to get a word in edgewise without much success.

In the bleachers, Rainbow Man stands with another one of his ubiquitous signs. This one says, 'Hebrews 12:1.'

For his own amusement, the announcer decides to let Murray have a go. "Okay, 'Unknown Announcer,' otherwise known as Murray Langston," he starts, "what do you think Rainbow Man is trying to tell us?"

Caught off guard, Murray stares blankly at the announcer for a long moment. "Uh... I'll just Google it— Hold on." Murray fiddles with his phone nervously. "Something about... I'll paraphrase, okay? Something about running the race with... Um... Perseverance."

"Well, my friend, yes," the announcer begins. "Rainbow Man knows, as we all do, that it's going to take plenty of that good old 'perseverance' here today with both teams set to play a doubleheader. How will they do it? It's going to be a very long day, indeed. But stay here, stay tuned, and find out with us."

Teri sits alone in the bleachers until her long-time best friends, Sarah and Catherine, join her. Neither of the women have kids on the field, but they both revere the importance of the national sport they grew up with. It felt like the entire neighborhood, families new and old, had come out to watch what was happening on the field that day. Everyone wanted that last glimpse of the hometown fields they had all known and loved throughout the years — surely, it was bittersweet.

Knowing this is the last inning of the game, the A-Team steps up with even more focus and passion than before. Regardless of the impending loss, they still needed to play on. Charlie hides his disappointment well, restraining himself from coming down on the kids like a ton of bricks. By the end of the game, each player on the A-Team had made it to the plate, and that was something to be quite pleased about for a team that thrives on democratic philosophies. Today was a day these kids would remember for the rest of their lives. Playing as a team together on these precious fields for the final time — now, that was something.

Michelle was the eighth batter to step up to the plate. The team had improved their score somewhat, but nevertheless they knew nothing but defeat was in reach; for this game, at least. She hits the ball way into the outfield... A potential home run! But one of the Giants' new *giants*, Benji, makes a flawless catch. On the scoreboard:

INNING #6

A-TEAM — 11

GIANTS — 16

And that's it. Hank cries out, "Out! Game!"

The Giants race into the center of the field, high-fiving each other. Then they run up to the A-Team and chant, "Losers! Losers! Losers!" Sportsmanship was apparently the one element left out of Herbert's curriculum at his bootcamp.

Charlie kicks at the dirt on the dugout floor. He was in need of a good pep talk right about now. The victory he had dreamed about was steadily slipping from his grasp. But all hope was not yet lost. There was one more game today, with the last and final one taking place tomorrow. No need to throw in the towel just yet, he realizes. Then again, the next game could very well be more of the same, and Charlie wasn't sure he could endure *that* much humiliation in a single day.

CHAPTER TWENTY-FIVE

Back at the snack bar, Charlie eats a hotdog. He throws pieces down to Shoeless Joe, who gobbles them up. Scores don't matter one bit in the life of a dog. Maybe Charlie should pick up a few pointers from his best mate.

Brian Ragsdale walks up and greets Charlie. "No hard feelings?"

"Nah. Congratulations, by the way... Your son *almost* pitched a great game. Too bad my players got some runs off him."

"Ah, no worries, he'll pitch a no-hitter soon enough. Oh, I should mention... David Evans of the LA Dodgers thinks it best for you to wait and try out again next year. Gives you more time to work on your pitching." He pauses. "Sorry about the tough break," Brian says when he sees a dark look come across Charlie's face.

As if on cue, Herbert strolls over and joins them in the already unpleasant conversation. "You struck out my batter with a fastball." He scoffs. "And we were expecting your stupid slushie pitch." Charlie smirks at the remark. "Clever."

Charlie shrugs. "I wanted your batter to go out swinging."

"Well, then," Herbert says with a huff, "we look forward to the final battle."

"I know you're nobody's fool, but maybe someone will adopt you one day."

"Sticks and stones."

"Don't thank me for insulting you... It was a pleasure," Charlie quips. Herbert and Brian leave Charlie behind just as Abe walks up. Charlie casts a long look at his brother. "What are we gonna do, Abe? Herb's team is stronger. I'm not sure there's anything I can say to the kids to turn our luck around."

"Grasshopper, a wise preacher man once said that you can lose the game and still win the battle."

Minutes before the second game of the doubleheader starts, Judy takes to the field. She stands on the pitcher's mound, holding a megaphone. She smiles toward the Giants' dugout, looking absolutely *smitten*.

"Herbert, come up here, sweetie pie," she says into the megaphone. Herbert pokes his head out of the dugout and walks up proudly. "I've already put this off for too long... Marry me?"

Herbert grabs the megaphone from Judy, and with the biggest grin this side of the Mississippi, he exclaims to everyone, "It would be an honor to marry the most gorgeous girl here!" He and Judy kiss. The crowd goes wild.

Abe lights a pack of fireworks and sets them off in the nearby parking lot 'in honor' of Judy and Herbert. They don't even seem to notice.

Finally, they step aside, and Nicky throws out the first ball to start the next game.

◊ ◊ ◊

Over in the announcer's booth, a local Miss Cleo type of personality sits in the guest chair. She holds a deck of tarot cards and begins turning them over one by one.

The announcer asks, "What's the point spread for this game?"

The woman turns over several more tarot cards before answering. "That's strange," muses the knockoff Miss Cleo. "Are you sure they are going to play baseball?"

Over in the A-Team's dugout, Charlie addresses the kids. "Hang in there. It's time to shake things up. We'll show them how to truly play the game of baseball. Let the circus begin."

"And now, time for plan B," Abe mumbles to himself.

Seth begins the second game on the mound, but he's looking more exhausted by the second. Charlie calls a time-out and switches pitchers. Emily, one of the young T-ball kids and also the A-Team's newest player, comes out of the dugout holding a large ball and a hitting tee. She approaches Casey, who stands at the plate, ready to take a swing. He looks bewildered as Emily walks up to him.

The little girl sets the tee over the plate and places the ball on top. "Batter up," she calls out.

Hank yells, "Play ball!"

"And there's the pitch," the announcer's voice says over the loudspeaker. Emily prances from the plate to the mound, overly pleased with herself.

From the Giants' dugout, Herbert signals in Charlie's direction.

Across the way, Charlie reads Herbert's signal aloud. "I thought we were playing baseball here."

Herb verbally translates the signal Charlie sends back in return. "Not anymore."

Charlie rushes out of the dugout, flailing his arms around like a maniac. His team laughs wildly. You'd think he was breaking their focus, but maybe this was what they needed, after all — to let loose.

Casey pops the ball high to center field, and the outfielders scurry to form a human pyramid. The centerfielder hops up and climbs between the other outfielders to catch the ball for an easy out.

Soon after, with the game still in progress, Charlie walks through the bleachers, carrying a tray of hotdogs. "Hotdogs! Get your hotdogs! I got your hotdogs!"

Abe walks up behind his brother and shouts to him, "I'll take two."

Charlie spins around to face Abe. "Shouldn't you be in the dugout coaching?"

"I thought you were coaching," responds Abe. The brothers turn to the dugout and realize that Shoeless Joe has taken over coaching the game.

Charlie quips with a grin, "Hey, they just struck out the kid! Maybe we *should* let the dog coach for a while." Abe nods in agreement after a moment, and the two take a seat, each enjoying their hotdogs in silence.

Back on the field, the A-Team's shortstop scoops up a grounder that comes his way. He positions himself like a football center and hikes the ball to the centerfielder.

The second baseman goes long to cover home, lying in wait as the centerfielder rockets the ball like a football toward the plate.

With one swift move, the second baseman catches the ball, tags out the runner at home, and does something reminiscent of a touchdown dance.

Over on the first baseline, Charlie brings out a group of cheerleaders to cheer for the Giants. "Herbie! Herbie! He's our man! If he can't do it, Charlie can!" The cheerleaders swarm around Herbert, sticking their pom-poms in his face. "Herbie! Herbie! He's our man!"

"Ladies! Enough already," spews Herbert, his hands flailing. He grabs a couple pom-poms and throws them to the ground in annoyance. Charlie chuckles to himself nearby as he watches Herbert's conniption.

Meanwhile, on the field, the second baseman throws the ball to first. The first baseman throws it home, the catcher throws it to third base, and the third baseman returns it to the second baseman. This continues for several rounds until Hank steps in and grabs the ball from the catcher at the plate.

Then the outfielders run to gather around the pitcher's mound together. They sing, swaying from side to side, while the basemen and the shortstop each mimic the motions of playing a violin.

They recite their song. "Three blind mice, three blind mice. See how they run, see how they run. They all ran after the farmer's wife. She cut off their tails with a carving knife. Did you ever see such a sight in your life as three blind mice?" The oddity of it all creates an eerie atmosphere, and Herbert's team is left unnerved by the whole turn of events.

Herbert's had enough and calls for a time-out. He, Charlie, Abe, and Hank get into a heated debate. "Hank, he's turning this game into a three-ring circus," screams Herbert, right into the older man's face.

Just then, on the field, the second baseman holds up a large hoop. The outfielders run and jump through the hoop while the pitcher imitates a monkey, jumping up and down, hooting and hollering. The catcher comes up, juggling three baseballs behind Hank and the rest of the adults.

Abe turns to Charlie. "We forgot the elephants." They watch as the first baseman cracks an imaginary whip at the shortstop, who pretends to be a lion, roaring and growling.

Hank gets into Herbert's face this time around and shouts, "Nothing in the rule book against players behaving like circus performers. Play ball!"

Now in the announcer's booth sits Shoeless Joe. The announcer calls it as he sees it. "The game looks like it's going to the dogs. What do you think, Joe?" The dog responds with a series of barks before the announcer continues. "I concur with your analysis. The Giants are playing a tight game, but their pitcher is starting to wear down."

The next Giants batter steps up to the plate. He gets a hit and makes it to first. Every A-Team player runs to first base and high-fives the opposing runner.

Herbert, extremely frustrated, squeals for anyone who will listen. "The man is making a mockery of America's favorite pastime."

Soon after, one of the Giants players attempts to steal second, but before he gets there, the second baseman grabs the base and runs off.

Over in the Giants' dugout, Guy stops Herbert from charging Hank. "You're wasting your time," he says.

Charlie moseys on over to their opponents' dugout with a hot dog in hand. "Want ketchup on it, Herbie?" He squirts ketchup all over Herbert's shirt.

On the field, the centerfielder snags a pop fly. The left fielder tackles his fellow player, and then the right fielder jumps on, followed by the rest of the team. Covered by a pile of teammates, the centerfielder suddenly sticks out his hand to show he's caught the ball.

The announcer calls it. "The A-Team has recovered the ball. It's first and ten — oops, wrong game," he quips with a chuckle.

◊ ◊ ◊

Eventually, Charlie calls for a time-out. It's already been a long day with still only more to come. The kids return to their usual positions and continue to play — for real. Benji takes the plate for the Giants. He stares down Seth, who is pitching again after the Emily moment. Seth does his windup and throws the ball.

"And another great pitch by Seth," booms the announcer. On the field, instead of making the call as per usual, Hank steps out of the batter box. The announcer continues. "Well, folks, I see it's time to play 'So You Want To Be an Umpire.' In this game, you lucky viewers in the stands get to decide if the pitch was a ball or a strike. Now, last inning, we passed out a double-sided card with 'ball' and 'strike' on either side. Majority wins." Moments later, the majority holds up their cards with the 'strike' side facing forward. "Well, there you have it. Majority says it's a strike! Thanks for playing 'So You Want To Be an Umpire,' where *you* get to make the call."

Over on the mound, Seth does his windup and a pitch. Benji slams the ball out of the park. Behind the scoreboard, Abe sets off fireworks. They fly high into the sky, erupting into a mesmerizing display. The crowd immediately goes wild.

In the Giants' dugout, Casey approaches Herbert. "Coach, my arm is hurting really badly. I don't think I can pitch anymore, let alone bat." The brutal man shows no concern for the potential injury to one of his own. Herbert points to home plate without a word.

"Can I at least have someone look at it?" Casey pleads. Herbert stands there, still pointing. Heaving a deep sigh, Casey grabs his bat and somberly leaves the dugout.

"A good soldier will fight regardless of how much it hurts," screams Herbert as he nearly chases the kid out to the plate.

Charlie signals across the way to Herbert, who translates it aloud. "The kid is in a lot of pain. You should bench him."

Then Charlie speaks Herbert's response. "Not until I achieve total annihilation." He scoffs at the remark of his nemesis.

"Do you know what a 'strike' is?" Herbert says, reading Charlie's signal in return.

Charlie stands by with a smirk plastered on his face. He whispers Herbert's response to himself even though he's already certain what said response will be. "What kind of dumbass question is that, moron?" Charlie shrugs and then nods in Herbert's direction. He blows his whistle, initiating the start of something even more wild than anyone could've imagined.

The A-Team kids run into the snack bar, where Teri meets them and hands out picket signs one by one. They return to the field, marching back and forth. Each picket sign reads something different in bold handwritten letters.

Teri returns to her spot in the bleachers and smiles as she takes a look at all the signs spread out over the field. The kids had spent the afternoon at her home, creating the colorful displays of protest. Soon, each of the players plant their selected picket signs into the ground where they stand, right next to their positions on the field.

Seth stands on the mound, next to his sign: 'No fun, no play.' On first is Michelle: 'It's not a crime to lose.' Toby stands on second base: 'Kids against out-of-control parents.' Grant plays third base: 'It's just a game.' In between stands Vanessa, the shortstop: 'If we lose, get over it.' Linda out in left field: 'Can't you see it's just a game?' Andrew, the centerfielder: 'We hate the ride home after a game.' Out in right field stands Kyle: 'My self-esteem is not tied to the results of this game.' Finally, the catcher's sign: 'Losing doesn't make us losers.'

Once the dust has settled, the kids resume their game. Seth prepares to deliver a pitch to Casey at the plate.

Before he gets a chance, Herbert comes barreling out of the Giants' dugout and charges Hank. "Look what he's doing to

MUTINY IN THE DUGOUT

me now!"

Kids from the bleachers trail onto the field, standing up for their own. Even Abe's youth group teens join in with their own picket signs, taking a break from fighting the big corporations to protect the spirit of an institution they had known and loved so many years ago.

Soon enough, the cheerleaders pile onto the field, doing backflips and cheers galore. "We don't, we won't play no more! Boom chicka boom! We don't, we won't play no more! Boom chicka boom! We're outta here!"

By now, the field is covered with kids — nearly one-hundred and with more on the way — all with their own handmade signs. Over the past few weeks, the team had invited neighborhood kids to come out and join in on the upcoming flash mob. Kids all over the area were eager to do their part and make this day one to remember.

Thankfully, Jack's technological wizardry across the miles was just what they needed to create a campaign that would both enthuse and appeal to the likes of the young people who'd shown up on the field here today. Otherwise, there's no way the adults alone could have created so much buzz to generate this many kids on the field, all of whom are actively campaigning for a new way to play the classic game.

Two kids with megaphones walk onto the field, chanting the following verse along with the others:

We won't play no more
If what you've got in store
Is fear and brimstone
Bring back your backbone!
We want to play like it's a game
Let's have fun and not fear or
We're... We're outta here!

A news helicopter flies overhead while another news van pulls up on the field, and a reporter and cameraman hop out the back.

Herbert storms onto the field and gets into Hank's face for what seems like the millionth time that day. "You've got to put an end to this!"

Hank pulls out the rulebook and shoves it right under Herbert's nose. "He's got three strikes, and then he's out. Play ball!"

Five or so reporters stand on the sidelines, each filming their own clips. One of them stares straight into the camera, with a harsh look and serious tone. "These kids have had enough. They are officially on strike. Out-of-control parents and coaches everywhere — take notice."

Casey calmly returns to the plate, stepping into the batter's box. He takes a warm up swing and nods to Seth, who stands on the mound. Seth winds up and delivers an easy underhand softball throw across the plate. Casey doesn't bother to swing.

"Strike one," calls Hank.

For the next pitch, Seth rolls the ball onto the ground. When it crosses the plate, Casey gives it his best golf swing and misses.

"Strike two!"

Herbert charges Casey, nearly knocking him over. "You will swing at the next ball that crosses that plate! That's an order. Do you understand me?" He stomps back into the dugout, enraged.

But despite the so-called 'order,' when Seth pitches another easy one right over the plate, Casey simply releases the bat, letting it fall from his hands into the dirt.

"Strike three! You're out!"

Herbert scrambles out of the dugout, yelling at Casey. "You're a disgrace to your new team! In fact, you don't deserve to wear that uniform. Mark my words, kid… You will never play ball again!"

Casey simply ignores Herbert as though he can't hear nor see him. Instead, he strolls over to Charlie, who hands him a picket sign. Casey joins the others on the field, partaking in the cheerful protest. The picket line grows every minute, with kids and teens from all over coming together to march around the field and stand for what's right.

Herbert signals from the Giants dugout for Frankie to take the next at-bat. Frankie steps up, but he doesn't swing at any of the three pitches Seth seamlessly delivers over the plate. He takes the quick out and somberly walks back to the dugout.

Herbert stops him, his feet firmly planted in the middle of the entrance. "Get off my field, you good-for-nothing kid! Benji, get your butt out here!"

From the bleachers, Frankie and Benji's mother Rosetta charges Herbert with the determination of a lioness protecting her cubs. "Excuse me, Mr. Herbert — no one talks to my boys like that!" She spits on Herbert, sending him careening back into the dugout with disgust. Frankie and Benji walk off with their mother in silence, both smirking at each other.

Across the way in the A-Team's dugout, Abe turns to Charlie. "Beer?"

"You have to ask?" Charlie replies cooly as they watch Herbert emerge from his dugout.

He holds a megaphone and stomps over to home plate. "We are victorious! I will go to the Youth Summer League World Series!"

Calmly, Abe says, "Eating a hotdog, drinking a beer, and watching baseball."

"As good as it gets," Charlie adds before taking a swig of his beer.

Nicky enters the dugout and runs up to Abe with a big grin on her face. "Grandpa's going to buy me an ice cream cone later for hitting the ball during my game!"

Meanwhile, Herbert continues his rant out on the field, still screaming into his megaphone. "We have achieved greatness today!"

In military precision, the Giants march in single file. Some exit the dugout while others gather from their spots on the field.

Teri stands just outside the dugout, handing each player their own picket sign.

Herbert spins around, bewildered, and takes it all in. "You fools! How dare you stand in the judgment of Herbert Turner!"

Still in the A-Team's dugout, Charlie and Abe calmly sit, watching the scene play out before them. Abe points to Gordon, who's now wheeled himself onto the field. "Look, Mr. G's got a picket sign too."

Charlie nods proudly. "Made it special — just for him."

On the field, Gordon sits parked beside his picket sign, which reads: 'Kids play. Coaches coach. Parents watch. Understand?"

Herbert maniacally spews words through the megaphone. "All I ask is for total loyalty — and in return, I offer great victories, the likes of which have never been seen!"

Unfortunately Herbert's too busy screaming to notice Shoeless Joe. The dog runs over with his travel bowl in his mouth and lifts his leg, relieving himself right onto Herbert's pants.

Attached to Joe's back is a picket sign that reads: 'Dogs like baseball. Let them play too!' He trots over to the A-Team's dugout and drops the dish at Abe and Charlie's feet. Abe pours a splash or two of beer into the bowl while Charlie strokes the dog on the head, whispering sentiments of praise to him.

"The fireworks were a nice touch," Charlie says to his brother.

"We should do it again next season on our new fields," quips Abe. A slow smile crosses Charlie's face.

Just across the way, Herbie continues spewing his rant to the unwelcoming crowd. "I refuse to steer off course in my determination to destroy all enemies!"

Abe looks at Charlie. "So much for going to the World Series."

"We'll be there. We're just going to earn it like every other team. Fight a good fight, and win. We'll make it to the playoffs, and then it's off to Williamsport." Charlie looks on proudly, watching his team march around on the field, refusing to give up.

Suddenly, Hank enters the dugout and takes a seat beside the brothers. Abe hands him a beer before asking, "Uncle, are you going to Judy's wedding?"

"Wouldn't miss it," Hank starts. "Any idea where they're registered?"

"I am the Messiah, and this is my crusade. My flock will rise above this and achieve the greatest victory of all," screams the still ranting Herbert, droplets of spit flying from his mouth.

Teri pokes her head into the dugout next. "What's wrong with this picture?"

Charlie looks dumbfounded. "Not a clue. Abe?" He turns to his brother with a questioning look. Abe passes Teri a beer.

"A lady shouldn't have to ask for a beer," Hank says, looking over at Charlie.

Charlie lets out a chuckle. "Sorry, Teri. But hey, I think I know something else that's wrong with this picture... We're the only ones without picket signs. I'll be right back." He gets off the bench and leaves the dugout. Teri stares after him, admiring his verve and love for life.

Soon enough, all three of them follow Charlie's lead and exit the dugout.

Charlie quickly returns to the group with a few picket signs. "I had some custom-made," he says, handing them to Teri. She looks down at the words on each sign — 'Yes,' 'No,' and 'Maybe.'

Teri looks at him, intrigued. "Yes, no, maybe... What's the question?" When she looks up, her eyes widen. She sees Charlie holding a picket sign of his very own. It reads: 'Will you marry me?'

Charlie smiles, barely able to contain his excitement. "Will you marry me, Teri?"

A huge smile breaks out across Teri's face. She drops the 'no' and 'maybe' signs onto the ground and holds the 'yes' up high. They both plant their signs into the ground before enveloping each other in a warm embrace.

"Yes," she shouts. As the two break apart, they high-five each other and then kiss as the A-Team kids march around them.

Abe and Hank stand by, watching the proposal play out. "Looks like you've got *two* weddings to go to, uncle," Abe says.

"Looks like it," the older man responds. After a few moments of silence, a small smile plays upon his lips. "Been a long time coming but they finally made it."

"They sure did."

CHAPTER TWENTY-SIX

Charlie spots Earl in the bleachers later that day. He's pleased to see that the older man had made the long journey in honor of the last day on these fields as they knew them. "Welcome to Mr. G's Fields, Earl. You're sitting on sacred ground here. Ground that in a few days will no longer be known as a baseball field."

"It's good to see you in action, my friend. Listen, I heard back from the LA Dodgers. Sounds like you might have a shot." Charlie's jaw drops in shock as he comprehends what Earl's telling him. The man continues hurriedly. "They're just shortlisting the next players right now, but looks like you might need to go in for another meet and greet. But believe me, it's all positive, my friend, all positive." Earl smiles as he gives Charlie the news.

Charlie manages to find his voice again. "Thanks, man. It's been a rocky ride, but let me tell you… Coming back home has been pretty positive too." The two men share a look and a brief moment of eye contact.

"Well," says Earl, "I'll let you get back to your family. I'll call you."

"Hey, I'll call you too," Charlie responds. He smiles and waves Earl goodbye. Not only had he been surprised by Earl's visit but even more shocking was the realization that the man had been sitting there in the bleachers, taking in every single shenanigan they had pulled that day.

In all honesty, it didn't matter to Charlie now whether he was seen as 'good enough' or *not* for the LA Dodgers. He knows deep down that he'd been good enough right here where it mattered. While he was glad to see out the last few weeks and have the chance to pay tribute to the life of Mr. G's Fields, Charlie found it hard to say goodbye. How could one truly say goodbye to the physical representation of a time and place that had meant so much? Shoeless Joe comes over to warm Charlie's heart, and together, they watch as the players leave the field for the very last time.

That evening, the sun sets over the horizon of the field. Charlie, Abe, and Gordon are the only stragglers remaining.

An excited Abe says to his brother, "Hold this." He stuffs a lighter into Charlie's hand before making a run for it. No one seems to have noticed the M-80 firecracker that Abe has lit under Gordon's wheelchair. "Hey, Mr. G, look out! Charlie lit a firecracker under your chair! Run," shouts Abe.

"He can't—" Charlie begins. His eyes widen in shock as Gordon suddenly gets out of the wheelchair and walks away. Moments later, the wheelchair explodes on the field into bits.

"Why, you little punk! I'm going to beat the living daylights out of you," Gordon screams in Charlie's direction.

Meanwhile, Charlie has a look of sheer confusion. "Mr. G... You can walk?" Abe and Gordon freeze. Abe looks at Gordon... Gordon looks at Abe... They both turn to Charlie.

After an extended moment of silence, Gordon shrugs. He looks back at Abe. "It was your idea. You tell him."

Abe grins and rushes over, putting his arm around Charlie's shoulders. "We made it up."

Charlie is purely bewildered with the whole situation. "You made *what* up?"

"Well, everything," Abe says. "The whole wildcard-slot-going-to-the-Youth-Summer-League-World-Series thing."

"What?" Charlie spins around to stare at Gordon accusatorially. "You mean you didn't have a stroke?"

Gordon sets a hand on Charlie's shoulder. "Yes, I did have a stroke, but I was lucky... I can walk. Asked a friend of mine at the Youth Summer League Headquarters to make something up and fool Judy while I was recovering."

Charlie still looks confused, looking into his father's eyes.

"But why? Why would you do that?"

Abe pipes up, shrugging. "Seth needs to be with his father. And you need to be with your son."

Then a worried look crosses Charlie's face. "And Herbert was in on it too?"

Gordon and Abe burst out laughing. "Ol' Snot Nose needed to be stopped."

Abe turns to Gordon, nudging the old man in the ribs. "You almost blew it when you moved your leg in front of Charlie when he first arrived."

The reunited family laughs together, hugging and finally tackling each other to the ground. Abe grabs Gordon's hat off his head, while Gordon swipes Charlie's, and they both slap Charlie on the head — all in good fun.

Minutes later, Gordon and Charlie walk off, leaving the field. Abe hangs back, catching a last look while a series of explosions destroy the dugouts and the backstops. He catches up with them moments later.

Charlie looks at Abe as his brother falls into step beside him. "So, there's no game tomorrow?"

"I think we can call it an end to playing Herb's team for a while," Abe says while another final explosion confirms the end to the games on what was once Mr. G's Fields.

"What about the gophers?" Charlie asks, sneaking another look back at the fields.

Abe cracks a smile. "There were never any gophers... I dug those holes myself. Besides, it doesn't matter. It's the end of an era."

As they reach the parking lot, the snack bar collapses into a pile of rubble behind them. Seth and Teri have been waiting, leaning up against Charlie's mustang. Charlie comes up and takes Teri's hand. His face says only one thing — he's over the moon. For the first time ever, Charlie feels like he truly belongs. He belongs to the Maddox clan, and now, he wants Teri to be part of it too.

When Gordon reaches them, Charlie says to his father.

"Meet the future Mrs. Maddox."

Gordon's waited a long while to hear this particular bit of news. He smiles gleefully at the radiant couple. They beam pure happiness. "We haven't had one of those for a while. Welcome to the team," he tells Teri.

"Thanks, Mr. G," Teri says, thrilled at the official welcome into the family.

"Call me 'Dad.' Look — everyone can just quit calling me 'Mr. G'! Or 'Gordon'! It's 'Dad' from now on."

In unison, all of them — even Seth — respond with, "Okay, Dad."

But Gordon isn't the only one who has recently been heralded with this meaningful title. Seth looks up at Charlie, his voice filled with an unusual shyness. "Dad." It sounds warm and right — the perfect word at just the perfect moment can bring immeasurable warmth to even the coldest of hearts, the coldest of souls. The family unites as the orange sun sinks into the purple sky above.

EPILOGUE

E verybody lucky enough to be a part of the Maddox clan has gathered at the beach to watch Charlie and Teri get married at sunset. Out in the parking lot, Gordon, Charlie, and Abe stand at the back of Gordon's old car. Abe pops the trunk, revealing a shotgun. With wide eyes, Charlie turns to look at Gordon and then back at Abe. He watches as his brother takes out the shotgun and taps it.

Gordon looks straight into Charlie's eyes. "So, son... What are your intentions with Teri now?"

Charlie hesitates for a moment as though the question was a trick one. "Marrying Teri, I think."

Abe taps the gun harder, and Gordon inches just a little bit closer. "Go on," the old man says.

"Dad, I love Teri. I am going to marry her, and I'm going to spend every day trying to be the best husband and father I can be." The three men stand in silence for a long moment.

Gordon stares absently at his son. "Good. This is yours now." Abe shoves the shotgun into Charlie's hand and starts walking toward the beach.

Charlie hesitantly takes the gun, nearly fumbling it in his shaky hands. He explains to Gordon, "You know, Dad, sometimes it takes leaving to find your passion was right in front of you all along."

Abe stops in his footsteps, overhearing Charlie's words. "Wait a moment, brother." He looks over his shoulder. "We freed you of your guilt so you could pursue your dream."

Charlie doesn't bother engaging and instead begins walking off toward the beach, leaving behind the others this time. "Well, how about we go make that dream come true right now?"

Abe hurries to direct them toward the proper walkway leading to the water. Gordon falls into step beside Charlie, and Abe comes up on the other side, putting an arm around his brother's shoulder.

Then Abe leans in to Charlie conspiratorially. "Gordon was gonna have me hunt you down with that gun and drag you back for a proper wedding, but I talked him out of it. Told him I had a better plan..."

◊ ◊ ◊

Soon after, Charlie and Teri stand under a wedding arch. Charlie's dressed in a tuxedo while Teri wears a beautiful bridal gown. They recite their wedding vows to each other as a performer strums his guitar, singing "Wedding Song" by Peter, Paul, and Mary, and "Photograph" by Ed Sheeran. The newly married couple kisses in front of the crowd to a massive round of applause.

From there followed a lovely breakfast reception at Charlie and Teri's favorite spot, The Park Bench Café, which was just as welcoming to Charlie's best mate Shoeless Joe as anyone else. They'd booked the entire restaurant for one-hundred of their favorite people, including the A-Team kids, the Giants, Hank, Shoeless Joe, Abe's youth group, and other family, friends, and thirty or so friendly canine creatures, who happily dined on the lawn together. It was quite a special event for the neighborhood, you see.

◊ ◊ ◊

Welcome to Williamsport... It had taken the rest of the summer to get there, and it was a time filled with remarkable changes, challenges, and rewards. But it had all been worthwhile. Now, Seth walks out of a tunnel and up the steps into the dugout. He smiles and looks up at the bright lights, taking in the sight of the wildly applauding crowd that surrounds him. His team is there to back him up, and nothing but excitement and energy flows through the air. Seth is surrounded by those who love him — but more than this, he is surrounded by those who *know* him. His mom and dad are there to witness and share in this glorious day, and he wouldn't be here without them.

Made in the USA
Las Vegas, NV
28 August 2022

54176055R00133